THE SHADOW ON THE MESA

**Center Point
Large Print**

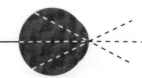

**This Large Print Book carries the
Seal of Approval of N.A.V.H.**

THE SHADOW ON THE MESA

JACKSON GREGORY

CENTER POINT PUBLISHING
THORNDIKE, MAINE

This Center Point Large Print edition
is published in the year 2004 by arrangement with
Golden West Literary Agency.

The text of this Large Print edition is unabridged. In other
aspects, this book may vary from the original edition. Printed in
Thailand. Set in 16-point Times New Roman type by
Bill Coskrey and Gary Socquet.

ISBN 1-58547-422-3

Library of Congress Cataloging-in-Publication Data

Gregory, Jackson, 1882-1943.
  The shadow on the mesa / Jackson Gregory.--Center Point large print ed.
    p. cm.
  ISBN 1-58547-422-3 (lib. bdg. : alk. paper)
    1. Large type books. I. Title.

PS3513.R562S53 2004
813'.52--dc22

                                                          2003023669

To my son
RODERICK
Who, being gifted with understanding,
will sense those unspoken thoughts
which flock about his name
as I inscribe it here.
December 24, 1932.

THE SHADOW ON THE MESA

CHAPTER I

ABATTERED OLD WRECK OF A MONOPLANE CAME wobbling up from the South, bringing a world-wanderer homeward after long years. Coming home! Jerry Boyne—to give him that name which he had worn so long now that it was his own more than any other—looked down from an altitude of several thousand feet, his eyes brimming with eagerness. Beneath him sprawled the ugly little Mexican border town; straight ahead lay an expanse of gray desert which was far from ugly in his eyes. For home was yonder, just a scant handful of arid miles where the little hills lifted up, clean and blue and inviting.

"Too bad I've got to land. I'd be at High Mesa in two shakes. Good old Dad! Gosh, he's nearly sixty now! Shucks, sixty isn't old for a man nowadays. Down we settle, old lady, and give you a shot of gas. We'd take a chance and rattle on and hang the government regulations, but it would be no fun getting let down in the cactus a dozen miles from home. Well, stop and all, we'll be there in twenty minutes."

Twenty minutes or so, after a voluntary absence of close to fifteen years, shouldn't have seemed long to wait, but did.

"Guess I'm homesick," grinned young Boyne. He picked out his landing place and nosed earthward.

The village turned out to watch the monoplane come down. The landing field—with a gasoline station on one side, a dilapidated, sway-backed hangar on the other, and an ancient biplane, belonging to the Mexican border patrol, being groomed close to the hangar—lay along the international boundary line and at the very edge of Nacional. Therefore, when the monoplane's bouncing wheels struck the earth, sending up clouds of dust, there were upward of a score of people, mostly children, lined up as admiring spectators. Jerry Boyne, attending for the moment strictly to business, scarcely noted the single figure on horseback, a somewhat flashily dressed young man riding a rarely beautiful black mare and conversing familiarly with a couple of half grown, dark skinned, white toothed village girls.

A moment later he did notice, however, and grinned broadly; for, though he must hold himself in some part to blame for the accident, his conscience did not in the least disturb him, and the thing *was* funny. This was the way of it: The ornate young gentleman on the black mare, scarcely less ornate with silver trappings on saddle and bridle, had been paying a good deal more attention to the two laughing Mexican girls than to the new arrival from the skies. He sat loosely in the saddle, one boot swinging free, the other carelessly supporting his weight in the stirrup, and was engaged in rolling a cigarette. To him planes were nothing new; to his mare this clumsy old wreck tumbling down from above was an altogether startling affair; and when it struck earth and then came trundling forward, taxiing across the field, the animal snorted, flung up a frightened head and spun about on a single hind hoof. As a result her rider sprawled in the dirt.

A whoop of joy rose from all the small boys at hand,

and a cackle of almost hysterical laughter burst from the two local beauties. Then it was that Jerry Boyne, seeing the fallen man leap up unhurt, grinned in evidence of his own appreciation of one of the unexpected bright moments of life. The monoplane jolted to a standstill; Jerry Boyne uncurled his long, somewhat lanky frame, and crawled out into the hot sunshine, disencumbering himself of his pack, tossing the parachute back into the place he had vacated.

"Sorry, stranger—" he began, but didn't look particularly saddened, and there was a chuckle in his voice. And that was as far as he got, for his off-hand apology was cut short by the wrathfully spoken words:

"I've a notion to knock your damned block off!"

"That so?"

Jerry pulled off his headgear, displaying a shock of dark-red hair; also he shook another kink or so out of his elongated frame and appeared a shade taller than the mere six feet he was. His eyes sobered briefly; then a smile twitched again at the corners of a generously wide mouth and made merry little crinkles about a pair of very keen, forthright eyes as he added:

"Well, I don't know that I'd blame you. You sure looked funny, and your lady friends didn't miss the humor. I've said I'm sorry, but I was sort of half lyin', at that. Now if you think you can get away with it and would feel any better, why, sock away, old-timer."

The girls, who had suspended all tittering to listen, now demanded of each other, *"¿Que dice?"* [What's he say?] and surrendered themselves to a fresh spasm of giggling. Jerry Boyne watched the face confronting his own turn a dull brick red, and noted for the first time that the disgruntled horseman was as red of hair as himself. It flashed over him that there would probably be a blow or two struck over this idiotic affair after all, for he not only knew the old adage that a red head made a hot temper, but subscribed to it. The Lord knew he had whittled away at his own fiery disposition for many a year—ever since the crazy explosion which had sent him wandering those fifteen years ago—and was still subject to bad moments.

The other seemed to hesitate, a pair of dark, reddish-brown eyes staring out moodily from under the dusty red thatch; then he swung on his heel. Jerry Boyne relaxed, considering the thing over and done with. But that spinning on a high boot heel was a matter of art—and of shrewd trickery; for the man spun all the way about and, at the unexpected moment, lashed out viciously, a hard brown fist landing square on the point of Boyne's unprotected chin. Jerry went staggering backward. He grew limp, and, in its own turn, his falling body sent up a great puff of dust. But where he fell he lay; to all intents and purposes he simply went to sleep.

"The dirty swine," he grunted a few moments later when he got to his feet and saw in the distance the lively black mare carrying an erect rider out of his ken. He felt his jaw gingerly. "Gosh, what a wallop! Hey, you!" he shouted briskly to a grinning Mexican leaning against the gasoline station. "Bring me a can of gas; on the run, amigo! What the devil are you laughing at?"

"You go for catch that hombre, no?"

"I'll land right square on top of him next time. Of all the—"

Then his eye chanced on a figure just emerging from the saloon across the dusty road, a broad, inflated-looking man in a light tan summer suit, with tan-and-white shoes and a glaring white straw hat encircled by a broad purple band, and Jerry Boyne's lowering brows perked up quizzically. Just then the nattily dressed individual saw him and came running, emitting a throaty sound of welcome as he charged across the dusty road.

"Hello, Crazy Fool!" clamored the throaty voice and broke upon a high note of delight. "Thought you was dead. Why ain't you?"

Jerry Boyne's grin came flashing back, for here was a man whom he liked, whom he had not seen for upward of a year, with whom at odd times he had lived life in some of its intriguing moments.

"Hello yourself, Succulent Squash," he called back, and the two shook hands warmly. "So Buenos Aires couldn't hold the accomplished Mr. Elmer Blodgett?"

"Thought you were anchored in the Argentine," observed Elmer Blodgett.

"Behold me just arrived from Argentina—and done with foreign lands, my boy."

"In that thing?" Blodgett nodded at the monoplane. "Guess it was your engine I heard just now; didn't sound so good to me." He stepped closer to the plane, regarded it curiously, encircled it and, at the end of his little tour, demanded: "Make it yourself?"

"Assembled it," grinned Jerry.

"At some city dump, looks like," grunted Elmer. "If I

15

was you I wouldn't bank much on that engine, not the way it sounded."

"I take no chances except getting off the ground and coming down. The rest of the time I keep high enough so if the old bird goes coo-coo, all I've got to do is step out and jump."

"Parachute?" Elmer Blodgett shivered. "Why on earth guys like you want to go sailing around up high when there's a perfectly good earth to walk on—" He broke off abruptly and a sudden look of lively suspicion shone in his eyes. "What's the game, Jerry?" he whispered. "Rum-running? Or dope or Chinks?"

Jerry smote him on a thick round shoulder.

"You couldn't see a gent with a walking cane without wondering whether he carried a knife or cocaine in the thing. If all your suspicions came true, what a rollicking old world it would be! And, by the bye, what do you happen to be doing in such a dump as this?"

Instead of answering the question as offhandedly as it was asked, Elmer Blodgett chose to look mysterious. Jerry laughed, for it was always Elmer's way to draw veils of mystery about him. If you asked him what he had had for supper, he would manage somehow to convey the impression that if you only knew the truth of that little matter you'd be fairly amazed.

"Come and have a glass of beer and we'll talk," suggested the stout man. "Their whisky here is vile, their wine filthy, but their beer, man, is tasty to the palate and soothing to the system."

"Can't, Elmer; thanks just the same. It happens I'm in a hurry— Confound it," he muttered as he observed the leaning Mexican still leaning. "How about that gaso-line?"

"What's the hurry, Jerry? Where to in this grand rush?"

Jerry started to answer, then checked his words and stared at his old friend almost blankly.

"Hanged if I know!" he chuckled as Elmer regarded him with a revival of suspicion.

"Haven't changed much, Crazy Fool," snorted Elmer. "Off on a dead run at the devil's beckoning, and before the devil himself has quite made up his mind where he's sending you."

"It's this way," Jerry explained. "Just two shakes ago I was promising myself that inside twenty minutes I'd be over yonder." He lifted a long arm, leather jacketed, to point to the little blue hills, inviting in the northern distance. "Then a nice friendly guy fell off his horse, poked me in the jaw and galloped away without leaving me his street address or telephone number. I've got a sudden craving to look him up."

"Stranger, Jerry? Just piled off his pony and popped you one and hot-hoofed it out of here?" That old knowing look came back into his lively blue eyes. He thought best to sink his voice to a whisper again. "I ain't been here long, Jerry, old horse, but long enough to sense things! Get me? Lucky for you he used his fist instead of a bowie knife. Some secret enemy of yours, old kid, advised of your coming, has his hired assassins looking for you. Let little Elmer Blodgett tell you that there are queer happenings pulled off along the border line. And if you're mixed up in something shady—"

But Jerry cut him short.

"Whether you've been here long or short, maybe you can tell me something. Know a man named Sommers? Gerald Hand Sommers?"

"No, I don't know him, but I know of him. Anyway, I've heard his name a few times. What about him?"

"You've told me that he's still here. Lives over yonder." Again he pointed to the hills. "At a place called High Mesa. I was on my way there when I had to drop down for gas—and got poked in the jaw."

"Here's where I can save you from risking your neck in that flying machine. I've got a car over back of the saloon. Come along; we'll have that beer and I'll take you where you'll find this Sommers guy."

"Man, I'd be at High Mesa before you did the first mile of desert."

"Only you wouldn't find your man there. He's over at the Empire."

"What's that? Another saloon?"

"The Empire, my boy, is a rancho—a regular rancho deluxe that stretches over half Mexico and some good bit of the old U.S.A. If you had ever come this way before, you'd know about it."

"I remember now. I'd forgotten—"

"It's got half a million acres to it," ran on Elmer Blodgett pridefully, being that type of man who always manages to extract some credit for himself from whatever large account he may be delivering, quite as though he had had a hand in ordering the things he speaks of. "A woman owns it, too; what do you think of that? A widow lady, young man, and from all accounts a heller.

They call her the Empress."

"They would," conceded Jerry. "Yes, I seem to remember having heard of her, too."

"Well, here's the point: There's some kind of big doings over at the Empire Rancho today and tonight and for a week to come; and among those present there'll be your bird from High Mesa. How do I know, not knowing him personal? I listen around, son. He's got some fancy ponies. He's entering one or two in the race at the Empire this afternoon. I know, because I'm placing a little money, and I only do that when I've nosed around a bit for scraps of info. The rancho is over that way a bit; there's a good road and we'll be there before you know it."

He in his turn pointed and Jerry observed that he pointed in the direction taken by the red-headed young man on the black mare.

"That road? Where else does it go?"

"Where else could it go? I answer you: Nowhere. Out that way, if you poked around all summer, you wouldn't find anything but Empire Ranch. Come ahead, my little one. Beer before business." He cast a last scornful look at the old monoplane. "It'll be safe here," he observed sarcastically.

Jerry let the words pass. His eyes no longer trafficked with the bright little blue hills but, brimming with eagerness, followed the way of the dusty road leading through sand and sage to the Empire Ranch.

CHAPTER II

IN A COOL GROVE OF COTTONWOODS THE DANCE platform, decked with evergreen garlands, stood ready for the gala occasion, and already some two hundred men and women from both sides of the international boundary line gathered in the grateful shade. This way came Jerry Boyne at such a swift, long-legged pace that his friend, who had not been able to catch up with him from the moment they left the car at the outer gate, was moved to gentle swearing. Jerry hung on his heel a moment but did not turn; his eyes were everywhere at once, seeking to single out one form from all this throng.

"What's eating you, Jerry?" muttered Blodgett, mopping furiously at his dripping brow with a pink-bordered handkerchief. "Follow me, can't you? I invited you to this party, didn't I? First we got to pay our respects to the Empress. Her name is Doña Luisa Blanco Fernandez, and she's no more Mex by birth than the Statue of Liberty is. New Yorker she was once on a while. If you'll listen to me," and he began whispering, "a lively little dancer and general entertainer until she led old Don Fernandez to the altar, and that was before you were born—"

"Later," said Jerry impatiently. "I'm plowing through this mob looking for somebody. Remember that. If you get track of him first, it's a man named Sommers; Gerald Sommers of High Mesa—"

"There she is; that's her," whispered Elmer Blodgett,

and froze on to his arm. "Tricked out like the Queen of Siam, sort of holding court on the platform. Come ahead."

But Jerry shook him off and went his way.

"Later," he said. "I've got something else on my mind right now."

"On my mind—and in my heart," he might have said, and spoken the truth; for of a sudden the fifteen years of wandering fell away from him and he was back among his boyhood days. He had loved his father, and his father had loved him; it was not coldness but heat which had separated the two. A fiery lot were the men of the Sommers tribe, good lovers, strong haters, staunch friends, eager strikers of lusty blows. With them it was no new thing for a father and son to come in swift passionate heat to an abrupt parting of the ways. It was "Damn you, sir," and "Hell take you, sir," a door slammed and the ending of an old, well-loved order of things.

Just now Jerry Boyne allowed himself a flick of pure sentiment. He recalled little things, the sort of things which are so often laid away as in lavender. He mused that a few minutes ago, while his monoplane circled high above, there must have been many eyes turned aloft if for but a moment; that among others his father had no doubt looked up, then down, with no thought: "Here comes my kid home again, back around the world to see me." Spots of color tinged Jerry's tanned cheeks; his eyes were very bright as he anticipated the moment when they would rest on the tall, erect form of his father, when his hand would touch the other's shoulder, when he'd say: "Hello, Dad. I hear you've got a horse in the running today. I'm betting on him."

Beyond the cottonwood grove he caught a glimpse of a very high, businesslike, white adobe wall. There were sturdy iron gates set in it near the corners, and through them and above the wall itself he saw something of the sprawling, red-tiled house. Here was a natural oasis which the almost unlimited wealth of Doña Luisa Blanco Fernandez, who used to be Louise White, a dancing girl, had made into a green place where spring-time loitered under a blazing summer sky. There were trees and shrubs and flowers on all hands. He saw the race course where a few men began to gather, and turned in that direction to look into the faces of men and women who strolled in couples or small intimate groups.

It was with an actual start that he recognized in one of these small knots of humanity the red-headed young fellow with whom he had had an encounter in Nacional. But this one's eye did not chance to meet his, and Jerry shrugged and went on. If he had forgotten the chap's very existence this long, it was just as well to ignore it a while longer; for, not only was Jerry burning with impatience to come upon his father, but also it struck him that any unfinished business between him and the sort of man who spun on his heel and smashed you while you were not looking was entirely a private and personal matter which, like his introduction to his hostess, could wait.

"He's somewhere in reach of my voice," he mused, hurrying on. "It seems funny to be so near each other again. I could yell out: 'Hey, Dad, where are you? It's Jerry come home!' and he'd hear me. I'll bump into him any minute."

And, looking off to the side where he had caught a glimpse of three men beyond a clump of young acacia trees, he did bump into someone. It was a girl who must have been paying as scant attention to her pathway as he. A startled exclamation burst from her, and Jerry whipped back, snatching off his hat and saying contritely:

"Hope I didn't hurt you? I am terribly—"

Only then did he get a good, square look into her flushed face, and he stopped in the midst of a casual apology. There are girls and girls, as Jerry Boyne very well knew; and still other girls, if you like. But never until now had it dawned on him that this everyday old world of ours held anywhere a girl like her. Not a girl of mere flesh and blood like all others, but one distilled from the essences of sweet flowers; there were roses in her cheeks and violets in her eyes—

"May I pass, please? Perhaps you haven't noticed that this path is very narrow?"

And still Jerry stared. That odd sensation which is so familiar to all of us at moments gripped and bewildered him; he told himself that of course until this second he had never laid eyes on her, yet it seemed none the less that already he had known her—somewhere—sometime, long, long ago—

She lifted her brows very slightly. He approved of her expression; also he saw her eyes better. They were far lovelier than any mere violets, not in fact to be spoken of in the same breath with that flower. Sweeter than pansies; gray; were there little golden flecks in them, or was that a trick of the sun?

"I asked if I might pass."

"I'll be all right in just a minute," said Jerry.

"Oh! You are ill?" she cried swiftly.

"Look here— I'm sorry I was so clumsy; I guess I was looking over my shoulder. But you're not hurt, are you? Fine! Tell me; surely I have known you some-where—"

"Oh!" It was quite another sort of "Oh!" altogether. Whereas the first had breathed a sudden sympathy, this one was a frozen "Oh!", as friendly as an icicle. And she elaborated: "I think that that is the very stupidest obser-vation that stupid men ever make, don't you? But I shall answer it. No, señor, we have never known each other. Not anywhere."

She slipped by him and, rapidly twirling the big straw hat in her hands, soon passed from his sight.

"I seem to feel," he remarked as he went on his way, "that today is going to be a day of days."

His search carried him down to the racetrack with its two grandstands, a tiny one for the chosen few who were invited to sit with quondam Louise White, dancing girl, now "Empress," a larger one for the riffraff. Half a dozen times he was treated to a start as some pair of straight, soldierly shoulders caught his eye, but each time he shook his head and sought on.

"A day of days," he told himself, and smiled. "And I can wait a minute or so. What a fool I've been, anyway! And now that I've held off all these years I'm fool

24

enough to get impatient over another five minutes."

A second time he saw the red-head of the landing field; the fellow now was in the midst of a laughing bevy of women, yet kept staring off over their heads as though he, too, sought someone.

A second time also he saw the girl of the gray eyes. She could have seen him, so close did she pass, but very obviously did not; so obviously in fact, that he doubted. She was hurrying, waving her big straw hat to someone, and Jerry looked sharply to see who that someone might be. When he saw he stopped short. There was a man who, once seen, was never to be forgotten; a man who somehow conveyed the impression of being tall, whereas he was nothing of the sort, an old fellow who carried himself with an air. Hair and imperial were snowy white, eyes as black as ink. He dressed all in white flannels with a white silk shirt and tall-heeled black boots and a broad-brimmed soft black hat. At a glance you knew him for what he was, a Spaniard and a gentleman.

"Señor Antonio Costa! And she— By thunder, I do know her! His little granddaughter. We played two whole days together, too! She must have been nearly ten, then! Wonder if she remembers?"

For it had been from Señor Costa that Jerry's father had bought the High Mesa. Memories clung thick about the whole affair. Jerry, the impulsive boy, had been deeply stirred; so much had happened. A day of wandering about with the little girl—a good-by—another day with her some two or three weeks later—the closing of the deal for the big ranch at High Mesa—and a cer-

25

tain explosion which had blown Jerry half around the world.

Well, he'd be talking with her again soon now, saying, "Look here, young woman, every man who says he has known you before isn't just trying to flirt with you!" Watching the light of memory dawn in her dear sweet eyes. Yes, all that soon. But where had his father taken himself? Why, among a mere handful of a couple of hundred people, was he so hard to find?

He began asking, stopping a man here and there.

"Pardon, I am looking for a man named Sommers; Mr. Gerald Sommers. Do you happen to know him? Have you seen him anywhere?"

It appeared that everyone knew Gerald Sommers.

"I saw him only a moment ago," said one. "Oh, sure, he is here." And another exclaimed: "Sommers? Of course! He was on his way, I think, to pay his respects to the Empress."

Jerry again circled the dance platform, looking swiftly and keenly into the faces of all men, ignoring many a bright curious glance turned upon him from some lively young woman who also hoped to find this a day of days. From a slight distance he made out the spot where Señora Fernandez stood "holding court," as Elmer Blodgett had said of her. There was no doubting which one was "the Empress." She would have attracted attention in any gathering, as vivid as a splash of crimson on a drab background. As proud as Lucifer, vain and arrogant, contemptuous of convention, a law unto herself and unto the many hundreds who in one way and another were dependent upon her, she carried herself in exactly that manner which a former cabaret dancer would almost inevitably associate with the resounding title which the border bestowed upon her.

She was a woman of fifty or thereabouts, but you did not guess that fact until you came close and looked straight into her eyes. Bold, cold eyes they were, an icy blue, as keen as knives, and a full half century old in shrewdness and disillusionment. But, before he looked into them, Jerry picked her out by her dress. She wore a scarlet jacket, made to her own taste, with a broad belt and a flashing silver buckle, riding breeches, and high, gleaming yellow boots, a low-crowned, broad-brimmed white hat with a long straight feather—and carried in her small, hard hands, a cruel looking riding whip. Beyond all this she was of medium stature, slender and sinewy and very light and quick upon her feet.

All this he took in at a glance, and his eyes sped on, taking stock of those surrounding her. They were the old Spaniard whom he had recognized a few moments earlier, Señor Antonio Costa, and his little granddaughter, a young man with a tiny silken black mustache and prominent blue eyes half-veiled by drooping lids, a burly looking brute of a fellow, dressed like a Mexican *vaquero,* even to the long spurs, and two others. These two were Jerry's old friend, Elmer Blodgett, and his more recent acquaintance, the red-headed horseman of the landing field. But nowhere did Jerry see his father.

He was just on the verge of drawing back and seeking elsewhere when Elmer saw him and called out to him so sharply that all those about the Empress turned and stared at him.

27

"Hi, Jerry! This way. I've been telling Her Majesty about you. She wants to look you over."

"Of all the asses," muttered Jerry under his breath; but, since there was nothing else to be done, he went forward to be presented. At least, he thought, there'd be a word or two spoken with old Antonio Costa's little granddaughter, the first of many, many words to be had with her before the promise of life fulfilled itself. He was conscious of her bright eyes on him as he drew nearer, then of the fact that she had turned her back and was saying something laughingly to the red-headed fellow at her side.

"Ladies and gents," Elmer Blodgett declaimed expansively, "meet Mr. Jerry Boyne, late of Argentina, friend of my bosom; Jerry Boyne that I've known pretty near since the time we were neighbors in our cradles." He grasped Jerry by the arm and dragged him face to face with the Empress. "Señora Fernandez," he ran on, "meet my old pal, Jerry Boyne, a wild boy maybe, but a square guy."

The Empress stared at Jerry coldly. It was clear that she liked to size men up for herself and that Elmer's effusive chatter was of no more effect on her liking or disliking the stranger than if it were a light wind blowing. Jerry, returning her look, saw the fifty years in her eyes and saw also the small hard lines in her face. Once, some twenty or thirty years earlier, she had been a very pretty woman; now she looked hard and coarse—coarsened, he judged her, not so much by the passing of time as by unbridled passions.

Of a sudden there came a strange softening to that

28

hard face, a quick smile to the red mouth and a flash of warmth to the keen blue eyes.

"Shake, Jerry," she said, and put out her strong hand to meet his in a powerful grip. "You're at home on the Empire. Take what you want; it's yours."

Jerry bowed and thanked her, and his eyes went involuntarily hurrying to Antonio Costa's granddaughter. If only the old Spanish phrase, adopted by the Empress, meant all that it said!

"I've just met a few of the Empress's friends," continued Elmer, still gripping Jerry's arm and steering him in the way he should go, "and I'll pass the introductions along. Mr. Costa, meet my old pal, Jerry Boyne. Miss Costa—"

"Beryl!" exclaimed Jerry, and made them stare, the girl most of all. "Not Miss Costa at all; Miss Beryl Blake!"

She looked at him wonderingly, then flushed hotly. Nothing seemed clearer to her than that the fresh young man who had bumped into her so awkwardly a little while ago had gone around asking who she was, and now meant to make some further pretence of having met her before.

"Right you are!" cried Elmer Blodgett. "My mistake. The name is Miss Blake. Miss Blake, meet old Jerry Boyne." Miss Blake inclined her head—or merely almost did so? Elmer rushed on with his introductions, still manhandling his captive. Confronting the youngish gentleman with the swollen eyes and lazy lids, a dandified young simpleton who effected a swagger which resulted in being only a mince, he announced: "Señor

Charles Fernandez, son of Her Majesty, widely and affectionately known as 'Prince Charlie.' "

Prince Charlie sneered and did not offer to shake hands.

Still Elmer babbled on. The brutish looking fellow in the cowboy outfit down to the long roweled Mexican spurs, was presented. It appeared that he was known far and wide as El Bravo. He too was an American and his name was really Frank Smith; he was nothing less than the Empress's right hand—

"Left hand, if you say so, old boy," snapped the Empress. "I'm my own right, by God, and I guess the world knows it."

"And now we're all friends," said Elmer, and beamed right and left. "I don't have to introduce you two red-heads, do I? This is the man you were looking for, eh, Jerry? You've known each other of old, I take it?"

Jerry's dark eyes for a moment rested on the reddish-brown ones of the man who so short a time ago had knocked him flat.

"Looking for me?" said the other coolly, and shrugged.

"Of course he was," broke in Elmer. "You're Gerald Sommers, ain't you?"

A curt nod said, "Yes," and a flash of the reddish-brown eyes demanded, "And what business may that be of yours?"

"I was looking for a Mr. Gerald Hand Sommers," said Jerry, puzzled, wondering how this fellow came by the family name.

"Looking for me?" said the red-headed fellow a

second time. Then he laughed. "I believe we did run into each other once, didn't we? There may be a little bit of unfinished business between us. I'll be glad to go into it at the proper time. This is hardly the time and place, is it?"

"You are Gerald Hand Sommers?" said Jerry dully.

"That's my name. You'll have no trouble finding me when you want me. I'm not skipping the country, you know."

Jerry stared at him incredulously. Slowly a strange feeling crept over him that the promise of the day was a lie, that eager hopes were coming down in ruins and ash heaps.

"There was another Gerald Hand Sommers," he said heavily, "an older man. He would be nearly sixty now. He lived at High Mesa—"

"He has been dead nearly five years. He was my father."

Jerry opened his lips to shout, "You lie!" but for the moment he held his peace. So great an amazement swept over him that he stared at the faces about him and was tempted to believe that this was all dream-stuff, faces in a nightmare. He heard the fellow who called himself by Jerry's own name laughing and talking with Beryl Blake; he saw her look a moment curiously back at him, then stroll away with her obvious admirer. He heard as from afar the other voices, the Empress saying something in an undertone to El Bravo, her "left hand," and Elmer's babbling voice entertaining the old Spaniard.

Dead. That, after all, was the thing which mattered—and stunned. The shock of it was all the greater because, during his search for his father here in this holiday crowd, Jerry had been so sure of him, had in his fancy seen him so clearly, a man hale and hearty, a man of the finest, the father he had turned his back on in wrath, the father whom through everything he had never ceased to love. Dead!

"I can't get it," he kept saying within himself, over and over.

Presently Elmer Blodgett gravitated to the Empress, and Jerry stepped swiftly to the side of old Señor Costa.

"Will you favor me with a few words in private, Señor?" he asked gravely. "I am sure you could answer a question or two for me if you would be so kind."

The old man regarded him calmly. He had the trick, while not appearing unfriendly, of holding himself aloof. His glance had the effect of reminding Jerry Boyne that a mere casual introduction by such a man as Elmer Blodgett meant a degree less than nothing at all. Yet, though he might hold himself apart, none comported himself with greater native courtesy than did Antonio Costa.

"Of course, surely, Señor," he answered simply, and strolled away with Jerry, excusing himself from his hostess with a profound bow. "It is something about the elder Mr. Sommers?" he asked presently.

Jerry nodded. Costa regarded him with a flicker of interest, so suddenly grim and bleak had the younger man's face gone.

"About his death," began Jerry.

Costa sighed.

"A very fine man. It was a tragedy. Nearly five years

ago as his son has told you. He was killed. Someone shot him. No one knows who did it."

Jerry stared away across the green fields of the Empire and off into the farther northern distances where the little blue hills no longer laughed and invited but seemed to withdraw and dwindle in a gathering mist.

"He was a friend?" asked Señor Costa gently.

Jerry started.

"Tell me about this young man who seems to have the same name. An adopted son? Taking the place of that other son who quarreled with his father and went away?"

"No, Señor; not a son of adoption. The real son. Yes, he and his father quarreled; he ran away. He was a boy then, perhaps twelve years old. Then his father died; killed as I have told you. He was wealthy; his son was his heir. The lawyers advertised. In time the boy, whom you met just now, returned. That is all."

"All? Good God, it's enough!" cried Jerry furiously. "Look here, Señor Costa, I—"

"Yes?" said the old man, his interest intrigued by Jerry's manner rather than by his insufficient words.

"Then this fellow," snapped Jerry, jabbing an angry thumb in the general direction taken by the red-headed chap who had just now wandered off with Beryl Blake, "is now the owner of High Mesa?"

"I see that you are strongly interested, Señor." Don Antonio proceeded to build himself a thin cigarette with quick slender fingers. "It is a long story, but for you I will make it a short one. The High Mesa was long ago my home, an old Spanish grant. I was born there, Señor.

33

I had a great affection for that place." He lighted his cigarette and shrugged. "Yet circumstances were such that I decided to sell High Mesa. I sold it to Mr. Sommers; that was nearly fifteen years ago—"

"I know," said Jerry.

"You know? Well, perhaps you know that I went away? To Spain, in fact. Later I— Circumstances altered, Señor. I returned here with the one purpose of buying back my old home. That was shortly after the death of Gerald Sommers, the elder, and the return of his son. So now I answer your question. High Mesa is mine again."

"You bought High Mesa—from *him?*"

"Yes, Señor Boyne. From the younger Mr. Sommers. Now have I answered all your questions? If there is anything else—"

Jerry surprised him with a short laugh so utterly devoid of mirth that the old man's fine white brows shot up wonderingly.

"Thank you, there is nothing else. Later? Perhaps. *¿Quien sabe?* Who, in fact, knows anything? You have been very kind."

Antonio Costa inclined his head and moved away. When abruptly he turned and looked back he saw Jerry Boyne standing very still, his hat crumpled in his hands, his head thrown back, his eyes turned with a strange light in them toward the far blue hills.

34

CHAPTER III

A T HIGH NOON, WITH THE SMELL OF BARBECUING beef heavy on the still air and the aroma of bubbling coffee stealing upward through the blue hazes which hung over the glowing pits, Elmer Blodgett came seeking Jerry, and finally found him perched on one of the cottonwood poles of a corral.

"Hi, Jerry!" he sang out. "What's eating you? I've been hunting you high and low. They're just opening kegs of beer like it was water. Hop down, young man, and follow me. What do you think you're doing up there anyhow?"

"Thinking," said Jerry, and looked keenly at his old friend, wondering somewhat vaguely what directions the circuitous Elmer's thoughts would dart off into if he knew just what the thinking was all about.

"Thinking!" snorted Elmer. "On a day like this? Don't you know there's times to ponder and times to pick your rosebuds while you can get 'em free for the taking?"

"The beer can wait, can't it? I want to talk with you."

Blodgett put his head to one side and narrowed his eyes.

"Something up?" he queried eagerly. He climbed puffing up to a place beside Jerry. "Yeah, it'll keep; the old dame sure knows how to do herself proud; they're hauling it up in trucks."

"How long have you been here, Elmer?"

"About ten days, around Nacional. Why?"

"What's holding you in a place like this? I asked that once and you just looked foxy. What's the answer—between friends?"

Elmer laughed and began rubbing his plump hands together.

"Between friends, I'm looking for an investment. Heard of an opening and have been just fooling around getting the lay of the land. It's this way, Jerry. There's a gent not so far away from this stock-corral right now that's got a reputation for losing money at any sort of game the other fellow cares to mention. If it was cards, horse racing, cock-fighting, dice or dominoes or checkers, he'd fall all over himself to contribute. Me, as maybe you know, I don't mind a little friendly game of poker now and then." He flung out his hands with a little gesture of, "And there you are!"

But when Jerry made no rejoinder but merely sat frowning into empty space, Elmer shifted, cast him a sidelong glance and finally burst out in full confidence:

"It's that old Spanish fandango, Jerry. The chin-whiskered hidalgo, would you believe it? Filthy with money, the old boy is, and a sport of sports, if you hear it all. He'd as lieve lose a thousand bucks as I would flick off a bit of fingernail I didn't need. Easy come, easy go, I guess. Anyway, here I am."

"Played with him yet?"

"Hell, no!" cried Elmer. "You don't know the old don yet if you think any hombre can go up and grab him by the flipper and say, 'Come ahead, old rooster, let's try our luck.' Ever hear the word 'exclusive,' Jerry? It means 'shut the world out and lock the door.' That word was made for this same old Don Spanish. I ain't had a look in. But now? Today we meet, Don Antonio Aranda Costa and Mr. Elmer Blodgett, moving in the same high circles, so to speak, formally introduced and all that. From now on, set back and watch. Come to me any time next week and I'll lend you a fortune."

"Exclusive?" said Jerry. "I'd feel that, too, if I didn't find him running with this bunch. This Empress of yours—nothing exclusive there, is there, Elmer?"

"You're wrong, boy. Friendly maybe she is in a broad and spacious, don't-give-a-damn way, but she keeps her head up and steps apart same as old Costa. Right now, for example, while the humdrum eats with its fingers and guzzles beer out of tin cups, where's she? In the castle over yonder, Jerry Boyne, foregathering with a bunch of the élite, picking chicken bones and swigging high grade liquor. Don't get her wrong; she's a mixer all right, but she draws the line of what they call *noblesse oblige*. Why, she says, 'Elmer, howdy!' to me as nice as you please out in the open air; but do you think I'd get any show to put my hoofs on the carpets? You just bet she's exclusive, the way you learn to be in a Broadway café. But I'm nosing in on 'em, Jerry boy, I'm nosing in; and, like I said, all you got to do is look me up next week and I'll lend you enough good long green to go buy you a new flying machine."

"Thanks for the offer, old-timer, and most of all for the full confidence. It would appear that you will have a little extra time on your hands, while waiting for the big game to come off; also I happen to recall that you told me a while back that you had been doing a little 'listening around,' picking up a few scraps of information."

"Right you are, Jerry. Before placing his bets, Mr. Blodgett always feels his way, so to speak. And am I correct in assuming that you have just developed a nice lively curiosity about something?"

"I've got a pretty messy sort of story to confide in you," said Jerry thoughtfully, and Elmer Blodgett leaned forward so eagerly to hear it that he came close to toppling off the fence. "No, I'll not spill it now; there's no time for it and besides I'd rather you didn't know a thing about it while you're making a few investigations. What you don't know, you can't give away."

Elmer looked both disappointed and hurt.

"I'm not the guy to snitch," he remarked with dignity.

"It isn't that." Jerry laid a firm hand on the plump knee. "I want a talk with you later on, maybe tonight. In the meantime, Elmer, will you in your own inimitable style glean a bit of information for me? There are reasons why I'd prefer not seeming interested."

"I knew it!" murmured Elmer, his voice hushed, his eyes bright with that old familiar suspicious look. "The minute I glimpsed you fooling along the border with a plane, I said to myself—"

"Yes, I know. You said it to me, too. Well, for the present you can suppose what you like—that I'm running booze or smuggling Chinks. Meantime will you gather all the information you can about—"

He hesitated. He couldn't bring himself to say "Gerald Sommers." But Elmer spoke it for him, swiftly supplying the name.

"It's that guy Sommers, ain't it? There's some mystery there, eh, Jerry? You knew his old man, and now you find him popped off, a bullet in his gizzard and the young fellow up to something shady? Am I right?"

"He's the man," Jerry conceded. "I take it that already you know something of him. You intimated as much."

"All I wanted to know was what sort of horses he owns. There's racing this afternoon, and I'm leaning toward placing a small, conservative bet or so. I'll hand you a hot one, kid. Bet a few beans on Lady Beryl; that's Sommers's pony for the second race."

"Lady Beryl, eh?" Jerry began hunting a cigarette.

"She's it. Named for Señorita Fandango, what? Well, that's no never-mind of ours. In the same race the old don has an entry of his own; so has the Empress. It'll be some race, boy. But take my prescription and clean up. Yeah, I've been listening around. Sommers ought to know horses, from what I hear, and he's backing his own mare in the good old-fashioned way; I'd say he was betting all the way down to his shirt on her."

But Jerry's interest had been a flash only; he was not concerned just now with horses and racing.

"That's all you know of him? Maybe, without seeming too particularly interested in the man, you could feel around and find out a good deal about him?"

"Sub rosa stuff?" Elmer laughed his soft, throaty laugh. "The first few toddling steps the baby Elmer took were in rubber-soled creepers! You say find out a good deal about this sport? I'll dig up everything; I'll tell you later if he's got a gold fill in his back molar or a hangnail on his little toe; how long he's been here and where he came from—"

"Do that!" said Jerry so earnestly that again Elmer was galvanized, a purely delicious thrill running down his backbone. "Exactly that, Elmer. And all about his inheritance at High Mesa—and the sale to Señor Costa."

"Leave it to Elmer! And— Sh! We're due for an interruption. And I'll add just this to the matter," he ran on in a voice for any to hear, "that no better beer ever came out of Germany. And I ought to know; for three months I operated a snug little brewery all of my own down in Mexico City, and— Hello, here comes Mr. Smith. I was just telling Jerry—"

The burly cowboy, known as El Bravo and acknowledged by the Empress as her left hand, his approach heralded by the clank of his long spurs, stopped at the corral.

"You, Jerry Boyne," he said curtly. "Señora Fernandez wants you up at the house. She is having some friends in for dinner and says to fetch you."

Jerry looked down on him curiously. He was thinking it odd that the Empress had invited him; also he was intrigued by the messenger himself. El Bravo impressed him as being at once the most powerful and most vicious looking brute he had ever seen, and he had encountered many a raw bucko mate and manhandling mine boss in his wanderings up and down. This fellow's shoulders were inordinately broad and thick, his muscular arms long and equipped with enormous, hairy hands; his thin-lipped mouth and cold eyes somehow managed to convey the impression of a snake, cold-blooded and treacherous and cruel.

"Me?" said Jerry with a start, realizing that he was staring.

"You," said El Bravo, who had stood staring expressionlessly. "Now. She's waiting."

"Gosh!" murmured Elmer Blodgett. "Hop to it, Jerry. You always were the lucky kid."

"Thanks," said Jerry to El Bravo. "Thank Señora Fernandez for me, will you? But you might explain to her that I'm with a friend I haven't seen for a long time."

"Don't be an ass," snorted Elmer.

"You can bring your friend with you."

"Not if he's not invited," retorted Jerry. There was something about El Bravo's manner that he resented; the fellow seemed to think that he, as the Empress's left hand, had but to crook a finger and have any man come running.

"Well, then, he is invited," said El Bravo, grown more surly than ever. If there was any reading a man's thought in such cold hard eyes it might be suspected that he agreed with Elmer in naming Jerry an ass, and further found difficulty in restraining himself from saying as much.

"Invited? Me?" exclaimed Elmer, and leaped nimbly down from his perch.

El Bravo shrugged and turned away contemptuously. Over his massive shoulder he said carelessly:

"The Señora said that if Jerry Boyne refused to come alone, then to tell him to bring his friend along."

Elmer's eyes rounded, then the left one closed in a wink behind El Bravo's broad back.

"Watch that dame, Jerry, old son!" he whispered dramatically. "Can she read a man like a kid gloms on to the Sunday comics? Can she peer into the future, knowing from the cut of a man's eye the way he's bound to jump? Watch her, Jerry, old horse. This sudden shining up to you, what's it mean? There's an Ethiopian in the coal bin, and maybe it's just as well I am invited, just to watch over you. Coming down? You ain't thinking of holding out on her, are you?" he asked in sudden alarm.

Jerry slipped slowly down from his place.

"Hardly," he said lightly. "Come ahead; let's follow the genial Mr. Smith."

El Bravo was waiting for them at the entrance through the high adobe wall. The iron gate swung open for the three to pass through, swung shut behind them; Jerry had a glimpse of the gatekeeper, a swarthy, Indian type of fellow, curiously garbed. He wore a sort of cloak or ample cape lined with scarlet, high glistening black boots, a peaked many-gallon hat—and Jerry saw a flash of steel at the fellow's belt.

"The Empress sure has got the swell ideas about things," remarked Blodgett affably. But Jerry only nodded absently and El Bravo appeared not to have heard, and the trio went on after that in silence.

At a long table in an open patio, lunch was already at its beginnings. Jerry saw the empty chair at the Empress's right hand and experienced a little flick of astonishment as he realized that she was beckoning him to take it. On her left was Don Antonio Costa who looked up at him

42

with just the hint of lifted brows.

"Squat, Jerry, and be one of the gang," Señora Fernandez invited with a pleasant, friendly smile. "There's a cocktail waiting for you. Drink hearty."

As he took his place he flashed a photographic look up and down the table. He saw young Charles Fernandez at the far end and noted that El Bravo was just taking a seat at his left elbow; also he marked that Beryl Blake sat at young Fernandez's right and was under the full battery of his prominent eyes, and looked flushed and uncomfortable under them too, Jerry thought. Half way between the two ends of the table, wedged in between a couple of young women whom Jerry did not know, sat the young man of the red hair.

It was a meal of much lively chatter, of three kinds of wine, of blaring music coming from a hidden but not sufficiently remote stringed orchestra, of reckless bounty in rich, highly-spiced foods. In effects, the wine and the boisterous music vied with each other, loosening tongues and lifting voices; before the end it was all din and babble, with shouts through the general confusion. For Jerry it was, most of all, an occasion for recording a number of queer, fragmentary impressions.

There were the servants; one wanted to count them! The former Louise White, now the relict of the plutocrat Ignacio Fernandez, had as Elmer Blodgett was so quick to note, "swell ideas about things." When she spent money, as she did extravagantly, it was her determination to have that money make a showing. Crystal goblets, cut glass, solid silver. Rare French wines and

43

brandies. Two men at the back of her chair. Liveries such as a Louise White, become Señora Fernandez, would invent.

At the far end of the table sat her son, "the beloved Prince Charlie," leering at Beryl Blake, twisting his glass, sipping, plucking at his loose lower lip, sipping—bending intimately close to her, murmuring—and Beryl, still flushed, leaning away from him. At his side El Bravo, silent, seeming to heed no word that was spoken the whole time, yet as watchful as a hawk. Watchful for what? Somehow—it was hard to say exactly how, yet there it was—he was like a bodyguard. Prince Charlie's bodyguard.

Marooned midway on one side of the table, the man of the red hair, who called himself Gerald Sommers and claimed to be the son of the man who had owned High Mesa, ate sparingly and drank with a rush. His eyes were forever straying to where Beryl sat and where Prince Charlie's eyes crawled over her.

Just across the table from Jerry was the old Spaniard, urbane, giving every attention to his hostess—yet on fire within. Now and then a flash of his night-black eyes betrayed him.

"Tell me about yourself, Jerry."

He started. Señora Fernandez had a little fan in her strong, sun-browned hand and tapped him on the arm.

"About me?" He shrugged. "Here, in this company, at the most interesting ranch I ever saw—"

She leaned closer and her words were for him alone, lost to all others in the general clamor.

"What's this about you and Red Handsome?"

"Red Handsome?" At first he didn't know whom she meant.

She made a gesture with her fan.

"Young Sommers. Nicknames settle along the border as thick as flies. His comes naturally enough. To begin with, he's the best looking man here. On top of that there's the name, Gerald Hand Sommers. It's only a step to call him Red Handsome."

"Yes," agreed Jerry. "And by the way, I understand he has a horse in the running this afternoon—"

"Damn his horse," said the Empress emphatically. "You don't switch me off the track that easy, Jerry. I asked, what's this about you and him?"

He stiffened. Did the woman have some uncanny sense of the things she could not possibly know? He had for the moment forgotten the encounter in Nacional.

"I don't get you," he said guardedly.

She looked at him contemptuously.

"Are you such a fool as to suppose one man can knock another down in the morning and word of it not be all over creation by this time of day?"

"Oh," said Jerry, relieved. Then, with an assumption of indifference he satisfied her curiosity. "I came down out of the sky in an old plane almost on top of him. His horse jumped and he spilled out of the saddle, whereupon some girls giggled and your Mr. Red Handsome took a wallop at me. When I came to he was on his way over here."

She seemed puzzled.

"You're a pretty hefty looking boy yourself," she said bluntly. "Not yellow, are you?"

45

"That's no question to ask any man," he smiled at her. "If he were, he'd not admit it, and—"

"If he wasn't, he'd dodge the issue like you're doing! All right, that's a good enough answer. Never saw him before, did you?"

"Never. I just blew in, you know."

"Why?" she demanded sharply. "What brought you here?"

"On my way," he answered easily. "Up from the south. Finished down there in the Argentine; fed up on it. Headed back north to the land where the eagle screams. Had to come down for gas, ran into an old friend—and here I am. For which," he added with a little bow, "I am duly grateful to a kind fate and Elmer Blodgett."

She narrowed her clever eyes to study him.

"A prowler, huh? A foot-loose bird with the itch in his heel? A boy who has been through things, or I'm betting wrong. Scars on the backs of his hands and maybe under his shirt. Want a job, Jerry?"

He hesitated but only long enough to ask himself what she was up to and to admit that he hadn't the vaguest idea.

"Thanks, if that's a tentative offer—"

"Tentative be damned. It's open and shut. I can use you."

"How do you know you can?"

"Men like you are no foreign language to Louise," she said with a snap of the fan. She tossed the thing from her, over her shoulder without turning, and one of her servitors caught it expertly. Jerry wondered whether that was a trick of hers and the man's. "And when I say

46

a job, I don't have a bunch of pennies in mind, either; nor yet a few Mex pesos. I mean money."

"Thanks outright, then. Right now I'm not looking for a job. I—"

"Heeled?" she demanded.

"Yes. Not so heavy with funds that I'm apt to sink deep in the sand, but in a position to take a little lay-off."

He reached for an olive and allowed himself a glance along the table; it was hard to keep his eyes away from the other end. This time he saw Beryl cast a helpless, almost pleading look toward Red Handsome, and saw Prince Charlie glare. Instinctively he turned swiftly to see whether the Empress had marked that byplay, and realized immediately that she had missed none of it.

"What have you got against Red Handsome?" he demanded abruptly, attacking the woman with her own sort of weapon.

"You are a clever boy," she said, and shrugged. She emptied her glass, watched it being refilled and lighted a cigarette. "Can you stick around a day or so as my guest? I might answer that question and we might find other things to talk about. I'm not so sure that you wouldn't like to work with me. You notice I pay you the compliment of saying with me, not for me?"

"I'm impressed. It would be interesting to know—"

"No, you don't, Jerry Boyne! No pumping unless you mean business. But if you'll hang around for a few days—"

"I'm full of appreciation, but it happens that I can't. Elmer Blodgett and I have had a little talk; he thinks he's spotted what he calls an investment—"

Just then there was a small commotion outside, angry voices muttering, and almost immediately one of the men in the red-lined cloaks came hesitantly into the patio, his troubled eyes turned to the Empress.

"Well?" she cried sharply in Spanish. "What sort of hell has broke loose now, Pedro?"

He came to her side and answered in a rush of words meant for her alone; still Jerry heard nearly all that he said.

"It's that ranchero from the Little Mesa, young Kingsbury. He is crazy, *por Dios!* He's got a gun; he swears he'll kill somebody unless he sees you right now."

"Kingsbury, huh?" She spoke with a strange, cold sternness; and her eyes, half veiled by her lowered lids, struck Jerry as being every bit as cruel and deadly as El Bravo's. "And they let him through the gate, eh, Pedro?"

Pedro shrugged elaborately; that was no affair of his and he was emphatic in making that point clear. But perhaps he had a kindly feeling for the guard who had let the rancher through, for he explained:

"Kingsbury is crazy, Señora. And he has a gun. He put it in the face of any who stood in his way."

The Empress sneered at him and named him a fat-head. Then she leaned forward in her chair and her eye met El Bravo's. He immediately pushed his chair back and came to her. The table was hushed; a few faces looked alarmed; all were stamped with curiosity. When Señora Fernandez spoke to her henchman, though she did not raise her voice, every word was to be heard clearly across the patio.

"It's that fool Kingsbury," she said, and fell to frowning thoughtfully. "He's outside; on the rampage, got me?"

El Bravo nodded as though here were nothing new, certainly no matter to bring a pleasant meal to a full stop.

"I'll step out for a word with him, Señora," he said, and turned to the door.

"You'll keep your shirt on, El Bravo!" she snapped at him. "Also you'll stand right behind my chair." She turned to the man Pedro. "Go herd that longhorn in— and you keep your eye on him, too."

But Pedro arrived at the doorway only in time to meet young Kingsbury coming in. The rancher barely escaped being a boy; twenty-two or twenty-three, he was a manly looking youngster with a fine, almost cameo face and the eyes of a dreamer—eyes, at this moment, of one whose dreams had led to madness. Dusty with desert travel, haggard, clutching a rifle before him in tense, hard hands, he had the air of being equally ready for murder or self-destruction.

"Well, Kingsbury," said the Empress coldly, "you're here. Speak your piece and let the ladies and gents listen in on the brayings of the pig-headedest jackass in two counties."

"Bob's dead," said the boy savagely, but with a break in his voice. "Know that?"

"And who the devil is Bob?" demanded the woman, with a voice as sharp as the crack of a whip.

49

"Bob! You know— Bob, my brother. He— Damn you! Damn you! You she-devil!"

"Better go slow, Kingsbury," said El Bravo quietly.

"Shut up, El Bravo!" she barked at him. "Let the boy rave on. I've been called a damned sight worse than a she-devil in my time—not by so many that I can remember to my face, though," she added almost under her breath. Then she grew businesslike again. "Shoot the works, kid. So Bob's dead? What's the rest of the story? Bob was a fool like you—"

"Damn you!" he screamed at her the third time, and the rifle began to shake terribly in his hands. Jerry, for one, thought to see murder done that moment—and was pretty sure that it would not be the sneering woman who fell, but the kid himself under El Bravo's swift fire. One just knew that El Bravo was ready—and that he would not miss.

But Kingsbury did not lift his weapon. He glared about him, then moistened his cracked lips and strove for control of his jumping nerves.

"You tried to buy me and Bob out," he said in a queer, hushed voice. "When we wouldn't sell for less than half what the Little Mesa is worth, you tried to hound us into it. You sent a pack of your dirty dogs to drive off our stock, to wreck our waterways, to burn us out—"

"I don't know what you're talking about!"

"Oh, you know well enough. Everybody else knows, too. You've got a cutthroat gang that robs and burns and pillages at your orders. And now—now," he cried chokingly, "you've got Bob, damn you!"

"Dick Kingsbury," said the Empress, her steady gaze

level on his own, "take a tip from me, will you? You're going nuts. You're half drunk, half crazy—" She shrugged. "Better watch your step, kid."

Half drunk? Well, perhaps he was, thought Jerry, watching him keenly. Poor devil. He had gone without sleep, without food, and had, just to keep going, poured too much raw liquor into his agony-shot body.

Young Kingsbury looked at her out of wild, red-flecked eyes.

"Where's Bob?" he demanded harshly.

"Why, man alive, I thought you said he was dead!"

"He is! I know he is. But your murdering curs have hidden him. I'll find him; I'll find him if you've buried him a thousand miles deep; I'll find him riddled with bullets." He pulled himself up, and seemed suddenly to grow as steady as a rock. "Then I'll know, and then I'll start killing. And I'll start at the top! You, woman; you, El Bravo, leader of border ruffians—"

The Empress made a slight gesture. Unnoted by most of the company, two of Pedro's red-cloaked fellows had joined him at the patio entrance. The three stepped swiftly forward, seizing Kingsbury's arms. An instant later he was hustled out and only his screaming voice came back to assure those who had heard that they were not just now awaking from an ugly dream.

"Crazy as a bedbug," said the Empress contemptuously. She stared at her glass a moment, lifted it with steady fingers, then turned swiftly and looked straight into El Bravo's eyes. "Yet he's more apt to hurt himself than anyone else," she concluded thoughtfully. "I know that kind; it wouldn't surprise me if I heard before the

51

day was over that the fool had blown his own brains out. He's a weak sister anyhow."

A queer nervous laugh greeted her words and drew all eyes to the one who laughed at such a time. It was Prince Charlie. His face was deathly white; he was cowering low in his chair as though he had been about to slip under the table; a twitching of his muscles showed him just coming out of the grip of terror.

The Empress created a diversion as she spoke swiftly, singling out Red Handsome.

"Funny about your meeting this morning with Jerry here, Red," she said banteringly. "He's just been telling me about it. How you fell off your horse! And I thought that you considered yourself a fancy rider?"

He shrugged and said coolly:

"Did he tell you the rest of the story?"

She stood up and the others rose with her.

"The rest of the story? How could he? It isn't finished yet, is it? Now, everybody, do what you like best. I've promised Jerry to give him a bird's-eye view of a ranch that is a ranch; any that like can stick along with us." She turned to El Bravo. "Some horses, Frank; and have the *Hawk* ready. Come ahead, Jerry."

Jerry, accompanying her, saw how hurriedly Beryl escaped from the vicinity of Prince Charlie; how Charles himself sat alone at the table, fingering a crumb of bread; how quickly Red Handsome stepped to Beryl's side.

They mounted, half a dozen of them all together, the Empress on a plunging, rearing devil-horse of superb lines and untamed, wild spirit. Two men held the animal

52

for her to mount, then sprang aside and the Empress, with strong hand and sure seat, brought the rangy, bit-fighting sorrel to some semblance of control.

"A ranch that is a ranch!" Jerry Boyne, knowing something of large holdings, of the enormous cattle ranches and plantations of South America, was still set wondering by what he came to glimpse during the next hour of this well-named "Empire." At the foot of the hill on which the big house stood, all but hidden among spreading pepper trees, was a small town with its three score of adobe huts, its store and saloon, dance hall, post office, blacksmith shop—all the Empress's creation, all pouring rents and revenues into her purse. She retained an army of cowboys and workmen; she paid them promptly and well; and with clock-like regularity the money came rolling back to her.

At the edge of the village, in a bare, level field, was a long shed. They arrived at it in time to see a big new biplane being trundled out, the *Hawk*.

"I'm modern," laughed Señora Fernandez. "Modern in an ancient civilization, no? That helps me to get the edge on things. Climb in and I'll take you for a ride."

Due south they sped a full twenty miles; due east forty miles; northward twenty; westward forty and returned to the starting place. "All mine," cried the woman with a flash of her eyes. "Over half a million acres, Jerry; a good eight hundred square miles, and what do you think of that? Think it over—and the chance I'm offering you to work with me."

During the flight he had seen great desert stretches which he fancied were not worth paying taxes on. But also he had seen fertile tracts, reservoirs, cattle innumerable, bands of sheep, tall silos like watch towers, irrigated alfalfa lands and, tucked away among little hills, two other clusters of buildings, villages sufficient unto themselves and keeping a broad stream of money rolling on and on.

"I married a cagy old don when I was only a kid, twenty-two and hoofing it on Broadway," she told him when they alighted and went up into their saddles again for the short canter to the grandstand at the racetrack. "I started in just to pull his leg, as any girl naturally would, and wound up—how do you suppose? Respecting him, that's what; he was all there. Could have been the head of the army; had his chance once and maybe twice to be president. Not him! He used his power, used his influence—and hogged land. It's mine now; yes, my boy, the power and the influence along with it. Go down to Mexico City, nose around with the high-ups and ask 'em about the Señora Luisa Blanco Fernandez! Will they pull off their hats? Well, they better!"

Altogether Jerry's "great day" was one of kaleidoscopic impressions. What had he to do with racing? The first race swept by and he was scarcely aware of it. There was Prince Charlie, lowering, plucking at his lip, sitting between two of the red-cloaked men. Beryl had escaped him and was with her grandfather, with Red Handsome leaning over her. The second race came; he caught Elmer Blodgett's eye endeavoring to remind him that here was the chance to do a little betting. Red Handsome had gone from Beryl's side; that was because he was riding his own mount. Señor Costa was all lively interest. He had a horse entered, also, and no doubt was backing it. The Empress said to Jerry: "Don't you ever bet? I've got the slickest little four-year-old you ever saw that's going to run away with the race. Go see if anybody'll give you a chance to clean up. Take any odds you can get. It's a sure thing."

He shook his head and yet felt a stir of interest as he watched the six horses get away for a red-hot half mile. It was a beautiful start marred only by the erratic behavior of the horse on the outside. It became unmanageable just as the pistol cracked, began a wild lunging, whirled—and charged off the wrong way. The Empress burst into such a stream of curses that Jerry, though he knew better than to expect soft words from her lips at such a moment, was startled. The boy up on the refractory mount wore a scarlet jacket. There went the Empress's "sure shot," lost at the start.

The field swept by and Red Handsome, doing a pretty bit of riding on a lean, powerful roan, led from the jump and to the end. Beryl was on her feet, waving her big white straw hat, excited and eager. Her grandfather looked up at her, smiled and shrugged.

"Here I lose two thousand pesos, and you cheer!" Jerry heard him say lightly.

"I had that race in my pocket," muttered Señora Fernandez angrily, "and that pock-marked son of an Indian dog threw it away. *Pedro!*"

"*Sí, Señora,*" answered Pedro, and was ready to start even before the Empress's swift gesture assured him that he had read her mind aright.

"I don't think the boy pulled the race," said Jerry, not

liking the cold gleam in her eye. "The poor devil just got rattled—"

"That's his bad luck then," she said curtly, and sat frowning moodily, watching Pedro as he hastened down to the race course and toward the slight, stooped figure in the scarlet jacket. He caught the boy by the arm, said a sharp word or so and came piloting him back to the grandstand.

"Before God, Señora, it was not my fault!" The boy's flat, deeply pitted face, redeemed from utter ugliness by a pair of large, limpid eyes, black and fathomless, was stamped with fear. He chattered rather than spoke. "Before God, Señora! You saw; a devil entered into him!"

The Empress smiled. Where Jerry had looked for an explosion, she merely smiled; but the boy, a youth of not over fifteen or sixteen, cowered and the blood drained out of his face.

"For the love of God, Señora!"

She looked away from him with a shrug and made a swift gesture to Pedro; the gesture consisted in raising both hands, the ten fingers outspread.

"No! No! No, Señora!"

Pedro's grip tightened on the thin arm and the boy was dragged away; one sharp cry of pure terror burst from him, then he went silently.

"You dispense justice, both the high and the low, I take it, Señora?" said Jerry grimly.

"You're damned right, Jerry—and you can call me Louise, if you like. The kid double-crossed me; you saw it. All right; ten fingers for him!"

"Meaning?" he demanded sharply.

She looked at him with smoldering eyes; he was sure that she was about to say one thing and at the last moment decided on another when she said with a shrug:

"I've got my own jail. Ten days. All right, here come the ponies for the next race."

Yes, a kaleidoscopic day. The other races went by rather like a blur for Jerry Boyne. The orchestra was playing under the cottonwoods. Couples began dancing. As through a smoke screen which now and then reveals red flashes of flame, Jerry glimpsed an order of things which he did not know could possibly exist upon this western continent; he caught fragmentary impressions more frequently than true glimpses, sensing power, the merciless, grasping power of a woman's strong hand: gun butts, sheathed knives under the red-lined capes; fear looking slant-eyed from morose faces; bodyguards as though indeed here one had to do with royalty; hatred flashing up unexpectedly, suspicion peering out. And always music and laughter and light feet dancing.

They dined gayly in an enormous room at a table seating sixty guests. There was an entertainment for these favored ones, provided by four couples of young Mexicans executing some of the more picturesque of their national dances. The Empress herself was delighted with them, chose to be most gracious, gave them gold pieces and sent them to the servants' quarters to be filled with wine and feasting.

"Señorita," said Prince Charlie, more than a little drunk, "I love you. You see all this; some day it will be mine. Will you, most lovely Beryl—"

Even this Jerry overheard; it was just as the dinner broke up and there was some slight, bright confusion. And he saw Beryl whip back, break away from those about her and run to Señor Costa, followed by young Fernandez's passionate look.

"You could play marbles with his eyes now, am I right?" whispered Elmer Blodgett at Jerry's elbow. "Come ahead, kid; snap out of it. We're on our way to the casino."

Luisa Blanco Fernandez had never been Louise White and foregone her opportunity to have a little gambling hell of her own. It was well withdrawn from the house, a sort of exotic curio architecturally, looking under the newly risen full moon like a Japanese nightmare. Inside were gambling tables, big chairs in red and deep-blue leather and a well-stocked mahogany bar.

"Here's the one place on the ranch where money talks," announced the Empress as those following her trooped in. "Nothing's free here unless your luck wins it—and now's your chance to buy your hostess a drink!"

Antonio Costa, knowing in advance the custom prevailing here, was first at the bar, spinning a gold piece, as with grave courtesy he invited all to join him in a toast to their most charming hostess.

Money blossomed on all hands; every table soon drew its devotees. Elmer Blodgett plucked at Jerry's sleeve.

"Watch my old hidalgo go into action," he whispered.

Señor Costa played roulette. Given a chair, he placed

58

a well-lined bill-fold before him—and from that moment it was clear to see that for him everything and everyone in the room, save the game itself, faded into nothingness. A warm pink crept up into his cheeks and a livelier light shone in his eyes.

Though nearly everyone present made at least some small contribution at one of the altars of the goddess Luck, there were only three who plunged. They were the old Spaniard, Red Handsome and the Empress herself.

Jerry found his chance at last for a word with Beryl Blake. She had gone quietly to a little alcove with a casement window looking out upon the white moonlight shimmering upon a tangle of vines. He thought that she looked lonely despite the many gathered in the room. As he came near, he sensed her distress. When she turned swiftly he thought that it was something other than the moonlight which brightened her eyes—a shining wetness.

"I have been wanting a word with you all day, Miss Blake," he said as she turned back to the window. "I was sort of a blunderbuss this morning, but I did not mean to be—fresh. I know that that's what you thought. I was in earnest. I did feel that we had known each other."

"Did you?" she queried aloofly. "By now, of course, you know that you were mistaken?"

"No. I was not mistaken."

She had to turn to look curiously at him, so gravely emphatic was his tone.

"Where, Mr. Boyne?" she asked, and did not strive to hide her incredulity. "When?" She laughed her disbelief. "It must have been very long ago!"

"It was. Long and long ago. Some day, if I may, I'll remind you; I'm sure you've not altogether forgotten. Just now—I'm rather in a queer dream, it strikes me— I'll just trust to your generosity and ask you to believe me."

"I don't like mysteries," she said swiftly. Then, in hot impulse: "I hate mysteries! I hate this place! That woman— God will need to be merciful indeed if He is to have mercy on her soul! This place reeks, I tell you! I shouldn't talk this way—to a stranger—should I?" She strove again for light laughter and failed signally, covering her failure with an elaborate shrug, very Spanish, reminiscent of her grandfather. "You are so obviously her oh-so-devoted admirer!"

"She is our hostess, isn't she? We have at least broken bread with her—"

"As at a public hotel," she retorted. "I, for one, pay my way and owe her nothing. Perhaps you did not notice; I put down a ten dollar bill just now on the roulette table and lost; it will go to her. Since I felt that I must come, I have paid my score."

"Soon," said Jerry, "I am going across the border and up toward the High Mesa. May I come to see you?"

"No!" she flared out at him. "I tell you—"

"You hate Señora Fernandez? Well, that is your privilege and no doubt you have reasons for your feeling. But I—"

"You are one to sit at her right hand; you are one of her sort! And her sort I'll tell you are not mine."

He bit his lip to check the retort to which he was

being stung by her rank injustice. Were not she and her grandfather here, they who knew so much more of the Señora Fernandez than he did? Was not that swaggering devil, Red Handsome, here and did she not lean toward him?

Just then, before he could find the words he wanted, the outside silence was disturbed by a faint, fairylike strain of muted harmony; someone just under the window was beginning to pour his heart out through the softly touched strings of a violin. Here was no such music as the roistering orchestra had offered but something very fine and subtle, the stifled crying out of some artist's soul. Gradually the strains grew louder and presently they filled the room. Voices were hushed. Jerry, turning, looked across the room into the face of the Empress. She stared, her eyes round; her mouth was slightly open; she seemed to be drinking deep of the stirring plaint of the violin. The violin yearned on. She put her head back, her eyes were closed now—and Jerry, amazed, saw two tears slip down her cheeks.

She ran to the window at the last throbbing note, thrusting Beryl out of her way and calling sharply:

"Who's there? Who are you that play like that? Come here! I say, come here!"

It was the boy with the pitted face and large, limpid eyes, the boy who had lost the race.

"Juanito! You! By God, boy, you play like an angel!"

She clapped her hand on his bent shoulder and he winced as though it had been a lash on raw, quivering flesh, an involuntary groan breaking from his lips.

"Oh!" she said contritely. "I'm so sorry, Juanito. I

would not hurt you for the world— Here. Here and here!" Her hands had been filled with coins brought from a gaming table; she thrust the money into the boy's pockets. "Go now, Juanito. Tell Ortega you are to sleep tonight in my house. The doctor will see you there. Go, Juanito, and you shall play for me all alone tomorrow."

"You know, Señora," wept the boy, "that I did not mean—"

"Go," she said not unkindly. "I know, Juan."

He snatched her hand, kissed it passionately and sped away, his scarred face radiant.

The play went on. Jerry saw the Empress win and lose, lose and win. He saw Red Handsome, a look of triumph in his red-brown eyes, win and win again and go on winning. And he watched the old Spaniard, always smiling and seemingly supremely indifferent, empty his wallet before the spinning ball.

"See it?" gasped Elmer in his ear. "Who'd think the old sport would dare carry that much of the long green in his pocket? It's just inviting murder, that's all. Know what he was pried loose from, Jerry? A clear two thousand bucks, and I don't mean Mex. Is he an investment? You come to me next week, like I said—"

A sinister whisper was going up and down through the room, and Elmer broke off, his ever ready suspicions quickened; something untoward had happened. The word had just been brought by a couple who had gone over to the cottonwood grove for a dance and come back to start the tale which would sweep along the border tomorrow. The young rancher, Kingsbury, was dead. He had been found with a bullet in his brain. It was said that he had killed himself. Just as the Empress had predicted. Where had it happened? No one knew. Who had found him? El Bravo.

"She commanded it done! We heard her!" It was a nervous scream from some woman, overwrought; her identity was lost to most of those present as her friends closed in about her, hushing her.

Of them all the Empress alone appeared not to have heard. She crossed the room to Antonio Costa.

"Too bad you didn't get the breaks today, 'Tonio mio," she said coolly. "Lost on the race and lost here again, eh?"

"It is nothing," he said curtly; but Jerry Boyne, observing him keenly, thought that there was a new grimness about the lips under the white mustache and a queer look—almost the look of the hunted and desperate—in the fine black eyes.

CHAPTER IV

T HAT MOON OF SOFT DELIGHT, THE BORDER MOON, drifting serenely above the raw edges of two countries where north and south impinge, where bright, steadfast spirits gather and sodden dregs settle, shone down on what was at the beginning like a cavalcade winding away from the gates of the Empire Ranch. Under the moon's sorcery the sage bushes became a fretwork of silver and ebony, the harsh sands were softened and glinted like rippling waters, smoke trees were like ghosts half real, half imagined; a barranca was filled with black mystery and a mocking bird in an old olive tree became the voice of the night's beauty. Through the silver glory of the night went the many departing guests and visitors, leaving the sprawling Empire Ranch to its own silver and ebony, its own scarlet and gray, its own menace and mystery.

These departing ones constituted at the beginning a heavily flowing procession, queerly quiet. As swifter vehicles, desert-scarred motors, found their places at the fore, a long line, vari-speeded, resulted, breaking down into the single items of car, horseman, harnessed team; akin only in their silences and in the black shadows they dropped upon the winding white strip of road. Close to the fore of the long line went Jerry Boyne and Elmer Blodgett in Elmer's dusty car; a horn blared and they turned out, two wheels churning the loose sand, to let a long gray closed car slip by them. There went Don Antonio Costa and his granddaughter, in great haste to return to High Mesa.

The spell of silence was broken by their honking horn. All along the lengthening line voices broke out. Elmer Blodgett, jockeying his car out of the loose sand and back into the hard-packed road, muttered throatily:

"It's murder! Damn it, man, it's murder. She as good as told El Bravo to go do it—and he went and pulled the trick." He shivered and muttered angrily: "That woman! That snake-eyed El Bravo! Grrh!"

Jerry lighted a cigarette, broke his dead match in two and stared after the bobbing red light of the gray car vanishing among gray ghostly smoke trees. He said thoughtfully:

"A man would be tempted to remark that they couldn't get away with a thing like that in a civilized world that's rolled as far as this one has from the Dark Ages."

"Then he'd be tempted likewise to be an ass," growled Elmer. "I thought that kid Kingsbury was coo-coo, like they said, when he shot off all that talk of his; now I'm beginning to think he didn't tell half of it. If you'll ask me, Jerry Boyne, we've poked in some places where the inhabitants thought themselves tough babies, but I've got a hunch they was just amateurs to this outfit. What's got you interested in this layout, anyhow? Not just that poke in the jaw Red Handsome gave you, was it?"

"Suppose you tell me what you learned about him during the day? For I take it you gathered some information?"

"If everything folks told me was true," grunted Blodgett, his eyes busy on the road ruts, "then I learned more in one day than a man generally absorbs in a year. About him and all and sundry, as you might say. The sum total of which causes me to remark that I'd rather go up to a head-hunting cannibal king and kick him in the shins than start anything with some of these hombres. You heard Kingsbury?"

"What about this fellow they call Red Handsome?"

"That's easy. Came into this country as a kid with his dad about fifteen years ago. His old man bought the High Mesa you been talking about, and about the same time him and his kid kicked up a row between them, which seems to have been the style in that family, and the kid ran away. Never showed up again until time came when someone popped his old man off—and if you're asking me about that part, I'd say go ask El Bravo or the old lady he takes killing orders off of!"

"Got any reason for that remark?" demanded Jerry sharply.

"Reason, you poor infant? What more reason do you want—"

"Go ahead. What's the rest about Red Handsome?"

"He came back only about five years ago, which was after old man Sommers was no more. Look here, Jerry, you're in on this mess somehow; you knew that old guy; you came drifting along to see him. And you know something—"

"Never mind, Elmer; I told you I'll spill my story in time. It's your turn now."

Elmer whipped a bright curious glance at him.

"All right," he sighed. "Like I said, Red comes back. He finds old Don Spanish on the job, bulging with money that he's just inherited from somebody in Spain, and all het up to spend the wad to buy back the old ancestral acres. So the minute Red gets title, he unloads; and who'd blame him selling any ranch for a measly two hundred and fifty grand! Gosh, some folks is lucky!"

"Two hundred fifty thousand? Cash, do you know? Or time?"

"I do know. Cash. Red asked three hundred thousand and came down to two fifty when Don Grandee shoved the cash under his nose. Do you blame him? Red, I mean?"

"Go on."

"What do you mean, go on? That's the tale, ain't it?"

"There's a small point I thought of. He had gone away, you say, when only a kid, and had never been heard of; then he pops back and says, 'I'm the man who owns High Mesa.' It would be interesting to know just how he proved his identity. Who'd know him, a man of twenty-five or twenty-seven, for the same kid of twelve or fifteen that ran away?"

Elmer's jaw slackened, his eyes rounded and he stared. With a snap his jaw came back into its normal position and he whistled softly.

"You mean it's a skin-game? Gosh! Say, Jerry, do you know the day I poked my nose into Nacional I just smelled strange doings smeared all over?" He seemed positively to thrill; no man ever had an eagerer mind for darting down dark side streets, for sensing mystery even where mystery played no part. Here was subject matter for whisperings, and in a hushed whisper he added: "You mean maybe Red Handsome ain't the right heir at all, but an impostor?"

"I mean," said Jerry curtly, "that I happen to be Gerald Sommers myself."

Elmer started, slewed his head about, his eyes bulging, and only Jerry's quick hand on the wheel saved them from swerving out into a thicket of mesquite.

"What a hunch, what a hunch!" the stout man murmured approvingly. "Two hundred and fifty grand! Whew! And you might get away with it at that! Shucks, Jerry," and he laughed as a man does who just becomes aware that the joke is on him, "you fooled me a minute.

But I know you for a square guy; you wouldn't pull a fast one like that, would you?"

Jerry shrugged. After all, he was keener for getting information just now than for giving it.

"The point remains: I wonder how Red Handsome proved himself to be the son and heir? But I don't suppose you chanced on that part of it."

"I did, though! Oh, you couldn't play that game even if you was serious, Jerry. He's solid o.k. It was the Empress that went to the bat for him. She took an interest in the boy, staked him to a loan to scout around and helped him locate several men who could swear to him."

"The Empress?" That, in view of a certain enmity which he had sensed to exist between the two, surprised him. "I'd say she'd rather see him flat on his back than sitting pretty."

"You got to figure on passing years and the fickleness of woman," replied Elmer sententiously. "Her and Red Handsome was as thick as thieves, but that was four-five years ago. I don't know what happened to spoil their sweet friendship, but it's sure a bad-spoiled commodity right now. He's a right bold bucko, I'd say. Me, if I was him, I'm hanged if I'd go prowling within reach of her hired killers."

They sped on for a little while in silence, then Elmer began to chuckle.

"You almost fooled me, old kid, the way you said, 'Me, I'm the long lost son!' And here I've known you more than a dozen years and know your name's Jerry Boyne as well as you know mine's Elmer Bashford

Blodgett. By the way, Jerry, what's the job the old lady was so anxious to hand you? Sounded like big money to me; why didn't you jump at it?"

"I've got something else on my mind right now. I don't know what it was; she didn't tell me."

"There's this," said Elmer reflectively. "She sure took an almighty shine to you—and she's a widow! Of course she ain't as young as she used to be—and I'm not saying it wouldn't take a brave man! You know, if that dame had a guy hanging around that got on her nerves, she'd just whistle and old El Bravo would come a-running, and she'd say, 'Bozo, bump this bird off for me,' and there you'd be. Still, I dunno."

They drew into Nacional, become under the moon a pretty little village with white walls gleaming softly and red tiles bright and clean, and Elmer was all for sharing his room with his friend. Jerry thanked him but shook his head.

"Stake me to some gas out of your tank instead," he said and had Elmer stop at the landing field. "I couldn't sleep tonight if I tried. I'll see you again soon, Elmer; tomorrow maybe or in a few days."

Blodgett regarded him with the liveliest interest.

"Maybe you will and maybe you won't. Going sailing, huh? It's my notion, Crazy Fool, that every time you go up in that butterfly you're taking one chance too many. Parachute? Brr." The very sight of the thing made him shiver. "Where are you going, that's what I'm dying to know? Short of a little trip to the moon, I don't know a place open this time o' night. Not back to the Empire, are you?" he demanded sharply.

"Little Mesa, this time." Jerry climbed in. "I ought to be there in twenty minutes. Give me a whirl, old party."

"I observe," remarked Elmer tartly, "that you're wise enough to say you ought to be there in that time; I note you don't say you will be there! What on earth do you want at Little Mesa? Last time it was High Mesa. A man would suppose that with you any old Mesa would do."

"You heard what young Kingsbury said? About his brother, I mean. The kid thought that Bob had been bumped off; he was trying to make it his job to find out. I've got a hankering to carry on from where he left off. Which you might keep under your hat, Mr. Blodgett, along with any other little remark I may have dropped during the evening. Got me? By the bye, I don't know what border patrol regulations I'm breaking, but if the racket I make getting away brings any Mex officials buzzing out, tell 'em who I am, where I'm going and that later on I'd rather buy 'em no end of drinks than go to their damned jail. And so, sweet dreams and *adios*."

His ancient monoplane went bumping down the field, rose a trifle crookedly and more than a trifle reluctantly and winged awkwardly into the air.

Little Mesa. He knew it well enough despite the fact that he had seen it but the once and that long ago when it had constituted a part of the larger ranch, High Mesa. He wondered whether it had been carved off and sold separately by that rarely officious individual known so

70

picturesquely as Red Handsome, or whether Señor Costa had sold it more recently to the Kingsbury boys? In either case, he fully expected to discover in the course of time that it belonged to none other than Jerry Boyne—at whom Elmer laughed for suggesting that he was any other than Jerry Boyne.

He piloted his craft into a long slow climb and breathed easier when he had attained that precarious distance from the earth which he was in the habit of considering a "safe altitude." A glance downward at the diminished moon-bright houses satisfied him, and he straightened out his course and at last headed toward those little hills which had invited so long.

"And some of this dirty pack got you, Dad, did they?" he said grimly. "And I, who should have been taking whatever came, shoulder to shoulder with you, was off somewhere half way around the world. God forgive me for the fool and worse that I've been—and no doubt am! Why didn't I turn back home any one of the hundred times that I came so close to it?"

What swift racing years they had been! Up and away from High Mesa in a burst of boy's passion, out into the great world where adventure ever beckoned to such as Jerry Boyne; up and away with light running feet and a heart beating high. Down to the surge of ocean where great ships were sailing off to all the luring ports of earth, where the sun set red far out at sea and the quick imagination saw it making a blazing red day on tropic beaches. Out across the ocean, meeting up with many strange men with stranger tales to tell, rocked to sleep each night in the arms of large dreams. Tropic islands at last were dreams come true, blossoming on the breast of blue water; strange trees and birds and flowers and men, strange smells and foods and customs. Friends chance-made, breezing into one's life, breezing out, gone with a nod and a wave and a devil-may-care swagger, fine fellows, stout fellows, and rogues of the quick smile and quick blow; all kinds. "Come to me! I will show you wonders! I will pour rich gifts into your lap!" always whispered some far port with a haunting name. Java! Borneo! Tahiti! Madagascar! Tripoli! Tierra del Fuego! Sirens all, until visited; then only familiar places where a restless boy went up and down, growing into restless manhood, hearing newer far voices calling: "Come to me! I hold the true wonders for you!"

And now and again sharp homesickness, a deep, deep yearning for his own flesh and blood. "Dear Dad, I'm going a bit deeper into Australia; I've made a little stake and am going to try to double it. There's a good guy named Elmer Blodgett that I've sort of teamed up with; we're after gold. When we make our pile— Gosh, Dad, I get homesick sometimes." But at these times home was so far away and the moments passed, and were recorded only in the infrequent, hastily scrawled notes to his father. And during all those years only two letters, almost equally brief, from the elder Sommers; he remained always ready to welcome his boy back home, but he'd have gone out and chopped his hand off before he would have put on paper either the yearning in his heart or a command. All men, according to the Sommers creed, were, thank God, free agents.

Yes, you merely put off from one day to the next the thing you meant to do, and it seemed that your intentions somehow oiled the swiftly spinning wheels of time, and the years ran by. You knocked about a bit, and were always an interested onlooker on life and many times an active participant of lively doings; you dreamed big dreams and whittled into solid achievement some fragmentary corner of each; you went down into mines, and tried diving, and learned to fly; you nibbled at schooling and got, because you were the sort you were, a habit of books; you found your youth an endless, pleasant, meandering pathway, and therefore took your time as your birthright. Suddenly you said, "Fifteen years!" and were all fever and rush and eagerness to get home. Too late! That melancholy bell tolling out the news that not even youth is endless, that there *is* such a thing as time and that it passes and having passed does not return.

In the moonlight the desert lands, like a section of some still, silvered ocean, slipped away, and the little beckoning hills seemed at last as eager as Jerry Boyne and came rushing along to meet him. He saw the reflected glow of the High Mesa car's headlights and obeyed the impulse to swoop down toward it, rising again sharply and soon leaving it far behind.

"That, if you only knew it, is saying 'Good night,' Beryl, my dear," he said aloud; "and is meant to inform you that, despite your having missed by a good sea mile being cordial in your invitation to drop in, that's exactly what I'm going to do right soon." He grinned and added: "It's a duty, you know, little playmate! For, as it seems to a man up in a plane, you're beginning to lean a little too far toward the sort of fellow who pokes a man while he isn't looking and steals another man's birthright—and then, damn him, cheats your own granddaddy out of a quarter of a million dollars!" His grin faded long before he got that far, superseded by an angry scowl. "It's a mess," he muttered disgustedly. "What am I to do? Go chase old Costa and a mighty sweet girl out and say, 'It's mine; too bad, but if you want anything back go take the matter up with your fine friend who played you for suckers.' Yep, Jerry-me-lad, as messes go it's a beauty."

Lights sprang up, far ahead and off to the left. That was High Mesa. In the bright moonlight he could see the lofty table-land where the old home stood, casting a long black shadow; he could make out the many white adobe walls, the walls of the house itself, gleaming white, splashed black with clinging vines. He regarded all this a moment musingly, then let his eyes run along a wavering silver line that was High Mesa Creek and swerved off to the right.

Here, though of no such mammoth proportions as the Empire, was a ranch to make a landowner's mouth water. It rippled away to north and south, east and west, sloping down into wide fields, breaking abruptly into deep-gouged, clean-cliffed hills, barren as bare rock in places yet cupping delightful little valleys. Not over half a dozen fleet miles due east from the big house on High Mesa were the ranch buildings of Little Mesa.

There were no lights to guide to Little Mesa, but there

74

was the bold upland on which the house stood, and Jerry picked it out from afar and circled about it, coming gradually lower until at last he could make out some detail. Ruin had swept the place. The house still stood, for it was an affair of rock and adobe, but out-sheds were black heaps and corrals were broken; a few tall thin lines of smoke stood up almost unwaveringly aloft from a smoldering heap of what had once been a big haystack.

Jerry was due for a surprise with a most decided thrill in it. Faring forth from Nacional he had come looking for Bob Kingsbury, yet with hardly any true hope of finding him. As he had told Elmer, he was in no mood for sleep; he must be doing something; he came then where his quick sympathies led, that was all. And yet, only a few minutes after he circled Little Mesa, he found the man whom young Kingsbury was so sure the raiders had butchered.

Not at the ranch headquarters, but off among the rockiest of the hills, some two or three miles distant, he saw a spurt of light signaling to him. He dipped lower, saw the bright flare in a black nest of bowlders, rose again, took his bearings and sought a landing place. Luck was with him and within a quarter of a mile he brought his plane down upon an open, treeless plateau. He climbed out and went hurrying toward the spot where he had seen the tongue of flame.

But before he and Bob Kingsbury ever gripped hands, Jerry Boyne came awesomely close to having his own life snuffed out. There was a second spurt of flame, this time from a rifle followed by a sinister scream of

75

lead close to his ear and a snarling report echoing away among the rocks. Jerry leaped behind a protecting mass of black lava rock, and yelled out angrily:

"Hi, you polecat! What have you got on your mind, anyhow? Or have you got any mind? I've a notion to start bamming rocks at you, same as you would at a rattlesnake."

A voice, trying to jeer, responded weakly:

"Come along; show your damn head once more—"

"If I show anything it'll be heels, unless you put that gun away," snapped Jerry, but peered out cautiously from his barricade.

He saw the dying embers of the little signal fire, and made out beside it the figure of a man lying among rocks. The figure stirred ever so slightly, moving painfully.

"Is that you, Kingsbury?" Jerry called.

"You know it's me. Why don't you come and try to finish what you started? I'm waitin' and I won't run away."

Then Jerry Boyne knew that the fellow, with sheer grit and will-power, was holding himself from sprawling into a faint, that Kingsbury had had to lick dry lips with a parched tongue to speak at all.

"I came looking for you, old man—"

"I know you did! I heard your motor and saw you, flying like the black bat you are. That's why I made a flare. Now what's holdin' you back?"

"Think I'm from the Empire, huh? Well, I'm not. Did it ever dawn on you that the *Hawk* isn't the only plane in the world?"

Thereupon he stepped out into the moonlight, lifted his hands high so that the wounded man could see, and stepped forward.

"Stop where you are, that's close enough," said Kingsbury, and Jerry came obediently to a halt not a dozen feet from where Kingsbury lay. "Now who the devil are you, Stranger?"

"You said it; I'm a stranger to you. I chanced to hear something of what had happened up here, didn't have anything particular to do, did have a plane raring to go, and hopped over. And, from looks of things, it's just as well that I came."

"How'd you hear?" demanded Kingsbury, still inclined to be suspicious. "Who told you?"

"Your brother. He couldn't find you. He thought you were wiped out."

"Where's Bud now?"

"He—he went down to Nacional and the Empire Ranch; he's there yet, I suppose. He was trying to get on your trail."

"Why didn't he come with you?"

Jerry looked down into a haggard face, one side showing gaunt in the moonlight, the other in black shadow, and decided swiftly that the worst of bad news could always wait. So he shrugged.

"I don't even know your brother; I was only one of a crowd that heard what he had to say—and it was in pointed language. He went his way and I went mine. Now if you're of a mind to have a stranger lend you a hand, speak up."

"Pull your hat off," snapped Kingsbury.

He reared up on an elbow and stared into Jerry's face, then fell back with a grunt.

"Haven't got any water on you?" he demanded as he let his rifle slip from his hands. And Jerry, about to answer, saw that he had fainted. There were blood smears on the man's face where he had mopped at his brow; otherwise the face was deathly white.

There was a canteen in the plane—for Jerry was too old a hand to go nosing across desert stretches without water and a packet of sandwiches—and he hastened back for it. As the precious stuff gurgled between the cracked lips, Kingsbury's eyes opened. Jerry poured a cupful over the feverish face, gave him a second drink and squatted down on his heels to build a cigarette and take stock of the situation.

"Hurt bad, old-timer?" he questioned the wounded man when Bob, too, was smoking. "Or just weak from loss of blood and lack of water?"

"Shot plumb to hell," said Kingsbury succinctly. He drew deep at his cigarette. "God, that's good! I'd run out." He tried to pull himself up. "I'll get 'em yet," he announced as he slid back, "and it's good news they didn't get Bud. I was scared they had."

"Strikes me," said Jerry hastily, "that you take a lot of killing, Mr. Kingsbury! Feel up to moving a bit? How'd you like to spread-eagle on a bed again? This is no man's sort of sanitarium up here."

"It's a good two miles; if you'll get me a horse—"

He proceeded to faint again, and Jerry though at first fearing that the man was dead, gathered him up into his arms and carried him the quarter mile to the plane. It

78

was a weird task, he and a man who might already be dead, moving heavily among the black rocks and through the white, ghostly moonlight; a back-breaking task, too, but Jerry set his teeth and carried on. The monoplane behaved itself rather nobly, rose clear of the uneven surface when in another moment it must have gone crashing into the bowlder-strewn slope, and a few moments later settled down in a field near the Little Mesa ranch house.

"That's one awful chance you've taken in this life and never known a thing about," Jerry confided in the unconscious man as he started to the house with him. "When you go riding with me you ought to have your eyes open and a 'chute ready. Well, we got away with it!"

The door stood open. Jerry passed through a shadowy room and in the adjoining one put Kingsbury down on a bed. He found a coal-oil lamp, added to the illumination with a couple of candles and bestirred himself about first aid. Man-style, he slit garments with his knife and soon had Kingsbury stripped.

"Good Lord!" gasped Jerry as he looked at the body he had exposed.

That the man still lived was a marvel to him. Altogether he was wounded in five places, each of the two graver wounds being bound in blood-soaked strips of his shirt. He had paid no attention to a furrow across his scalp, a notch in his shoulder and a cut along his shin. "Shot plumb to hell," the rancher had said, and Jerry as he frowned at the gaping, inflamed hole in the man's side wondered that he had not died long ago.

And yet Bob Kingsbury lived. Further, when bathed with warm water from the kitchen stove and rebandaged with a torn sheet, he regained consciousness.

"Slip her here, old-timer," he said and put out his trembling hand. His eyes roved about the room, found it familiar and came to rest on the face above him. "I forget your name—"

"Jerry Boyne."

"Thanks, Jerry."

"Forget it, Bob."

"There's a jug in the kitchen cupboard. I could do with a drink and maybe you'll have a snort—"

Jerry, going to the kitchen which had open windows all along one side, was surprised to note that already the night was at an end. He caught a glint of the rising sun, fiery red and angry looking. A new sudden wind had sprung up, harsh and dry, shrilling around the house corners.

"Wonder how long the poor devil lay out there in the hills? A good twenty-four hours at least, maybe forty-eight and maybe longer! And still alive! But if I don't find him a doctor in a hurry, all his gameness is going to be for nothing."

He brought the jug and gave Kingsbury a good stiff drink.

"Where's the nearest doctor, Bob?" he asked. "He might take an interest, you know, in looking you over. And for all I know there may be enough good lead left in your carcass to make it worth a man's while digging it out."

Kingsbury strove to grin.

"Did we fetch my rifle along?" he asked.

"We forgot it, I'd say. But shucks, man, you've had enough of that sort of thing to satisfy you for a day or so, haven't you?"

"Some of those jaspers are apt to come pokin' back," muttered Kingsbury. "If you're thinkin' of goin' off and leavin' me flat here, I'd just as lieve have something handy—a monkey wrench is pretty good, you know, when a man hasn't got a gun!"

"I've an old forty-five in my plane; I'll leave it with you if you like."

"Fine. Only don't rush off right now. Since you're electin' yourself to a sort of nurse job, how'd you like to make some coffee first? Did I dream of coffee out yonder? Coffee and cigarettes? And, havin' lost a drop or two of blood, how about something to make some new? There's a pot of stew; maybe if you'd set it on the fire I could suck up some of the gravy? Damn it, I hate to ask favors—"

Jerry, anxious to be upon his errand, could not up-and-away without doing what small things lay here at his hand; he strove to do what common sense told him a physician would order; also he strove in small things to humor a man who had moments of feverishness in which he lost his grip and grew querulous. An hour passed and another, and Jerry at last grew restive with a fresh anxiety—the wind came in stronger and stronger gusts; the climbing sun was blood red in a sky filled with whistling sand.

"If we're in for a sand storm, I'd like to be on my way before it kicks up much more devilment," he muttered, and went to tell Bob that he was on his way.

Kingsbury lay in a heavy stupor, plunged, Jerry thought, into a profound sleep. So Jerry softly drew a table close to the bedside, set water and whisky and coffee on it, closed all windows against the wind, and went out. The wind tore at his flapping coat; fine sand particles lashed his face and hands. He squinted his eyes at the red ball of the sun.

"I'll make it all right," he said, and meant to have a good try at it. "The wind will help me get under way; I'll ride it out until I can climb up where it's smooth sailing. Yep, Jerry-me-lad, we'll ride high this trip. Looking at it square in the face, we've got to make it."

CHAPTER V

JERRY BOYNE WAS NOT TO BE THE ONLY ONE THAT morning who went charging off into the threat of a sand storm. When he had, some hours earlier, swooped earthward over the car making what speed it could along the High Mesa sandy road, and had said something to himself about Beryl Blake "leaning" toward her red-head friend, he had been much closer the literal truth than he could know. For with Antonio Costa and his granddaughter was this same red-head, having eagerly accepted the girl's invitation to ride with them. One of his hired men who had been left behind at the Empire Rancho was following with the horses. And the red-brown eyes, as the red head was thrust out of the car window, watched the monoplane recover altitude and go on about its business.

Beryl shivered. To her as to Bob Kingsbury, the roar of an airplane's motor spelled the *Hawk* of the Empire.

"Why have they followed us?" she asked nervously. "What are they after up here, at this time of night?"

"It's not the Empress's plane," was the answer. It came only after a little silence during which the speaker, no less than the girl, was wondering what brought it here. "It's that fellow Boyne."

"Jerry Boyne! What do you suppose brings him up our way?"

"The Lord knows. Here's hoping he's simply on his way somewhere else—and forgets the road back."

The three sat in the roomy tonneau, Señor Costa's chauffeur at the wheel, Red Handsome with his back to the driver and thus facing the Spaniard and his granddaughter. The moonlight was all about them gloriously bright; there was a sort of crepuscular glow within the car, and eyes, were they intent, could make more than a mere blur of a face so near. Antonio Costa, regarding his guest, observed briskly:

"You are enemies, then? You and this Jerry Boyne, no? There was talk of trouble in Nacional."

"Nothing." It appeared a matter to shrug away. "No, hardly enemies, Señor. Strangers, rather."

Beryl laughed and drew Costa's wondering eyes. It was not like her to laugh at trouble between any two men, least of all when one of them was a friend. Yet she was not altogether like herself tonight. She had had moments of such sheer, bright gayety that her companions were puzzled, so deep had been her previous abstraction, so almost frantically eager had she been to hurry home, so quiet and distraught had she seemed at times. What they did not take into consideration was that she was overwrought, her nerves keyed up like violin strings; laughter and tears in such a mood lay very close together. Herself hardly knowing what ailed her, she felt queerly reckless. In such a mood a girl can drive a man wild, and Beryl sensed something of that lively power and felt an impish zest in employing it.

"What is it, Little One? Why do you laugh like that?" demanded her grandfather.

"Oh, nothing!" There she told the perfect truth and was gleeful in it—or rather that no one would know it for the truth.

"I see nothing funny," said Costa almost stiffly.

"No?" asked Beryl, and smiled enigmatically. "Isn't everything in the world funny? Isn't it funny, for example, when one man falls off his horse and then two men start fighting?"

It would be a long day before Red Handsome heard the last of having fallen from his horse. He flushed hotly now as he had flushed a time or two already.

"The fool with his crazy old monoplane dropped down under my nose while I wasn't looking," he said, his words falling crisp and savage. "I was rolling a cigarette. He thought it was funny, too, and got his face slapped."

"Do you know, Señor," said Costa soberly, "that is the thing that they told me and I found hard to believe? This Jerry Boyne, now; I talked with him; I looked at him in the eyes. I did not think him the kind who takes a blow and runs away."

"I too looked into his eyes, *Papagrande,*" said Beryl, now peeping covertly at her goaded admirer. "He did not seem a coward when I was fierce with him!" Again, and over "nothing," she laughed gayly. "He looked ever so bold."

"Bold with the ladies, I've no doubt," said Red Handsome swiftly. "He and Señora Fernandez hit it up like a pair of long separated lovers. Or did you notice?"

"Did they?" said Beryl innocently. "How nice!" And now it was he who smiled. But he was merely storing up trouble for himself.

For, arrived at High Mesa, where he found that moment he had counted on, when he had her all to himself, he got little solace from it. A couple of servants were astir; the headlights of the car had been sighted miles away and the house was illuminated, coffee ready, bottles, and glasses set out on the sideboard. The three entered at the ancient, deeply-recessed door, Señor Costa remembering to say a courteous, *"Gracias, Vidal, y buenos noches,"* to the driver, Beryl forgetting poor Vidal utterly until too late. The old man had a glass of wine, a cup of hot coffee and was off to bed, suggesting that the others, unless they were mad as most young people were, had best follow his example. They watched him go, then proceeded to have breakfast.

"It will be day in no time," said Beryl, "and I'm as hungry as a wolf."

They breakfasted in a little bower of a place, a tiny room with spacious arched doorways, one of which looked to the rugged, rocky hills while the other gave upon a delicious bit of the garden. Before coming to the table, where she was to eat nothing despite her declaration of wolfish intentions, Beryl went to look out across the tangle of pomegranate and olive and roses, out and out across the billowing miles streaming away as far as the border and beyond.

"Did I ever confide in you, Mr. Red Handsome, that I am something of a witch?"

"Bewitching," he said emphatically, taking the obvious opening. "And I wish you wouldn't call me that. You know I loathe it."

"A witch," said Beryl without turning, playing at being deep in earnest, making her voice hushed and somehow far away, "can read what is written in the stars—and she can see a scarlet patch on the moon."

He laughed and said, "How about that appetite of yours?"

"And," she went on dreamily, "she can see a black shadow like the shadow of an enormous bat! The shadow of an airplane!" She turned then quite suddenly and he could see the still candle flames reflected in her eyes. "You were wrong; Jerry Boyne will come back! Did you notice how unusually dark his eyes were for a man with such red hair? The effect is striking, isn't it?"

"Beryl, why are you like this tonight? You know how I love you; you know—"

"It is still night, isn't it? But almost morning. How silly the candles begin to look."

In Señor Costa's home were only candles; no electric lights had come to invade his old-world atmosphere, and he hated the smell of kerosene. On the table were tall silver candlesticks, very old and very Spanish. Beryl tried blowing the little yellow flames out, one at a time, and noting the effect. The fine tremulous light of the dawn was coming on swiftly and, as solemn about it as though she was sacrificing the lives of these little fires on the altar of the true day, Beryl extinguished the last.

"You know I love you, Beryl; and I thought—"

The table was cozily small, yet when she sat at one side and he across from her it joined forces with her in thwarting him.

"Do you know," she interrupted him, peering down into her coffee-cup as though witch eyes might read the future there too, "that I've often wondered about love; true love, my dear."

"I love you truly—"

"And I always dreamed that love came at first sight!"

"It does. From the first day I saw you—"

"That was so long and long ago, wasn't it? When we were just a little girl and boy."

She looked at him, lifting her eyes suddenly and as suddenly began laughing again, her brief solemn mood gone. A quick involuntary frown fleetingly darkened his red-brown eyes. It seemed rather a habit of hers, here of late, that harking back to a time about which, as far as he was concerned, the least said, the better.

"Every time I start to say anything— Why do you always say that, Beryl? Why do you so love to tease?"

"But I'm not teasing! And why shouldn't I naturally think back to that first day? Just consider what it meant; the very first time I ever saw you, when, if you are in earnest and not just trifling with a country maiden's affections, you fell in love with me!"

"I did!" he maintained stoutly. "You know I did. Oh, I know what you are going on to say. If I don't happen to have as lively a memory for details as you do, if after fifteen years I have forgotten some little thing—"

"And I remember everything!" She put her elbows on the table, her chin on her hands and eyed him provocatively. "Let's see; when we climbed that old tree behind the stable—"

"It was a great day; I remember the high lights of it all right," he said hastily. "We had a ride on your pony, didn't we? Both at the same time. A funny, roly-poly pony; her name was Mariana—"

"You do remember some things, don't you? How splendid!" But her eyes mocked him, and he stirred uneasily as she concluded innocently: "Even that ride—is it that you remember it, or did I happen to burst out with it, reminding you all over, that next time we met?"

"Of course I remembered— But now, Beryl, all that's a long time ago. Today is today."

"How true!" she laughed at him. She sipped at her coffee, appeared to grow thoughtful again and observed, this time without looking up: "When we buried our treasure—"

"Pennies in a tin tobacco box," he said promptly. "Under a piñon tree in the pasture."

"Did I blurt that out, too? Or is that one of the things you do actually remember?"

"I'm sorry I've got a memory like an old sieve; but I

wouldn't think you'd hold it against me. A man can't help a thing like that."

"But not keeping the one I gave you—the bright, particular penny! It was to have been a keepsake. You say you remember that! And if love really began then, at first sight as all the poets say—"

"If, over a period of fifteen years I lost it— Hang it, Beryl, when you know I am eating my heart out for you; when you have known it so long; when you've let me think that you, too—"

If she wanted some small revenge for his lack of memory of a bright day so long ago, for his failure to cherish a copper penny down through the years, she came by it to the full in the merry laughter with which she taunted him. But, amazing an already bewildered man, her whole mood of a sudden and with no slightest warning, was exchanged for its antithesis. There was no simulation now in her downright unhappiness.

"I feel stifled! How can you talk to me of—of love? How can I listen to you and chatter as I have done? I can't get that poor boy out of my mind! I can see him all the time, his poor eyes so terribly wild and sad. They said he was crazy. Crazed with grief, with an agony of fearful uncertainty—"

"Oh. You mean Kingsbury?"

"And he is dead already." She shivered. "Did El Bravo kill him?"

"Who knows? After all, Kingsbury was half drunk and all nerves. I'd say that no one will ever know."

"I know! It was El Bravo. It was at that horrible woman's command, too."

"With your witch instincts you ought to know!" he chuckled.

"How can you laugh at such a thing!"

"Great Scott! Here you've been laughing half the night!"

"And what about his brother? He said that they had killed Bob. What if Bob Kingsbury is lying somewhere wounded, suffering—"

"I don't believe it. If he's been killed, he's dead, and there's an end of it. But if you're anxious, Beryl, I'll see what can be done. Little Mesa, you know, is on my way; I'll be starting off to my place pretty pronto if you'll lend me a horse, and will comb the hills above the ranch house."

"Do!" She jumped up from the table, all eagerness. "Are you ready now?"

He was not ready. He wanted to linger over a cigarette, to have her alone, to strive to draw her back to the one subject which interested him just then. But he said, "All right," and rose with her.

She went with him to the stable; it was almost day and a harsh dry wind was blowing.

"Beastly wind," he said, hunching his shoulders against it.

"I love it!" She could not have loved it, so rasping was it, so did it irritate the skin and sting the eyes. Yet, because she was all storm within, she welcomed this storm without and leaned her body against it.

"You're a funny girl," he said from the saddle. "You'd better tumble into bed. Sweet dreams."

"Be careful!" she called after him, and he swung

about at this first sign of any solicitude on her part, only to have her add tauntingly, "Be careful and don't fall again!"

"Damn!" he muttered so that she heard him, and jammed his spurs viciously into his horse's sides.

"Cruel!" she whispered. "He was cruel to the horse—just as I was cruel to him! Maybe I am 'funny.' I don't know what is the matter with me. Maybe it's just always seeing that poor boy—and that wicked, wicked woman staring at him. Oh, I feel as though I'd stifle!"

She whirled and ran back to the stable door, her light dress whipping about her in the gusty wind. Just inside, against the nearer wall, was a steep staircase leading to rooms in the loft. She had just put her foot to the first step when a narrow door at the top opened and a small, slight man appeared dimly outlined in the obscurity.

"Uncle Doctor!" she called softly.

"Coming, Miss Beryl." He came nimbly down the steep stairway, fumbling with the black bow tie at his soft white collar, his small, tight boots glistening in the half light.

"You are always coming when I need you, Uncle Doctor!"

"Yes, Miss Beryl. You're upset, ain't you? Yes, yes; I know. But everything's all right, you know."

He smiled at her now, his eyes on a level with hers, the kindly, strangely sweet and childlike eyes of a man of fifty, looking out of a clean-shaven, rounded, boyish face.

"Will you have a horse ready for me, Uncle Doctor?" She put her hand gently on his thin, black-coated arm.

"I have to get off for a ride, all by myself. But that isn't why I wanted you; I could saddle for myself, couldn't I? But there's something else. It's about the Kingsbury boys." The whole story, as far as she knew it, came with a rush of words, "Uncle Doctor" shaking his head over it and looking deeply pained. "Will you send some men out as soon as you can? They must look everywhere."

He stepped outside and looked at the sky.

"It's a'most day now. Yes, I'll send right off, an' I'll go myse'f. It's comin' on to blow bad. It might be better, Miss Beryl, if you— Oh, I guess it won't hurt you. I'll have a pony saddled time you're ready."

Since she had asked it, of course he'd have it done. He was a simple, kind, faithful little chap whose supreme happiness lay in loving and serving. He would rather have done some small thing that found favor in this girl's eyes than to have been loaded down with much fine gold. It had been "Uncle Doctor" who had saddled the fat pony, Mariana, that day fifteen years ago when for the first time he saw the little girl, Miss Beryl. For he had come to High Mesa with Mr. Sommers, for whom he had worked in the capacity of general handy man and veterinarian upon occasion. Even then he was "Uncle Doctor," the title having been bestowed on him by the little boy who was Beryl's playmate during two days. After the death of the elder Sommers, Uncle Doctor lingered on here with the ranch and his horses. When Señor Costa bought the old place back, Uncle Doctor stayed on. He was one in whom there was an innate need for the expenditure of a fine loyalty. That loyalty was for years for any of the house of Sommers, and during the recent years it had been transferred to Antonio Costa and to Beryl. Most of all to Beryl.

Now it was his small, hard hands which groomed her favorite saddle animal, Silvermane, and had the mare in readiness when Beryl came running out to the stable again. Uncle Doctor looked his bright, birdlike approval, exclaiming:

"That's the niftiest little ridin' rig that ever come up out'n Ol' Mexico, where they like fine things; and you sure do look pretty in it, Miss Beryl. Up you go." He held his hand for her to slip her foot into and she flashed up into the saddle. "Don't you worry none; I'll have the boys out in two shakes, an' I'll go along. Ride lucky, Miss Beryl."

The light words she tossed back to him were all blown away; she and her horse, off with a rush, seemed also carried by the wind.

"It's goin' to be an ugly day," the little old fellow said, looking after the racing figures, "but I guess she'll be all right. She's all upset. Times like that a good fight does a feller good, even if it's only a fight ag'in a mean day."

It was not yet sun-up when Beryl went racing out across the fields, heading up into the rocky hills which defined the eastern limit of High Mesa, now that Little Mesa was shorn from it, and which constituted a wild and savage no-man's-land between the two ranches. Her own destination was not in the least clear to her; she might ride only as far as the heart of that rugged demesne of lava rock and spiked cactus, or she might ride on and on and so come in time to the place she was thinking most about, Little Mesa, the Kingsbury ranch.

But the wild morning itself was to decide the question for her. At first she gloried in it. As Uncle Doctor had said, it was a fine thing at times to have something to fight. Stronger and stronger grew the gusts; swifter and ever swifter came the rush of wind through the passes among the hills; her horse's mane and tail were flying; Beryl's tight little hat was whipped away and her hair lashed across her face; fine sand came streaming on the wind, swirling about her, making thin hissing noises.

She saw the sun thrusting up beyond a wildly blown thicket of mesquite, blood red and ominous, the weird sun of a day of sand storm.

"I'm a ninny; I ought to go back and to bed," she told herself, and pressed straight on.

The wind grew stronger and fiercer all the while that she sped across the open fields, deserted by all save herself and Silvermane, the herds having already taken shelter where they could find it. She was glad to come under the sharp, sheer shoulder of the first of the lava hills, thinking to find a quiet haven if only for a moment or so. But here it was as gusty as out on the open, and among the sharp-edged rocks wailing voices screamed to the leaden heavens above.

Half a mile farther on she dismounted and led Silvermane into a bowlder-ringed hollow, protected somewhat by a fringe of desert willows which were wildly tossing their branches like the arms of men, their hard leaves rattling in the dry torrent of air. She tethered the mare here and, stooping against the wind, went on; for at last she began to realize that this was no such mere blustery day as she had mistaken it for, but one to take quick shelter from, and a few steps more would carry her to an ideal vantage spot from which she might watch, protected and yet in awe, an episode in the ancient battle of the elements.

With sand filtering into her clothing, entering at her neck, gritty in her sleeves, sifting in everywhere, in her hair, in her boots, in her eyes and ears, she pressed on those last few steps. Before her was a great rift in the breast of the hills, a steep-walled gorge with cliffs rising sheer above it, a place known rather far and wide as Indian Gully and thick with legend. To her it was a favorite haunt. In the rock walls were places where the wind could not come. Here in the forgotten long ago some tribe of cliff dwellers had made its home.

As the sinister ball of the sun rose higher, an unearthly, lurid light lay over the world, a dull reddish light against the cliffs, a wan umber glow over the rims of the cañons, a pale, sickly murk down among the shadows. She was grateful that she had only a few steps to go. Head down for the most part, looking up with eyes narrowed to mere slits now and again to make sure of her way, she battled with the wind about a monster bowlder and snatched at it frantically to keep from being blown into the sharp-edged ravine. A little farther on was the higher cliff overlooking all this wilderness. She hurried to its base and to a worn, crooked stairway in the rock. Laboriously, clinging tight, she wormed her way upward a dozen steps or so and threw herself flat down. Here was a wide ledge, the ruins of crude masonry walls still standing, and in this spot, behind the broken wall, she came into comparative stillness.

She rested a moment, then peered out through the ruined doorway. She could scarcely see the farther side of the cañon, so thick was the air with hissing sand. She spoke to herself aloud, and could not hear her own voice for the shouting, screaming, whistling, jeering wind voices raging among the rocks.

Thinking the storm must blow itself out soon, so great was its fury by this time, she crouched and looked out with fascinated eyes. The sun rolled higher and higher, and took on stranger, deeper tones of red. Now and then, sucked along the great aërial current, some blurred object sped by and was lost from sight, a sage bush whipped from precarious moorings, a dead branch flying like a monstrous bird.

An hour passed and another and still another. What with fatigue, sleeplessness and nervous strain, what with the mad orchestration of a thousand shrill trumpetings and a far-away, dull, booming roar, there was induced in her a heavy sense of unreality, an aloofness, a feeling of body and soul being detached, the soul standing somewhere above and looking down upon the body and upon the world in tumult, a sense of remoteness from this battle ground, though she lay in the very heart of it. She thought of the Kingsburys and was mildly concerned that they and their troubles seemed very far from her own life; it was as though they dwelt upon a distant planet. She mused upon the ancient people who had dwelt here and in whose place she now brooded; they in some queer fashion felt nearer to her than her own people. Was it because, perhaps, she was at the moment experiencing an adventure which had been a part of their tribal life? How often had they taken shelter, as she did now, in this very place, watching the dull sky as she now watched it—wondering about things?

Suddenly, out of that smothered sky as she turned her moody eyes upon it, something at first formless began taking form. It caught her attention and at first meant nothing to her. Then of a sudden she was on her feet, staring wildly, icy cold with horror. She saw a blurred thing falling, swinging, twisting, a thing that had unfolded in the menacing sky like a great blossom, that was being hurled along like a gigantic thistledown. A raging gust caught it, plucked it upward, dragged it down; it went by her with a rush, sucked down into the cliff-bound gorge, and only as it vanished did she know that she had made no mistake and that it was a man dropping in a parachute.

CHAPTER VI

BERYL HAD SMALL HOPE THAT THE MAN SHE HAD seen hurled along by the storm could have lived through so terrible a fall. In a breathless, horrified fascination she had watched the pendulous body lashed back and forth, flung against the cliff and slung at a furious speed into the depths of Indian Gully. Yet the instant that both man and parachute vanished in that raging inferno she took the first impulsive step to go to him.

With the wind snatching at her, making every inch of

progress fraught with danger, her body pressed tight to the rocks, her hands clutching desperately, she made her way down the steep, uneven stairway and so came to the big bowlder brooding over the cañon's rim. From here there was no straight way down into the ravine, at least none that a human being could hope to travel on a day like this. She drew back from the edge and ran with the wind, blown along so that twice she stumbled and fell. But five minutes brought her to a pathway of sorts leading downward, one that she must have missed entirely in all this pandemonium were it not that she knew the place so well. It led into a flinty cleft and thereafter zigzagged among spiked yuccas and sharp-edged fragments of rock and sparse, wiry grass down into the bed of the gorge. Down this outworn roadway of a long past age, half blinded, snatched at by invisible hands, she made what wild haste she could.

On the floor of the ravine the sand under foot was sweeping onward in whirls and eddies, hiding the thin stream of water which usually flowed in so crystalline a stream from Indian Spring; shifting mounds piled up and were in another second whisked away, and the air was so choked with sand that she could scarcely breathe. She used both hands to hold her handkerchief tight across her nostrils and, blown along by the wind, raced on in the direction where the savagely jerking parachute had been lost to her view.

It was the parachute, still flapping and tugging at its moorings which drew her to the fallen man, half buried in a heap of sand. Down on her knees she began scooping the sand aside. A cry of distress burst from her when she saw the white face, unrecognizable at first with grime and the blood which had trickled from a wound on the brow. All the while the parachute, as though endowed with a malicious will of its own, kept tugging crazily. Her hurrying hands found the straps buckled about the lax shoulders and got them loose; the parachute fluttered, was caught up in a swirling gust and was carried away.

"It is Jerry Boyne—and he is dead—"

She was utterly at a loss. She was not sure that he was dead and did not know what to do, and so knelt, staring at the closed eyes, trying not to look at the ugly cut at the roots of the red hair. Then she realized that, if this was only a deep faint, water was the thing. And there was water near at hand.

She sprang up and, with flailing grit particles lashing at her, went staggering against the wind to the shallow stream. She drenched her handkerchief, filled her cupped hands, and buffeted her way back. The water she let trickle down upon the upturned face; with her handkerchief she gently wiped the blood and sand away from eyes and lips. It was only after she had made her second brief journey for water that Jerry stirred, ever so faintly.

Again she was at a loss. That he still lived meant that he might go on living, if only she could somehow help, if only she could move him into shelter or bring someone to aid her. She wondered fearfully whether he would die while she went groping her way to High Mesa and then back to him again with good old Uncle Doctor.

A third time she brought water. This time from her palm she poured a few drops in at the corner of his mouth, and he swallowed. She felt for his heart; it beat steadily. She got her arms under his shoulders and lifted him a little. His eyes opened; he looked at her dazedly and tried to sit up, only to fall back heavily with a groan, his eyes closed once more.

She put her lips close to his ear and said hurriedly: "I am coming right back. It's going to be all right."

Once more she made her way up out of the cañon, this time to hunt the spot where she had tethered Silvermane. She found the mare looking utterly dejected and miserable, head down, tail to the wind. With flying fingers she untied the rope, and then began a new task filled with difficulty. There was no leading Silvermane down that pathway which she herself had trodden, but a few hundred yards farther along was a place where Silvermane had carried her before, many and many a time. The thing now was to persuade the animal to take any path save that which led the shortest way back to a snug stable.

But in the end it was done and Beryl brought Silvermane by the longer, easier gradient into the storm blast raging in Indian Gully.

"Now if he has the strength—if he can only help me to help him into the saddle—"

As for Jerry Boyne, he scarcely knew what was going on. His body had been scraped and battered against the cliff and was shot through with pain; there was a fearful dull ache in his head. He had his moments of confused consciousness when he seemed to feel the earth heaving under him and realized that someone, some busybody it seemed to him, was doing all sorts of things to him to make discomfort over into torture. For him the next hour was a crazy quilt of flashes of groping consciousness and other periods of black nothingness. Thus he knew that he was struggling for mastery of a saddle and that someone was helping him, and that there was never another saddle like it for elusiveness—he knew that he was moving through some wild din and uproar—he heard far muffled shouts, a clearer, excited shout at his side—there were many hands reached out to him—wind-blown voices all about him:

"Oh, Uncle Doctor, thank God!"

"You're all right, Miss Beryl?"

"Yes, yes. Hurry!"

"On each side of him, boys; hold him up; he's goin' to make it in great shape."

He felt himself floating through space and looked curiously about him. He was being borne through a big, lofty room—oddly familiar this place—plastered walls, lofty, beamed ceiling—tiled floor seen through a far, high arch—a heavy, beautifully carved chest—wrought iron things—a curving stone staircase—a tiny balcony jutting out over the big room—

He floated up and up, above all this—a door slammed like a cannon shot—the roar in his ears was suddenly softened and deadened—he could hear shuffling feet—

He became suddenly conscious that the floating sensation was done with, that his body was softly supported, that voices were discussing him.

"It's a man named Jerry Boyne—a stranger. He was at the Empire Ranch yesterday—last night we saw his plane—he must have been caught in the wind and had something go wrong—I saw his parachute—"

"Fine, Miss Beryl. Lucky for him you did see; lucky for you, maybe, that we came lookin' for you. Now let me have him. Send Vidal up to me with my kit. I may need some hot water and bandages."

Jerry opened his eyes but at first could see no one. His glance roved the room and found it, like the more spacious chamber downstairs, hauntingly familiar. He could see a window, deep set in a thick wall, with a grill and a vine with red flowers. There was a tall-backed, leather-cushioned chair that looked as though it were about to remark, "Hello, Jerry, old man; don't you know me?" An arched doorway in a wall three feet thick—wrought iron candlesticks of a queer, unforgettable quaintness—a bit of tapestry on a wall and a tall mirror reflecting still another window with a balcony—an iron-bound chest with a sheet of leather thrown over it—

A man leaned over him, a chap of indeterminate age, the face suggesting an acorn for ripe coloring and polish, the eyes childlike. Jerry stared at this face for a little while, then strove to smile and said faintly:

"Hello—Uncle Doctor!"

"Hello yourself, young feller," said Uncle Doctor, beginning in his rough-and-ready way of diagnosis to hunt out the sore spots with horny thumbs. It meant nothing to him that this chap seemed to know him; it was to be supposed that he had heard Beryl call him Uncle Doctor.

"Don't know me, do you?" demanded Jerry.

"How should I? Hurt much right here?"

"Ouch! Think I'm a sick horse?—Good God!"

"What's the matter? I ain't killin' you."

"No, of course not." Jerry squirmed about and managed to sit up, though dizzy and wavering. "It's about Kingsbury—I'd forgot—"

"Kingsbury?" snapped Uncle Doctor. "What about him? What Kingsbury?"

"Bob. I left him at his house. He's all shot to pieces. I was on my way to scare up a doctor when I ran into the storm and came to grief. Clear out of this and go to the poor devil. I'm all right, and he needs help the worst way. You can maybe hold him from slipping while someone goes for a real doctor."

The old fellow stood back and looked at him to make sure that he wasn't raving. Jerry's eyes were clear enough now though filled with anxiety.

"All right, all right, young feller; I'll step along. Lay back there, will you? You're all right, huh? Jus' a few busted ribs, if I'm any good guessin' an' a head damn near knocked off your carcass. But I guess that's nothin' much for a guy that goes aroun' jumpin' out'n the sky. Lay still, will you? I'll have ol' Vidal in to wipe the gore off'n you, an' to bust you with a club if you don't keep quiet, an' I'll go out an' buck the storm as far as Kingsbury's. Shot all to hell, huh? Who done it?"

Jerry, as limp as a rag from starting up, only shook his head and muttered:

103

"Snap into it, Doc; the poor devil's got five bullet holes in him. And send somebody for a doctor."

Later Jerry had rather a comfortable time of it, all things considered. That was, perhaps, because of the drink which they had given him. Vidal, chauffeur and other things, one who had aided the old Doc in many a first-aid treatment, had undressed him, tidied him a bit, bound strips of a sheet about his ribs, topped him off with another bundlesome bandage about his head and left him to doze in a big four-poster bed. Still later Jerry awoke, wondered at a headache and general lassitude, stared a bit and got his bearings.

"My own room," he mused wonderingly. "That's funny. The old chest right there, the giant's walnut wardrobe yonder—and the same iron table on the balcony. Nothing changed. It seems as though I'd lived here half my life, but a mighty long time ago—and I was at High Mesa only about two weeks all together."

Still later Beryl looked in on him. She had changed from her riding things to a pretty dress, a frisky little thing, thought Jerry, orange colored. It was short sleeved, and her arms were as lovely as he had known they must be. As she came tiptoeing across the room a pathway of sunlight streamed across her and struck sparkles from her swinging jade earrings.

"Thought I wasn't to come to see you?" said Jerry, smiling up into the eyes bent gravely down on his. "Then, when I wasn't in any condition to defend myself, out you came and kidnaped me and brought me in!"

"I saw you falling—" She shuddered. "I don't know how you lived through it."

"I've a mighty confused recollection of it—your part, I mean. But I'm clear enough on one point; but for you I'd have been done for."

"If you feel strong enough to talk—"

"I feel strong enough to get up and run a race!"

"Then will you tell me about Bob Kingsbury?"

His eyes grew sober enough then and he demanded sharply:

"They've gone to help him? Uncle Doctor, I mean?"

"How did you know that he was Uncle Doctor? I am the only one who calls him that."

How easy it would be to say: "And it was from me that you learned that name for him!" What a look he could bring into her eyes! At first, to be sure, she'd not believe; but when he recalled this and that to her, when he went into detail concerning a so-well-remembered day, what then?

So easy to say these things—and impossible! For there was the inevitable conclusion, whether or not he spoke the words: "This place is mine. It is you who are the guest here, welcome as you are. And, expelled from High Mesa, you and your fine old granddad are, I fancy, just two penniless babes in the wood!" Instead of all this Jerry, holding his tongue, thought swiftly: "Here you go, tying my hands all the tighter, saving my life for me—and every time you look at me making me adore you just seven times as much as I was already doing!"

All this while she was waiting for his answer, looking

vaguely puzzled. Hurriedly now he replied:

"Didn't I hear you call him that while you were getting me here? And you want to know about Kingsbury? First, they have gone to him, haven't they?"

"Yes. How they will get through the storm, I don't know; it's worse than when you came down in it. But they will."

"Fine. He's worth it, that Bob Kingsbury. Some day maybe there will be a gamer sport turned out in human guise, but I doubt it. You see, down in Nacional, not being sleepy and being a nosey animal, I got the hunch to mosey up this way and look for him, and I was in luck. He spotted me and lighted a flare. He was back in the hills a couple of miles beyond his house. We flew back to his place and there I left him; I didn't like taking any more chances carting him around than I had to, the poor devil being so nearly dead. If I had known where to find a doctor— Well, I didn't. So I left him there— and he ought to be dead by now—and if ever a man could pull himself through with sheer grit, Bob Kingsbury'll do it."

"Did he tell you who shot him?" she queried swiftly.

"He did not. Nor did I ask. But I think I could guess."

He told of his landing and of the shot he drew from the wounded man.

"He thought I was someone come back in a plane to finish a job I had started."

"And that that plane was the *Hawk*! Is there no limit to that woman's wickedness? Oh, I know this is her work, just as I know that that other poor boy, Bob's brother, is dead now at her orders."

106

"They are friends of yours, these Kingsburys?" he asked.

"I hardly know them. It is just recently that they came here, you know. My grandfather sold them Little Mesa only two months ago."

There he had one question answered. It had been Señor Costa, then, and not the fellow who posed at being Gerald Sommers who had sold Little Mesa. Well, what difference—

Why, this difference! The old Spaniard, poor devil, had sold something which did not belong to him, and could be held responsible. Jerry, his quick sympathies engaged, felt like squirming all over the bed—yes, and up and into his clothes to "start something." Just what and how to start anything he was very far from knowing, but he held it rather more than merely clear that the time was not far off when he would want an accounting with Red Handsome. What a skunk that good-looking devil was, not for his outright robbery of Jerry himself, but for victimizing a pair of dear innocents like old Antonio Costa and his little grand-daughter.

Beryl was looking at him curiously, at loss for any explanation of the deep meditation into which he appeared plunged; and when he looked up suddenly he saw that she was doing a bit of thoroughgoing wondering.

"Why not put it into words?" he said lightly, inviting confidence with a good-natured grin.

She flushed and bit her lip, then said swiftly:

"Very well, I will. What did you mean yesterday, Mr.

Boyne, by saying that you and I had met before?"

"Just that. We had." He chuckled. He enjoyed mystifying her and had no fear of her guessing the truth. That was a thing to which her mind was just naturally closed.

"Will you explain?" she asked, with a little narrowing and darkening of the eyes which, thought Jerry Boyne, was an indication that here you had to do with a young woman who on occasion might display all the earmarks of a blazing hot temper.

"You've traveled a lot, haven't you?" he said evasively. "Back and forth across the briny deep, into Spain and into various other parts of the world? Well, so have I."

"I met you on a steamer, perhaps?" She shrugged. "One meets so many that way—and it hardly counts as acquaintance, does it?"

"Not anxious to claim me?" he asked while his grin broadened. "Not even now after you've saved my life? You realize that now it belongs to you, henceforth and forever."

"That's nonsense, you know," she retorted.

"But it's nothing of the kind! Didn't you know? Why, when you pull a fellow back from the Great Beyond, he's just sort of reborn into this jolly old world, you know—and you're responsible. As much responsible as the mother who bore him. Like it or not, Beryl, I'm yours for keeps."

He had watched many different expressions dawn and pass and merge in her expressive gray eyes, but now for the first time saw a hauteur which may have been inherited from some very *grande dame* among her southern ancestresses.

"Perhaps you don't know the word 'presumptuous,' Mr. Boyne?"

"If I presume, it's on past friendship; remember that. For we *were* friends once, you and I."

Having absolutely no rejoinder to make which at all fitted the occasion, she was about to leave the room when her grandfather came to the door. Dressed as Jerry had seen him the day before, all in snowy white flannels and tall-heeled, shiny black boots, he constituted in the frame of the doorway the picture of elegance at ease. About to speak, for an instant he held his silence and his eyes spoke for him, very eloquent black eyes under very eloquent white brows which were elevated just the merest yet most emphatic trifle. Though he had lived on into the twentieth century, nonetheless his instincts were with his traditions, rooted in the nineteenth. Or in the eighteenth? The fact was that he did not altogether approve of finding Miss Beryl visiting in a gentleman's bedroom.

Jerry got that. Also, as Señor Costa's brilliant eyes rested on him, mild speculation in them, Jerry grew fully conscious of quite another matter, one to which he'd given little thought—and realized that he had been made as gorgeous as a bird of paradise in a suit of purple and gold pajamas. "The old don's, of course, but I'll bet a horse Beryl brought 'em home for him!"

All this in a mere flash of time. Señor Costa came into the room, smiled at his granddaughter and slipped his arm through hers. He turned to Jerry with a gracious expression of delight that Mr. Boyne had not been seriously injured, and voiced the hope that they here at High Mesa might be privileged in making up to him somewhat for the harrowing experience which had befallen him.

"I think, my dear," he said to Beryl, "that Mr. Boyne had best be kept very quiet; at least until the physician arrives and gives us orders for him."

"I'm as right as rain," Jerry proclaimed. "I must be up and around in no time."

But Costa piloted his granddaughter to the door. There he stopped again and looked at Jerry so intently that for the second time he grew pajama-conscious. "For if it isn't the pajamas he's looking at like that, then what?"

"Mr. Boyne," said Costa very gravely, very much the old-fashioned gentleman and very, very Spanish, "we are honored in having you under this roof. All that we have is gladly at your disposal. As our people have a way of saying—High Mesa is yours."

A moment longer he stood regarding Jerry eye to eye. Then he bowed deeply, said, "Come, Beryl," and the two were gone. And Jerry, propped on an elbow, stared after them; most of all did he stare at the back of the snowy head as he asked himself curiously:

"What did he mean by that? Did he mean anything? The Empress said almost the same thing: The place is yours—" The old familiar grin flashed back. "If the old chap only knew!"

CHAPTER VII

DESPITE JERRY'S ASSURANCE THAT HE'D BE UP and abroad in no time, he found himself for the moment drained of all power, as weak as a baby and as incapable of any independent action. His body was bruised from head to foot and became a patchwork of black and blue areas which, turning a lovely purplish color, went well with the gorgeous pajamas. Furthermore he had two cracked ribs, and a head which ached and reeled whenever he stirred. During the day a physician, summoned from twenty-mile-distant San Juan, a crisp young chap lately escaped from his internship and bristling like a field marshal, manhandled him, bandaged him and issued his ultimatum that his prisoner— Jerry couldn't help feeling like a military prize of war to this very military medico—was to have absolute rest and quiet, and a whole lot of it.

"How's Bob Kingsbury?" Jerry demanded the moment the physician came in. "You've looked him over, I hope."

"I have. He's alive. Some of these leathery chaps take a lot of killing. Five wounds, drained white of blood, two nights out in the rock-piles! Alive when I left him; that's all."

"Any chance for him?"

"The same chance you'd have right now if your parachute had decided not to open at all. If he'd had any chance I wouldn't have left that ass of a horse doctor with him." He shrugged. "The sooner he dies now the more mercy there'll be in it—and maybe the horse doctor will speed his parting guest. Of all the asses!"

Jerry obeyed orders, lay quiet and spent a thoroughly miserable day, save for the three or four hours of heavy sleep. All day when he heard anything at all he hearkened to the rush of the wind; even with windows and doors closed sand drifted in and overspread the old dark floor and mahogany wardrobe with a gray veiling of grit. Toward sunset however the storm died down and in the heavy stillness which followed the world seemed a very peaceful place.

A silken cord hung at the head of his bed and he was instructed that if he pulled at it a bell would ring downstairs. But he wanted nothing; he thought that he had never wanted less in his life. A Mexican house boy was in and out of the room all day, pretending to set things to order, tiptoeing and peeping at the bed with a most depressing sick-room expression, and from him Jerry had the cooling drinks which were his only solace during the long hours. Several times Señor Costa came as far as the door, spoke a courteous word, repeated that the thing to do was rest, sleep if possible, and went away.

There was ample time for pondering, but Jerry came to the end of all thinking in ten minutes, finding himself with a job on his hands that he did not like. The logical thing to do, of course, was to announce his identity, cast about for the proper steps to prove his contention—and let the chips fall where they would. Logical enough but decidedly not to be thought of until he had looked the ground over pretty thoroughly, with many a thought to the future. To put a red-headed impostor in the peniten-tiary was a thing which one might anticipate with relish; to break the news to Beryl's grandfather that he had been swindled out of two hundred and fifty thousand dollars and now had nothing but a worthless deed to show for it, was altogether a different matter.

Beryl herself he did not see again until so late that night that he had given up all hope of seeing her at all. Then she came alone as before and her foot at the threshold quickened his heartbeat. She had dressed for dinner, no doubt to please her grandfather; perhaps, with her mind filled with so many other things, it was all mere chance that she had chosen her newest and most effective gown; she wore her pearls, too, which she may have donned in a mere moment of abstraction. She wore black adorably and bracelets as though they were Cupid fetters.

Jerry, bethinking himself earlier in the day that she might once more take mercy on him, had vowed to be circumspect, neither to plague nor to presume; he'd guard his tongue and hope to prolong a golden moment. Now he blurted out involuntarily:

"Beryl! You knock a man's eye out with all that beauty!"

She laughed just as he was wishing that he'd clamped his teeth down on a darned fool tongue. There is a chance that she, too, had found the day long. It didn't happen every day that you saved a human life, the life of a decidedly good-looking if impudent young man. You couldn't do a thing like that and dust your hands off and forget about it. And when you sensed that there was something under the surface with the fellow—who by the way claimed that you were responsible for him, and who vowed that the life you had saved was now yours—well, it was neither more nor less than human nature to wonder about him.

"It would appear to the unprejudiced," she remarked while he hunted dimples, knowing full well that he was confronted with their very habitat, "that you have endured enough physical mishap without having an eye knocked out too. Therefore I'll haste to withdraw my fatal beauty, merely saying good-night and asking if there is anything that might add to your comfort for the night?"

"There is! Won't you sit down and visit with me for five minutes? I'm horribly lonesome. It would be too bad, wouldn't it, if, after all you have done to pluck me back from the tomb, I should up and die of loneliness?"

She laughed as she warned him:

"Remember you're risking an eye!"

She sat on the extreme edge of the severe, high-backed chair in a line between his bed and the open door and in such a fashion that every second she seemed on the point of getting up to go.

"I can't help calling you Beryl, so why not forgive me at the jump and we'll get on to other things?"

"How interesting! You really cannot help it? I suppose it's like a disease with you, like the utter inability of a drug taker—"

"It's like this: You know a rose? All right; would you ever think of calling it anything else? Take a—a water-melon, for instance; you wouldn't call it a bicycle, would you? If you gather my meaning—"

"You were unconscious when I found you," said Beryl with an assumption of deep gravity, though her eyes danced and he was sure of the dimple from actual discovery. "That blow on your head—"

"Since there was not as much inside as without, let's hope that more got knocked in than got hammered out! Thanks a lot for forgiving me. By the bye, I have a present for you; I've brought it back to you from half around the world. May I give it to you now?"

"A present for me?" The way she lifted her brows was reminiscent of her grandfather. She decided to frown, was not highly successful and finally smiled ruefully with a shake of her curly brown hair. "If I really had taken on any responsibility such as you insist on, I am afraid that I'd have to begin at the beginning and do a lot of making over! Why do you insist on such nonsense?"

"Then you'll accept it now?" He groped under his pillow for the wallet which Vidal had placed there after the change from dusty clothing to purple and gold. "It's only a little thing; something you're bound to like, though. And you'll mark how it proves every one of my words true! Put it to your ear and you'll hear it whisper that I've carried it more than twenty thousand miles to bring it to you."

"The world grows larger," said Beryl as if in awe. "When I was a little girl in school—"

"But I didn't come in a straight line with it! Why, that thing's been in my pocket for years."

"I do grow curious," she confessed, "even though I

never dreamed until now that sheer nonsense could affect one so."

"Tell me the latest word from Bob Kingsbury," he said, while opening his wallet.

"The doctor today said that the poor fellow could not possibly live a dozen hours. But a little while ago Uncle Doctor sent a man to High Mesa for some things he needed and sent word along that Bob Kingsbury was still alive and that the doctor from San Juan was a fool."

"Let's bet on Bob and Uncle Doc. And here's your present. Please like it—and keep it. I've a superstition about it."

He proffered a tiny parcel the size of her little finger, wrapped in a bit of tissue paper. Had it not been for the wrapping she might have found it so much easier to deal with him. As it was, the prickling of curiosity grew insistent. With a shrug which as good as said, "Oh, well, we must humor this insistent nonsense maker," she took his gift from his fingers and undid it.

"Oh!" she gasped, and that prickling sensation took on something of the nature of a pleasurable little thrill. "Why, they're beryls!"

They were. A pair of earrings of pink transparent beryl with a flash of tiny colored fires like soft hues in a sun-shot spray.

"But I couldn't possibly keep these!"

"Only you could. They're yours anyhow. I knew they were yours the very minute I took the rough crystals out of the mother earth that bore 'em. I had 'em fashioned in China, and I told the old Chinese gent that they were

116

for you, so he made 'em up like that with you in mind. And—"

She looked at him wonderingly.

"Why do you pretend this way?" she asked, insisting on the truth.

He judged that wisdom lay in wariness and said lightly:

"It's fun to pretend, isn't it? If you'll just pretend with me that we're old friends and the best in the world— why, that's what we'll be."

"I don't understand you, Mr. Boyne. I have a queer feeling that— You didn't merely drift this way by accident, did you? There was something that brought you; you have some interest here you don't speak about. Bob Kingsbury, for instance—"

"I never heard of Bob Kingsbury until yesterday," he answered promptly. And, discretion discarded for characteristic daring: "Whether I have some interest, whether something drew me here— You know how it is between steel and magnet? Can you blame—"

"Thank you for showing me the earrings; they are very pretty." She rose and placed them on his bedside table, adding casually: "And it is a queer coincidence, isn't it, that they should be beryls—"

"How do you spell that last word?" he interrupted. "Should be with a capital B and an apostrophe s. I told you they were Beryl's—"

"And now that our five minutes are up—"

"Lord! I should have brought you a clock instead! You haven't been here two seconds! Aren't you going to keep them?"

"Of course not," she laughed. "Good-night."

"When I grab my good and faithful crutches and hobble off into the desert to die of a broken heart, right there on the table those beryls that are Beryl's are going to stay!"

She had got as far as the door where she whirled to say laughingly:

"You haven't seen our cook yet? She is Maria and she is very dark Mexican and she weighs more than two hundred pounds. Furthermore she loves jewelry and I am sure would steal for pink earrings! If you leave your treasures there you do it at your own peril."

"Good-night, Saver of Lives. And remember that mine—"

"*Buenos noches,* Mr. Boyne."

She vanished and Jerry settled down philosophically to wait for morning and another glimpse of her.

But another irksome day dragged by and he did not even see her pass by his open door. A fine day it was, of open doors and windows and a slumbersome, tranquil, golden warmth pouring in, yet a day for all that which pleased him little. True he had word of her; Señor Costa came to see him three times, stopping once to sit down and chat. He said that his granddaughter had slept late, being much in need of sleep; that later she had ridden over to Little Mesa, superintending the conveyance of such trifling delicacies as she supposed a sick man might partake of; he gave the impression that she had, oh, a number of things to do, such as young women occupy themselves with—and drifted to other and unimportant matters.

Jerry progressed rapidly. The soreness began to go; the general stiffness departed with it; his head no longer ached, and he came to the conclusion that the doctor didn't know what he was talking about when he said that there were a couple of ribs broken. In any case, what did a cracked rib or two amount to when a fellow wanted to be up and about?

Meantime he amused himself with bribery. At a time when the Mexican house boy was pottering about the room, Jerry beckoned him to the bed.

"See those earrings on the table there, Tommy? It's that new pair of Miss Beryl's; she left them here when she came to call on me. You take them and put them on her dressing table. Just put them there when she's not about, and say nothing. Now hand me my trousers; if I didn't scatter my loose change all over High Mesa, there are a couple of nice new *pesos* there that belong to you."

Tommy showed his fine white teeth appreciatively and the thing was done.

Another perfectly good day was wrecked because there was no Beryl in it, but its fag end was somewhat redeemed by a call from Uncle Doctor.

"And how's the high-jumper?" he wanted to know.

"Squat," commanded Jerry. "For God's sake squat and fill my ears with conversation. Man, I like to look at you!"

"Complications set in?" snorted the little old fellow, eying him sharply. "That ass of a doctor from San Juan wasted his time on your staves when it was a mental

119

case. Why'n-'ell should anybody like to look at me?"

"That's part of the mystery," grinned Jerry, and reached out to smite his visitor on the knee. "When I tell you, you'll rare up on your hind legs and fall over backward like the miller's old sow when she went into a swoon. So the San Juan doctor is an ass, huh? You two sure agree fine! How's Bob?"

"He's pretty bad hurt; worse'n that, he laid out in the open two nights. Just a few bullet holes alone through a man that's got stamina, shucks, that's nothin'. He'll be up an' stirrin' in time. And know what I'm goin' to make him do?" A fine mesh of wrinkles gathered about the bright, eager eyes. "I'm goin' to say, 'Looky, Bob; I sweated over you and now you pay!' And he'll goggle at me and git red and start to say how of course he was goin' to ask how much is it. And I'll say, 'I'll let you work it out. You jus' climb into the saddle and ride over to San Juan and look that fool doctor up and hand him one swingin' kick to show him how much dead you are.'"

"Tell me some things," said Jerry abruptly. "What sort of folks are Antonio Costa and his granddaughter?"

A cold eye was cocked at him and he had a forthright answer.

"Any man as says a single word about either of them two is a dirty liar!"

"That sounds as though you meant it. Next, old party, what sort of a bird is that young, red-headed friend of theirs that they bought High Mesa from?"

"You're a sort of free and easy jasper, ain't you? Kind of offhand and don't-give-a-damn and mebbe nosey?

I'd say, if you want to know all about young Sommers, you might go ask him. I c'n see you ain't bashful."

Jerry grinned impudently into the puckered face.

"And I seem to note that you don't hop to the bat for him as lively as you do for our friends here at High Mesa. Don't like him, eh?"

"Whether I do or don't is nobody's business—unless it's his, and I'll try to answer up when he asks."

"Used to know him when he was a kid, too, didn't you?"

"What if I did?" The words were fairly snapped at him, and the good-humor crinkles about the shrewd eyes changed subtly into furrows of a different order.

"What if I said," continued Jerry placidly, "that he's a low-down, egg-sucking crook?"

A shrug which was intended to be the sole answer was immediately followed by a snort of disdain and then the contemptuous words:

"You're the kind of so-called man that I'd like powerful well to wipe my feet on after trudgin' in a dirty corral. Whyn't you stand up to him and sock him back when he walloped you down to Nacional, stead of belly-achin' to me about him behind his back? Whyn't you mosey over to San Juan and get you a job sweepin' and cleanin' spittoons for that feller that lives in a house that's got a M.D. sign hung over the door? You'n him would make a team."

"Whoa!" cried Jerry, and sank back among his pillows, enormously gleeful. "Do me a kindness, old-timer, will you?"

"I'll see you in hell first! Honest, and speakin' for

121

publication, I can't stomach a man that slinks and does his fightin', near as nature'll let him, like a polecat does. *Addy-ose!*"

"You darned old fool!" laughed Jerry in high delight. By now his mind was fully made up; he was yielding whole-souledly to temptation, and was downright certain that for once he was doing the right thing. "Toddle over to the door; it's a mite open and we want it shut tight. Then toddle back here, fix yourself good in your chair so you won't fall out—and I'll ask you three questions. You won't have to answer a single one of them aloud, either; just answer them to yourself. Hop to it, pal o' mine!"

It was a thoroughly mystified little man who, dubious yet intrigued, closed the door firmly and returned to the bedside.

"I'll take it standin'," he said irritably. "Better make it snappy, too. What's on your mind?"

"Question Number One," said Jerry, smiling up into the unsmiling eyes piercing at him as though they meant to excavate the shortest way to the truth. "You hadn't clapped eyes on the aforesaid red-headed pilgrim for a good ten years when he came back from parts unknown some five years ago, had you? Mind, you don't have to answer."

"Shoot!" growled Uncle Doctor. "Eve'body knows that."

"Question Number Two: You looked him over and you said to yourself, 'Shucks, unless he said so, I'd never have known him for the Sommers kid. Time did sure make a lot of changes in that kid.'"

The narrowed eyes merely narrowed a bit further. Jerry, still smiling, concluded swiftly.

"Number Three: Has it ever dawned on you—you who had taught him to ride, who had cared for his dog that time old Bounder got caught in the steel trap, who gave him his first rifle and showed him how to shoot holes in old tomato cans, who used to loll out in the shade with him and tell him tall lies about scalping Injuns—has it ever dawned on you, you old horse-doctoring reprobate, that our red-headed friend didn't even remember any of those little things?"

The old fellow's face, from being screwed up in puzzlement, of a sudden went as blank as the plastered wall. Then there came a flash of light into his eyes, a flash of understanding into his brain.

"Good God!" he gasped, and sat down in his chair as abruptly as if his legs had been mown away beneath him.

There he sat, open mouthed and limp bodied for perhaps all of five seconds. Then he came erect with a jerk.

"Man alive!" he gasped. "This thing you're tellin' me—if I ever heard a cock-and-bull yarn—"

"Back up!" Jerry laughed at him. "I haven't told you any sort of yarn. You can't blame me if just a plain question or two—"

A snort cut him short. Uncle Doctor jerked forward and stared him in the eye, and certainly never did a man stare harder, never did eyes seek deeper. Of a sudden those eyes brightened joyously and a flush spread over the acorn-polished old cheeks. Out shot a hard hand to grip Jerry's in a mighty squeeze.

"It's you, Jerry-boy! Damn if it ain't!"

"It's me all right," grinned Jerry. "Howdy, old-timer. And now you know why I said you're good to look at. Gosh, it's been a long time."

"Yep, it's you all right. I know it; I c'n feel it. Changed? I grant it. But now that I look at you—you're your dad's own, kid. And—and that other red-headed son of sin!" Click went his teeth savagely. "What he's done? Why, dammit!" he exploded and sat back to stare afresh. "It ain't you he's robbed! It's the old don and Miss Beryl! He's robbed them of a clean quarter of a million! I always knew that devil for a polecat—"

He pulled out a small black pipe and rammed tobacco in it viciously, whereupon he shoved it back into his pocket.

"Them two," he blurted out, half angrily, his thoughts boiling up, his eyes becoming belligerent, "I've told you they're the finest. And here you come crawlin' back to make 'em trouble!"

He got to his feet and went stamping up and down, frowning and muttering. He came back to the bed, and by that time had worked himself up into a small fury.

"Why'n'ell didn't you show up sooner, a long time sooner—or not at all?" he demanded truculently. "Now look you, Jerry Sommers—if you are Jerry Sommers, and I guess you are—I ain't goin' to stand for your knockin' all the props out f'm under old Antonio Costa and his little granddaughter. Got that? Get it right, feller. If you come pokin' home late, after all the fat's in the fire, that's your loss. Don't count on me lendin' you a helpin' hand to puttin' the two best I know in the pore house. Help you—against them?" He cackled derisively. "By gravy, I'll go to the bat for 'em; I'll swear you're no more Gerald Sommers than I am. How's that strike your funny bone, you pestilential troubleshooter?"

"Look here; you can't blame me—"

"I do! It's all your own pesky fault. I—Lord, Lord, Lord!" he burst out and again fell to trotting around the room. "It's a mess."

"So far we're agreed. Now suppose you sit down and keep your hair on; it might even help if you lighted that unlawful old pipe of yours. There's a lot I want to dig out of you if you can come down to earth again."

"Maybe you ain't Jerry Sommers at all!" It was only a feeble flare and in the next words, "Maybe you're just stringin' me," there was no conviction.

"I haven't said I was Gerald Sommers, have I? Remember that first day at High Mesa? How you saddled the fat little pony for Beryl and me? How we ate sandwiches out in the pasture—and you sat on a piece of blackberry pie and ruined yourself with it? How you shot a rattlesnake's head off on the way up that morning? And the next time we came, the day we took possession and Señor Costa and Beryl went away, how he wouldn't look back—and she did, and was crying and shook her fist at us? How—"

"Oh, dry up, Jerry Sommers," groaned the old fellow and from under his scowl shot forth a bright and tender look of affection. "Lord love me, but I'm in a whirl!" He stiffened and said, very much after the fashion of a thoroughgoing villain of the old-time melodrama days:

125

"I'll go into court and swear on my immoral soul that you're no more named Sommers than I am!"

"You old sinner," chuckled Jerry, "I believe you would. Now get this first: I'd be as sorry as you would to make trouble for these people. I haven't done a thing or said a word so far, have I? Like you, I've realized that things were in a confounded tangle. But there's always a way out of any maze, you know, if a man can only find it."

"Mean that, Jerry? You see old Costa's side of it, too, and ain't all hell-bent for lettin' him down?" At Jerry's emphatic nod he sat down, unpocketed his pipe and lighted it. "I might have known it," he said as the first puff of smoke rode away on a long sigh. "It's in the blood, I guess, that a feller turns out to be fine stock or reptile. I begin to think that it won't be necessary after all for me to strangle you and then diagnose you as havin' choked to death on a piece of rib that worked free." He beamed all over; reaching out swiftly he rumpled Jerry's red hair in a way dear to them both. "Let's talk big talk, Chingagook!"

"Big talk it is, Hawk Eye!" They grinned at each other, remembering.

"Where'll we begin?"

"At the beginning." Jerry's face sobered and he demanded curtly: "Tell me about Dad."

"You've already heard somebody mowed him down? Well, that's pretty much the tale, my boy. Nobody knows who did it and nobody ever will. It's one of them things. There are those who don't like that Fernandez woman, of the Empire Ranch; there is talk that there

126

was trouble between her outfit and this one; it's said she was sore at your dad account of him buying High Mesa in the first place. You'll recall it was heavy mortgaged before Antonio Costa was forced to sell to your old man? And that the Fernandez woman held the mortgages? They say she had her heart set on rakin' High Mesa into her pile." He shrugged. "Folks talk a lot. Me, I dunno. If some of her crowd wiped him out— Why, we'll never know."

"That El Bravo is a killer if I ever saw one. Was he with her then?"

"He was. What's more he come pokin' up here once in your dad's time—and got kicked clean off the ranch with advice to stay off." He sighed. "Still you can't hardly go out and shoot him for that, can you?"

"But you think—"

"If I'd had any rights to think it, I'd have gone out and gored him long since, wouldn't I?"

Jerry dropped his eyes moodily to the cigarette which was now keeping company with the pipe.

"Let's get along to other things for the moment," he said presently. "This red-headed hellion that's trying to wear my shoes, what about him? Who is he and where'd he come from?"

"Search me. I thought he was you." He began feeling thoughtfully for any fresh stubble on his yesterday's-shaven chin. "He blew in about six months after your father's death. *You* was advertised for and he upped and proved that's who he was. He'd coached himself pretty good; he must have nosed about from under cover pretty considerable before he declared himself; he's foxy and as I seem to remember he kept his mouth shut and let the other fellow do the talkin' as far as possible. Why, he even fooled Beryl, and I guess he did it by lettin' her do most of the chattin' about the time they'd had together as kids. I kinda reckon, Jerry-boy, that he's a right smart young man."

"Looks that way, devil take him. Well, what about him now? What for a man is he anyhow? And, most of all, what has he done with the two hundred fifty thousand?"

"Aha! That's the talk! We'll take that polecat by the back o' the neck and *squeeze!* What did he do with his wad? For one thing, he's got him another ranch; it's the old Cadwallader place; they call it the Alamo Springs, 'count of the poplars. Maybe you'll remember it? Just the other side Little Mesa. Say, he's got his nerve, eh? Squattin' right down here instead of takin' what he had and shootin' to some other nice far-away place. Reckon he figured you was dead, hey, Jerry?"

"How much is the Alamo Springs outfit worth?"

"That's right; hold me down. Glory be, Chingagook, this is like old times, ain't it?" His body contracted to the impulse to rumple the red hair again, but he controlled himself and added briskly: "How much for the Alamo? I'd say about seventy-five thousand; dunno just how much he's done to it or what stock's runnin' on it. Maybe a hundred thousand."

"Well, there's a recoverable slice of our two hundred fifty thousand. What about the rest of the money? Suppose he's got it banked? Or had he shot it?"

"Do you know—I'm beginnin' to git a hunch!"

"You mean the Empress, don't you, Hawk Eye? I know she helped him make good his bluff."

"She did, that's a fact and that's what I had in my mind. Now, why? If she thought he was the real goods, why kick in? It's pretty close to bein' a Bible fact that she and your dad was enemies, so why should she turn a hand to help your dad's kid? But if she knew, the wise old hoot-owl, that he was a rank outsider hornin' in, then what? In said case she might chip in to help him, hey? And I guess she'd figger her share was half the gate receipts and maybe more."

"Guess work," said Jerry, though he leaned a long way in the direction the other indicated. "We'll make it our affair to try to check on him, anyhow. Incidentally I'd like to know where he banks and what sort of a balance he keeps. And, here's a bright and shining thought: Do you suppose that a low-life like him, having got away with so fruity a crooked deal once, would shut his eyes to other chances in the world? Or, being the kind of a man we know him to be, and thinking it was all dead easy, wouldn't he be keeping his hand in?"

"I don't see how he can. Still, I dunno. If he was still runnin' with the Fernandez woman, I'd say that he was bendin' all energies to go from bad to worse. But he's broke with her and—"

"Do you happen to know why?" Jerry interrupted sharply.

"I happen to know why. And you're gettin' me in a state of nerves where I feel an itch to go git my old double-barrel shotgun, load her to the muzzle with buckshot and cut glass and rampage around killin' folks.

Why, boy—and maybe it don't mean anything to you but it does to me—the Empress has a rat for a son that she thinks the sun was made to shine on, and that pop-eyed son of evil has got it in his head to marry our Beryl; on top of that the Fernandez woman makes it her filthy job to give him everything he rolls his slimy eyes on; and on top of that the red-head that calls himself you has also got it in his mind that he means to have her. That springs war in camp; that's the first step to make old lady Fernandez start sharpenin' her bowie knife for Mr. Red."

"And Red, as it happens, finds some slight favor in Beryl's eyes?" asked Jerry, once again examining his cigarette.

"Why not? She didn't know— Wait until I git through tellin' her what sort—" He broke off as he saw where his own words were carrying him and groaned. "Only I can't tell her a damned thing, can I?" he ended miserably. "But I would, though!" he exploded violently. "Before I'd let her marry that pup I'd spill all the beans, no matter what it cost Antonio Costa."

"I fancy he could lose a good many thousands and not break him?"

"You're a fancy fancier then," snorted Uncle Doctor. "You'd think he'd learned his lesson, wouldn't you, losin' High Mesa once already? But there's folks that hasn't any more business with money than a kid has playin' with matches and gasoline. It cost him pretty close to all he had, buyin' High Mesa back. Oh, that was fine with him; he'd make a lot of money on the place this time, sure! *Seguro, señor!* Only it's been breakin' him. He spends money like it was water when he's got it, and when he's broke he goes out and borrows. Next year, he's always sayin', the luck will change. He's mortgaged right up to the eyebrows now. And, if you ask me, he's beginnin' to git scared."

Jerry was amazed.

"Why, I saw him drop four thousand at the Empire, on a race and at roulette, and he never turned a hair."

"That's Señor Antonio Arenda Costa for you."

"Whew! That means that if I did close him out—"

"To the pore house, like I said. Or, him bein' Señor Antonio Arenda Costa, under the sod. One of the finest, too." Then he shot one of his piercing looks at Jerry. "How come, old son, that you're all for bearing down so easy on the old scout? You don't hardly know him even."

"My one ambition in life," said Jerry promptly, level eyed and hard about the mouth, "is to marry his granddaughter."

Conversation languished after that and both men stared off into vacancy. At last Jerry observed abruptly:

"I'm going to need money, all the money I can get my hands on. I'm not on my uppers; I've got a few thousands stuck away in a Los Angeles bank, but if I'm going to tie into this game, bucking a man that owns a seventy-five thousand dollar outfit—maybe bucking the Empress's millions before the play's over—I'm going to need money."

"I'll play. Bein' kinda thrifty myse'f and with not

much overhead, I've got a tidy little pile put by."

"The sinews of war. Thanks, pardner. We'll see. Meanwhile, I'm wondering whether maybe Dad left a little something that would be—well, mine now, I guess."

"I know what you mean, Jerry. I've thought of that of course a hundred times. You mean his 'Sure-enough Money,' don't you?"

Jerry nodded. The elder Sommers, though a man always of some considerable means, indulged all his life in a habit which he had copied from his own father, Big Dan Sommers. Big Dan, making his own pile in a day when many men, and with reason, looked askance at banks and bankers, maintained that every man ought to have, always at hand, a stake of sorts which he called "Sure-enough Money." Let banks break all they pleased and bankers hop to Canada, Big Dan could always reach out to a handy place and show you, in gold, a sum ample in the eyes of the more modest to grant a life of leisure.

"If we only knew where your dad planted it," sighed Uncle Doctor. "It's never turned up, so far as I know, and I reckon it never will."

"I happen to know where he put it," said Jerry quietly. "He never made a secret of it with me. Just the day that we— What an infernal jackass I was! Flew into a rage, both of us—"

"Two of a kind, boy."

"And all about—what do you suppose? About that very same 'Sure-enough Money.' We'd been smol-dering, I guess, ever since the day we moved into High

132

Mesa. Kid that I was, I couldn't get it out of my head that we'd broken old Costa and little Beryl all up in business; I felt that just because Dad had money it wasn't fair. And he sort of felt that way himself; that was the devil of it. It bothered him the way the old man looked when he went and the way the little girl looked back and shook her fist, crying all the time. Well, that last day, he had shown me where the 'Sure-enough Money' was tucked away, and I boiled over with something about it being a fine thing, him with money hid where he didn't even see it, and them going out to starve. Before we got through— Well, I was on my way."

"Folks is funny," said Uncle Doctor. Then he demanded briskly: "So you know where it is? Where it ought to be, anyway?"

"Yes. By the way, Dad left a will, I suppose?"

"Yes. Everything to you."

"Then if there's anything where he put it—"

"Why not? Whose, if not yours?"

Jerry smiled crookedly.

"It's in the house here. And Antonio Costa bought, or thinks he bought, the house and all in it!"

"I said it was a mess, didn't I? You can't hardly go to Costa and ask him to please let you go rummagin', that's a fact. How the devil—"

"Leave it to me. It's a deed for the stilly night, Hawk Eye. Can you get me a flashlight? And a good strong screwdriver?"

"I can! Also, if you say the word, a black mask, rubber soles and—what else do burglars use anyhow?"

Uncle Doctor departed soon after, coming back twice to shake Jerry's hand. He was chuckling, when he did go, over his parting shot:

"I'd sure like to be lookin' on, you night-prowlin' thief, if you happened to get caught! Wouldn't you look funny, tryin' to think of things to say? And mind you, if you got yourse'f in trouble, you couldn't be hollerin' for me to come and git you out. You'd say, standin' like Napoleon, 'Tell 'em who I am, Uncle Doctor!' And I'd squint at you and slap my leg and say: 'This feller does look sorta familiar. Why, Great Snakes, it's Mexico Red, a feller that the last I heard of him was in the pen for bank robbery.' Well, ride lucky, kid."

CHAPTER VIII

AT AN EARLY HOUR IN THE MORNING JERRY Boyne was in possession of flashlight and screwdriver. His fellow conspirator, on his way bright and early to spend the day with Bob Kingsbury, tore himself away when he wanted nothing better than to linger and chat.

"Here's the tools of your evil trade, Jerry," he said, producing them from under his coat and hastily shoving them under the bed covers. "I ought to have brought you some brass knuckles, a jimmy and a piece of gas pipe, but the other burglars was all workin'. *Addy-ose,* Thug—and luck."

"My respects to one Bob Kingsbury," Jerry called after him. "Tell him I'll be looking in on him before long. Tomorrow, maybe."

He disposed of his newly acquired implements by taking them into bed with him, and awaited the events of the day. When Tommy appeared with a well laded tray from which steamy fragrances arose in most delectable wisps, Jerry greeted him like an old friend. When Tommy went away with empty plates rattling, Jerry slipped out of bed, donned a dressing gown which was a thing of glory—the old señor's, doubtless, and no doubt purchased by Beryl—and tried out his battered body.

For one thing, he could walk; for another, that was about all. He winced with pain and found that shifting his weight from one foot to another did not greatly help; his whole body was sore. None the less he persisted in his brief journey and crossed the big room to the open window from which he looked down for the first time in years upon the old gardens surrounding High Mesa. Cool and fragrant and delightful, the tall poplars and trailing pepper trees, the oranges and olives and pomegranates seeming to him to be dripping with pleasant shade, altogether the grounds embowered the fine old home in such a fashion that no one could draw the line where art carried on from nature's stopping place. Splashes of color were everywhere, a crimson rose against a yellowed wall, a yellow rose dropping flecks of gold upon a green sward, warm red tiles glowing through the sheen of vines—and a still murmur which may have arisen from the vibrant wings of bees or may have been the garden breathing languorously. Then, too, there was the sparkle of clear water, quivering silver where it overflowed a fountain and drifted away in a tiny brook which sang as it went and invited to drink.

"No wonder the old chap loves the place! It's a part of him and he's a part of it. Beryl, too. Born here, bred of all this, putting herself back into it."

One knew that it was love which had created so fine a beauty. Other places were the recipients of money lavished freely; consider the Empire Ranch, for example! Yet how hard and crude was it compared to this oasis, mellow and fragrant, like an old home in Spain.

Beyond the stables, low walled, red tiled, he looked across wide fields to the rugged sky line where the hills already quivered with the morning heat; from this window he could not look out toward the south and the border, but how well he recalled the view! One approached High Mesa by a winding road which came crawling up from the lower lands at the rear; in front the table-land broke off abruptly in an escarpment comparable for sheer steepness and height to that which characterizes Stirling's castle. Thence southward the eye might run far out across the richest fields of the entire hacienda, irrigated and abundantly productive, and on and on across the miles of further sage and sand, to the distant hills of Mexico.

"To have lost all this once," mused Jerry, "was enough to break a pair of splendid hearts. To lose it again?"

He quitted his window and limped up and down, bound on working some of the soreness out of him and on getting his strength back. When he tumbled into bed

136

again he was profoundly grateful that he had a bed at hand.

Tommy returning brought him an armful of books and magazines. Jerry eagerly exclaimed:

"Fine! Who sent 'em, Tommy?"

"It was Señor Costa," said Tommy.

"Ah! Thank him for me, Tommy." But something of his enthusiasm was gone.

"Bueno." Tommy began his leisurely tidying. "Miss Beryl, I heard her tell him."

"I'll thank her, then," said Jerry, again as bright as a cricket.

But when she came he forgot all about the books. As he first glimpsed her it required no end of self-control to refrain from shouting out his extreme satisfaction; being an impulsive young man it was really quite an achievement for him that he appeared no more than conventionally pleased. For there was a look in her eyes of that sort which in a general way may be termed provocative; there was mirth in it, warmth, perhaps, certainly a dash of challenge and, if Jerry saw aright, a fillip of daring. She had never looked so pretty, and that was not because of the very charming little white sports costume; the fact was that from her ears hung a pair of pink earrings. Ah, what a difference a little touch of pink did make at times!

Having given Jerry full credit for his commendable reserve, it must be admitted that Beryl did not come alone. Antonio Costa was with her and they came arm in arm to visit their patient.

Their visit was all too short. No, they would not sit;

137

Señor Costa was so well assured that utter quiet was the thing for a sick man.

"But I'm not sick!"

"But, Santa Maria! is it not even a graver thing than a mere sickness? To have endured such a fall from Dios knows how high up, to have been tumbled around in the air in a storm, to have been hammered against the sharp rocks of Indian Gully!"

"I haven't properly thanked your granddaughter; I don't know how. If it hadn't been for her I'd either have been buried in the sand—or, if I had managed to get to my feet no doubt that 'chute of mine would have run away with me again, and by now I'd be skimming along with it off the tip end of Tierra del Fuego!"

He loved to hear Beryl laugh. Yes, during the short while of their being with him the air was drenched with sunshine. But they went so suddenly. The old man bowed from the doorway. Beryl had a little way of dancing through doors, quite as though borne gaily along to some new joy. The pink earrings twinkled softly. Jerry summoned Tommy to him and presented him with two more pesos.

Twice again during the day did he don the ornate dressing gown and take his exercise. When his tray came at noon there was a pink rosebud on it. Jerry, with a fine assumption of casualness, spoke of its beauty and opened the door to explanations. Tommy confessed that it was his own idea; he thought the señor would like it. Jerry regarded it rather more critically; it wasn't much of a flower after all. And when it happened to fall into his bowl of hot soup there was no such ado about the matter as there might have been under slightly different circumstances.

If he hoped during the afternoon that his host would be called away on business and that Beryl would feel it her responsibility to take that host's place, it was merely hoping for the moon. But he did have a visitor just about sundown.

"Elmer!" he exclaimed in surprise. "What brings you to High Mesa?"

"So you went and did it, like I said you would!" retorted Mr. Blodgett taking that same satisfaction from his observation that so many mere human beings do when an "I told you so!" works out in a way they never expected. "You're just the guy to go climbing a cyclone when men that use their brains to think with hunt cellars. Maybe some fine day you'll start in to treasure some of the pearls of wisdom which rattle down like hailstones when Mr. Elmer Bashford Blodgett opens his mouth."

Jerry laughed and seemed, to the piercing regard of his visitor, very far from being down in the mouth; there was, in fact, a look about him of a man very decidedly contented with things as they are. That puzzled Blodgett, who had heard exaggerated tales and who came to be one of the mourners. From puzzlement he went in a flash, the Blodgett way, to lively suspicion. For him, there never was a woodpile without its Ethiopian.

"Aha! So that's the game, huh?" he observed in his whispering voice. He hung his hat on a bed post, preempted a chair, clasped a plump knee between plump hands and, all this done deliberately, as deliberately closed his left eye to register sly comprehension. "Flew high and watched your chance, did you? Spotted the *señorita* taking a little *pasear* and did a high dive right into her arms! Made it so that even the old grandee couldn't say, '*Raus mitt um,*' but had to invite, '*Entra, Señor,* and the house along with my Sunday pajamas is yours!' Fox!"

"Don't be a baboon," laughed Jerry.

"Fox!" repeated Elmer, eying him in unstinted admiration. "Why couldn't I think of a fast one like that? Here I've been all this time trying to horn in, and your first day along the border lands you in the bosom of the family, so to speak. Still, thinking it over," and he pursed a full lip dubiously, "I dunno. On good old terra firma I'll take chances with the rest; but to go up in the sky—and jump—and twiddle my thumbs until I've counted whatever the count is—and pull the string and wonder whether the damn thing's ever going to open— Nope; my way's good enough; just wait for the right chance and hop in."

"As now!" Jerry said quickly, and glared balefully at his friend. "You make an excuse of coming to see me, just to insinuate your oily carcass into High Mesa!"

"They was nice to me downstairs," Elmer admitted complacently. "A feller took my bag and another feller come running with the cold drinks; the Conquistador himself made me a bow that somehow makes a man feel at last his real worth is recognized. By the time—"

"Your bag?" Jerry demanded.

"Old Costa may have a whole wardrobe full of nighties; then again maybe there's only two pairs." Elmer leaned over and fingered the texture of the purple and gold raiment. "Those things come high."

"You haven't any idea you're going to stay here?"

"It's darned sure that if I'm invited I'm not going to let the old don down cold. Those birds are awful sensitive, Jerry. Want a cigar? Must have broke yours when you high-dived."

"How'd you hear about it?"

"Cordial, ain't you? Want all High Mesa for your own? How'd I hear, you ask? Why, they sent for a doctor, didn't they? Do you suppose a fact like that isn't known in two shakes through every village, hamlet and town? And when there's news in the air—" He tapped his shirt front; the thing was of blue with green stripes in it. "They had it around that you were horribly mangled."

"Your concern for an old friend is touching, or would be, rather—"

Elmer chuckled good-humoredly.

"I was concerned, kid, and that's one reason why I packed my bag. Then, of course, it was a good chance to crow over you, after you'd spilled out of your flying machine. That's two things." He began now checking on his thick fingers. "Three is, I wanted to know all about Bob Kingsbury; I guess you know the whole of that. Four, I'll admit, here was a wide-open chance to visit with Señor Don Antonio Arenda Costa. And five, having nosed around as per your request, *amigo,* I blew in to report. So you see I didn't go off halfcocked like

141

an impulsive young red-headed Crazy Fool I know—"

"What's the report, Elmer?"

"Well, not so much; still something. The other Red-head— Of course you know what he's up to right now? No? You see! Without me you're without just exactly what you need in your business." He beamed and waited for Jerry to ask particulars. When Jerry just stared at him and asked nothing, Elmer shrugged and continued caustically: "Right under your nose, and you don't know! Why, at this minute, Gentleman Red is down in the flower garden; and who do you think's with him? If you guess it's the dame he names his race horses after, you'll guess right."

Jerry frowned but strove to say carelessly:

"Here, is he? Well, I suppose that's hardly surprising."

"Just the same you look like you tasted something bitter. Well, since you're a friend of mine, I'll cheer you up. Poor old Red was in a sweat trying to square himself. You see, he'd told her he'd go look for Bob Kingsbury, the morning of the high wind, seems like. And, not knowing you had Bob back at Little Mesa, Red ducks for home and let's it go at that. Later, hearing what had happened, he had to come back and fix things, pretending—"

"One wonders at times how you know so much!"

"What did God give us ears for?" asked Elmer, lifting his brows. "Anyway, Lady Vere de Vere was making out that she was an icicle with frost on it and he was getting warmer all the time. Will that bring the roses back to your cheeks?"

"Confound you, Elmer, I won't have you spying on these folk! What they do—"

"Why, I thought you wanted me to nose around?" said Blodgett innocently. "You're like a guy that says, 'Bring me some water in a cup but don't let the cup get wet!'"

"I do want a bit of information and if any man can get it, you're that man. But lay off Antonio Costa and his granddaughter. You can't stay here, Elmer."

Blodgett's jaw dropped.

"Can't? You say I can't? Why can't I? There's room, ain't there, and beds aplenty? If there wasn't, you and me could bunk together as we've done before."

"Want to make a little money, Elmer?"

"You know I'm looking for money."

"I don't know the state of your finances. I've known you flush and I've known you hungry. If a hundred a week—"

"Sold out. Want me to kill somebody? How many?"

"I want you to go over to Little Mesa; that's Bob Kingsbury's ranch only half a dozen miles off. Wait there for me. They can give you some kind of a shake-down. I'll join you soon; maybe tomorrow."

"I knew you wasn't hurt like you pretend," said Elmer triumphantly. "Well, now I know the pay I'm drawing, what's the job?"

"Gathering information absolutely on the quiet. I want to know all that is to be known about that chap they call Red Handsome. What he does with his spare time, how he lives, who his friends are, how much land he owns, whether it's paid for, what he's got in a bank,

143

how many banks he has—and a lot more."

"Lovely," nodded Blodgett. "I've got a job that ought to last quite a spell. It's all fine with me. But let's begin drawing pay tomorrow. That is, if the old matador downstairs asks me to spend the evening getting acquainted, and says, 'Stay all night,' and maybe says, 'Let's have a little game just for fun.'"

"No," said Jerry firmly. And then, as his friend's eyes began to harden, he put out a hand and laid it on Elmer's heavy shoulder. "Do as I ask, old-timer; not for the money in it for you; just because I ask you. Can you? I'm in earnest about this."

Blodgett sighed and nodded. And a little later when Don Antonio, at the urge of his fine hospitality, did ask Mr. Blodgett to honor High Mesa with his presence over night, the stout man sighed again, made a heroic struggle, pressed Costa's hand fervently, murmured a string of excuses, and in the sacred name of friendship went mournfully away.

"And I'll best I could have had a thousand pesos out of the old rooster, too." Almost tearful by that time, driving off in his dusty old car, of a sudden he perked up and brightened. "Jerry's got something big on, something that'll make a thousand pesos look like a string of wooden beads. Fox!"

How Mr. Blodgett's all-seeing eyes would have protruded, what an exquisite thrill would have rippled along his backbone, could he but have looked in on Jerry Boyne a few hours later at the beginning of his nocturnal adventurings! Long after the whole house was hushed and dark Jerry threw back his covers, donned his

144

dressing gown, took up flashlight and screwdriver and crept on bare feet to the door. Had Elmer Blodgett been permitted one swift glimpse, how simple an affair it would have been for his racing fancies to make of that simple household tool a most deadly variety of Spanish dagger!

In Jerry's room was a wan glow from the moon. The long corridor, however, was so dark that when he stepped into it and softly closed his door behind him, an utter blackness blotted out all detail. After a moment of listening—there was never a sound—he flashed his light along the corridor. Out of the nothingness leaped plastered walls, arched doorways, deeply recessed; seeming a long way off, the wrought-iron handrail for the curving stone stairway which he must descend; a polychromed dado of tile, a mirror reflecting the light, a painting. As he turned off his light and stole along the passageway, it was the painting which he continued to see even in the dark; some Señora Costa, no doubt, of a time very long ago; white haired, stern faced, yet with young, merry eyes. Those eyes he felt following him in the dark.

With a hand on the iron rail he paused again, peering down into the high-vaulted, generously spaced main *sala* of the house. Curtains were drawn over all the windows save one; at the far end of the big room a narrow, grilled opening admitted a dim pathway of light. But the stairway from top to bottom and all the nearer end of the room where the fireplace was, and where Jerry's errand led him, were pitch dark.

There was a runner of carpet up the middle of the

stairs, but Jerry, one hand always on the rail, trod with silent bare feet on the cold stone. He went with a caution ever tending to increase, ready at the slightest sound to whirl and dash back to his room. But there was no sound and he descended steadily.

Once on the main floor, still in darkness, feeling his way at first along the staircase, then along the wall, he made his way without mishap to a point near the fireplace. In this brief journey he found cause for gratitude that in a home like this there was no clutter of silly furniture against which to crack a blundering shin; those of the breed of Antonio Costa regarded floors as floors rather than as spaces crying for messy bric-a-brac. It was really quite simple to make his journey both silent and expeditious. Nevertheless a little sigh of relief escaped him when he reached his objective.

Not even yet did he need to make use of his light; his hands served him as well as eyes could have done. On each side of the fireplace, only a foot or so above the heavy stone mantel, was an ancient bracket-candlestick of massive iron beautifully wrought, produced by late seventeenth century skill and ardor. It was the one at the right of the fireplace with which he had his affair.

Placing his screwdriver and flashlight conveniently on the mantel, he employed his hands in a preliminary investigation. How well a fellow could remember a thing like a candlestick through the years—when it masked a secret! He fingered the heavy iron plaque affixed to the wall. From its middle sprouted the two graceful iron stems, one curving upward and being crowned with a wax taper, the other drooping slightly and terminating in a shallow dish whose purpose Jerry, the boy, had supposed to be to catch candle drippings, but which his father had explained had been intended as a receptacle for flint and steel. Jerry's fingers, in the first superficial examination, found all this familiar; they ran over the plaque itself more carefully, seeking and finding the heads of the two long screws which held it in place. His task now was merely to take the sconce down, grope in the aperture which his father's hands had contrived there in the adobe wall, take out whatever "Sure-enough Money"—if any!—might be awaiting him, put things back as he had found them and so to bed.

He was anxious to get his job over and done with, yet guarded against undue haste. Thus first of all he removed the candle, to insure against its falling to the floor; he investigated the shallow dish lest during his operations some object that might have found a resting place in so convenient a catch-all clatter to the hearth, making all sorts of racket.

His precaution was wisely taken. What a clinking, chinking din he might have made had he neglected to investigate the iron cup's contents! For the shallow receptacle, as though here were a sort of money-blossom thriving on what the iron roots had found deep in the wall, was half filled with coins.

As he began removing them, all in silence save for one slight unavoidable clink, he passed from surprise at finding them here to understanding. He recalled the old Spanish custom of having small sums of money openly at hand to the need of any who cared to help himself from the supply. When it was all gone there would always be more forthcoming, for was this not a world of plenty, and was not bounty a command laid upon such as Antonio Costa?

Faint as was that soft chink of silver, Jerry twisted about anxiously. He found it no pleasant sensation, yet one of which he could not rid himself, that everywhere in the dark there were eyes watching him. How other eyes could see where his could not he did not in the least understand; yet there the feeling was. And now, when he slewed about guiltily and distinctly saw a curtain stir gently at the far end of the room where the faint light was, he forgot to breathe.

He listened intently, straining his ears against a silence without a ripple in it. He watched the curtain unwinkingly. It was as still as everything else about him. A puff of air, maybe? Perhaps a window had been left open.

A moment later he saw the curtain move again and, what was very much more to the purpose, realized that there was someone else in the room, someone as silent as he, someone standing now by the far window. Just then could Jerry Boyne have had his wish he would have been safely back in his bed—and the "Sure-enough Money" might repose, for all he cared, at the bottom of the sea.

There came a tiny spurt of flame where someone had scratched a match. It was held a moment only, then extinguished. And now more than ever was Jerry anxious to be anywhere rather than here. That match, held a moment before a window, could be nothing other than a signal meant for someone outside.

"I'd rather be caught as a thief than as a spy," Jerry told himself, and wondered if he might retrace his steps now before he either saw or heard anything further—and before he could be seen or heard.

Then the curtain was thrust back and he saw who was standing there, outlined against the outside night. It was Costa. Costa had opened a window which looked out upon the garden. From the terrace rose a man's form, cloaked and hatted and unrecognizable, yet plainly that of a thick-set, burly visitor. He might have come and gone, unknown to Jerry, were it not that as he stooped and came in at the window his hat was brushed off. Against the revealing outer glow the flat ugly face of El Bravo, the Empress's left hand, was not to be mistaken.

What passed between the two men was, much to Jerry's relief, conducted in undertones so that no word of their talk reached him. For the greater part it was Señor Costa who spoke. His utterances were swift and earnest. El Bravo heard him out in silence or with short words, accompanied now and then by an assenting nod. Something passed from Costa's hand to El Bravo's; the thick, cloaked form passed out through the window; the window was closed, the curtain re-drawn. Soft footfalls of slippered feet passed swiftly through the room to the stairs and, dying away, left Jerry with the dark and the silence.

He put his left hand to his forehead. His right still clutched the coins from the cup in the iron candlestick. His brow was thick with drops of sweat.

"I'll finish this job while I'm at it, and if ever again in

149

my life I start plying the trade of a burglar I hope to get caught at it."

But there was no need to commit himself to any subsequent furtive expedition in order to be apprehended; already he was found out. He knew it the instant a second match scratched, spurted blue, and flowered in a small yellow flame. The match dipped to a nearby candlewick; the candle revealed Beryl in dressing gown and slippers, her eyes looking big with wonder, then, as she took him in from head to foot, bright with angry contempt.

"Evidently, Mr. Boyne," she said in such a fashion as to cause him to recall Elmer Blodgett's description of her as a well-frosted icicle, "you took quite literally my grandfather's invitation to consider High Mesa your own!"

"Beryl!"

"Don't you dare call me Beryl!" she flamed out at him. Then, with a queer, nervous laugh, she pointed at him, crying warningly: "Careful! You're about to drop something!"

It was a gold piece, slipping through his fingers.

"Damn it!" he exclaimed, and grew hot with anger in his turn. He slammed the coins down on the mantel. "If you'd simply ask for an explanation instead of judging a man out of hand—"

"An explanation? Is one needed? Very well. I am listening."

He opened his mouth to blurt out the truth, since at that hideous moment anything seemed better than the present misunderstanding. The words were formed to

150

say: "I was only going to take something which belongs to me," when he realized that to make his explanations was equivalent to saying: "Look here, this place is mine, not yours." How long would she remain after such a thing was proved to her?

"Well?" said Beryl, seeing only confusion in his look and guilt in his silence.

"I can't explain after all. Not yet. Some day—" He took a quick step toward her. "I know it looks as though I were an ingrate, a thief and a spy—"

She started and a new look of distress came into her eyes.

"Will you go please?" she said unsteadily.

"You must not think what you are thinking of me now. Good God, I couldn't do a thing like that! I am no thief and I am no intentional spy. If I can't explain at the moment, it's simply because of a devilish sort of tangle that things have got into—you wouldn't believe the truth if you heard it. But before long—"

"Will you go, please?" she said again, and he thought that all of a sudden she looked pale and weary.

"You've some trouble of your own!" he blurted out. "It has to do with your grandfather and his meeting with El Bravo."

"If you feel that I have any trouble of my own, perhaps you will go and leave me with it," she said coldly. "And, as you go, you are welcome to take with you the money you threw down so dramatically."

"Damn!" said an infuriated Jerry and, summoning what dignity he could in a flapping dressing gown, went his barefoot way up the stairs.

CHAPTER IX

ACROSS THE BREAKFAST TABLE SEÑOR COSTA bent a pair of very keen black eyes upon his granddaughter.

"Our guest has taken his departure," he observed carelessly, as though that were a matter of less importance than the unfolding of his napkin.

Beryl showed unmistakable signs of a sleepless night; she was pale and looked weary. The eyes which she lifted and then let fall rather hastily were unhappy. She made no reply to Costa's words but sighed faintly. His lips twitched into a smile. Where she appeared moody and troubled, he was inclined to be lively and full of zest.

"These oranges are excellent," he informed her, and added lightly: "You do not appear surprised that Mr. Boyne has left us?"

Although she had had long hours to ponder the happenings of last night, such was her distress that she did not know which way to turn or what to say. For no reason at all, it seemed to her as she strove to grow logical, it was going to be difficult to tell her grandfather of the disgraceful behavior of Jerry Boyne—a mere stranger. Nor was it easy to dwell upon that other matter, her discovery of El Bravo coming in the dead of night for that whispered interview. That this was not the first time the two had held secret parley, she knew right well. When she had cried out to Jerry, "I hate mysteries!" she was thinking of that inexplicable part which somehow Antonio Costa was playing in them.

"What is it, my little Beryl?" asked Costa softly when she sat still, neither speaking nor eating, just staring before her.

"I—I didn't sleep well." Again she lifted her troubled eyes to his face, trying so hard to read those eyes of his which at times were as guileless as a child's, at other times as unfathomable as a professional gambler's. She sighed again, but added: "You are sure that Mr. Boyne has gone?"

"Some time during the night, evidently. Oh, you Americans!" At times, generally when he felt like teasing, he used the expression, "Oh, you Americans!" implying that some Western trait or other was altogether beyond the comprehension of a sane Spaniard, and that his granddaughter was as bad as the rest. Her father, Captain Richard Blake, who had lost his life in the War, was so very "Western" that Costa had not entirely approved of him when he came wooing his daughter. "Some people in this world do have quaint ways, eh, my Little One?" Costa continued gayly. "At first, when I looked in on my way downstairs, I was afraid he had gone without even a word of farewell. But he left a letter, a nice big fat one, too. For you. No doubt it is full of fine thanks for our entertainment. Perhaps, since it was you who found him and saved him and brought him here, he did not remember that I lived. American style, *no?* Or did he by any chance set down the postscript: 'Please thank your most excellent grandpapa for his hospitality and beautiful pajamas!'"

"Why do you call him 'our mysterious stranger'?"

153

she asked with the first sign of any lively interest.

He gave her a Spanish shrug, as typically Spanish as anything that ever came out of Spain.

"But are not all strangers, coming from nobody knows where, arriving for nobody knows what, tumbling out of the sky most literally, are they not all mysterious? And mysteries, are they not enchanting?"

While laughing at her he took the letter from his pocket. Jerry, writing at fever heat upon small pages torn from a memo book, had required many of the inadequate leaves for his running scrawl. Beryl regarded the packet in silence, and for once gave her grandfather as inscrutable a face to study as ever he had turned bafflingly on her. She noted how the thing was addressed simply: "To Beryl." She saw that it was intended to be a private matter; it was tied about with a purple thread which could have come from nowhere save from the tassel of an ornate cord of certain pajamas; a blob of candle-wax sealed it and was pressed down by Jerry's thumb in a way that spoke of emphasis and perhaps a final, good-night "Damn."

"Funny folk, *Americanos,* no?" remarked Costa, disposing of the last of his orange and thereafter nicely brushing up the ends of his white mustache. "He writes, 'To Beryl!' His compatriots make for themselves, I believe, the word, 'Fresh'; is that not it? One would think that he had known you all his life!"

"He said that he had known me! Of course—"

"He said that?" demanded Costa sharply. "Tell me. Did he say where? And when?"

"He would not. I think that he—lied!"

154

But Costa brooded. Of a sudden he laughed again.

"I will tell you something," he chuckled. "This fellow Jerry Boyne, he is what you call a Romantic! *Seguro que sí!* Oh, I am very sure. I would not be surprised some day to find out that he had a grandmother or maybe a greatgrandmother, who was a Spanish lady!"

"But I thought you did not like him! At any rate, he is a common thief!"

"Eh!" ejaculated the old fellow. "A thief! Now that is a terrible thing to say. How do you know? Who has told you that? Aha! it was your young other red-headed friend! The one who quarreled with Señor Jerry Boyne?"

Suddenly Beryl drew the letter to her and broke the absurd seal. Jerry last night had spoken so earnestly, so spontaneously about an explanation— No, there was nothing of the sort here. Denial, yes; violent, angry denial; explanation, no. The penciled note permitted of a hasty skimming:

"Beryl, just get this clear: I am no thief. Hang it, why do folks always have to jump at conclusions? . . . If you saw a hen standing by an egg, you'd swear she laid it; and if the hen turned out to be a rooster, well then you'd swear he was up to something shady anyhow. . . . You were so adorable today in those pink earrings that I knew there was nothing in the world that I wanted but you . . . and then, the way you looked at me by the fireplace, I could have bit you! . . . I'm on my way right now.

I am going to borrow a horse; *borrow,* I said. I'll send the darned thing back. Thank Señor Costa for me; I'll hope to thank him later. I dare you to tell him your confounded suspicions of me; he'd howl at you. . . . And howl at you now, my dear. . . . Now listen to this: I love you.

"Jerry.

"PS. Wrote this before getting dressed. Dressed now and laughing! What a silly thing it was. I adore you. . . . Also, I am glad now I didn't bite you. Please keep the earrings; if you give them to Black Maria, I'll creep in during the stilly night—you know how good I am at that!—and strangle her."

"Perhaps it's just that he's mad!" gasped Beryl.

"Shall I read and judge, my dear?"

"Yes!—No!—Grandfather—"

Actually Señor Costa looked uneasy. That "Grandfather." It was so seldom used; only when he had been caught at something reprehensible. He assumed an expression of mock terror, but it availed him nothing; Beryl was not to be turned aside nor were smiles easily coaxed up this morning.

"I saw you with El Bravo last night," she said bleakly.

Up shot his heavy brows; down they came again and down they remained, drawn into a scowl such as Beryl seldom had any opportunity to see darkening his face.

"Well?" he snapped coldly.

"Not I alone saw," she continued, eying him as

156

steadily as he eyed her. "Our guest, this Jerry Boyne, he too saw."

Costa stiffened in anger and in arrogance.

"Am I then in a nest of spies?"

"Of spy and—and thief," she retorted. "Yes, I spied. I did once before. I knew there was something wrong; I felt something was troubling you. I knew you were not sleeping; I heard you stirring about. And I followed. So I saw you and El Bravo—"

"And listened?" he sneered at her.

"No." Though she flushed hotly she returned defiantly: "I could not hear. But I saw."

He regarded her fixedly a long while. Little by little his expression altered; his brows came back into their normal positions and a tight little smile barely broke the straight line of his lips.

"*Bueno*. You saw El Bravo. You heard nothing. So you have but a small thing to do in forgetting that you saw him. Do you understand, Beryl? You are to forget. We will not refer to this again. Now that we speak of it once and for all, I want to tell you that there are things in this world that you know nothing about and that it is best you should know nothing about. If you want to ruin me, run around and talk like a foolish thing. If you love me, keep still. No!" he said sternly as she was about to ask him something, "I will answer no questions! Not one. You are my very dear little granddaughter and I love you very much—but this is a man's work and no little girl's; it is my affair and—you will excuse me for speaking in simple little words?—it is none of your business."

In ten years he had not once spoken to her so harshly, and now, despite her determination to face all unpleasantnesses unflinchingly, her eyes misted over with tears. She dashed them away and said bluntly:

"If it is a matter in which there is possible ruin for you, Señor, is it not best to remember that Jerry Boyne, too, saw?"

He got to his feet; she could hear him swearing under his breath. Antonio Costa swore as readily and fluently as another, yet not in the presence of that softer sex toward which he unvaryingly comported himself with so rare a gallant deference.

"You upset me, child! You make me swear like a stable boy. *Jesus, Maria y San Jose!* What was Boyne doing there?"

"Stealing," said Beryl firmly. "I told you he was a thief."

"Stealing?" He looked amazed, seeing how serious she was. "What on earth was there to steal? Did he take my grandfather's Cadiz chest or Doña Elmira's Turkish rug?"

"It was the money that you keep by the fireplace."

"Money? Those pennies!" He stared more incredulously than ever. "I think there may be all of seven dollars there; maybe twenty-seven! You mean that he took that handful of beggar's pennies? Am I mad, then?"

"He did not take them. He threw them down."

"He did not take them? Then what did he take?"

"Nothing. You see—"

"No, I do not see. A thief steals; this thief of yours stole nothing! You have made me irritable, I fear." He sighed and began making a cigarette, forgetting his breakfast. "What you mean to say is that there were three of us prowling at the same time last night—you trying to catch your grandfather doing something wrong; your grandfather entertaining his little playmate, El Bravo; Señor Jerry trying to steal pennies. And you scared him away before he could get his hands on the money!" His tone had grown lighter, but now of a sudden his frown came back. As though it were himself that he addressed, he muttered softly: "What I think Señor Jerry was doing was the same thing that occupied my little granddaughter! Spying on me! Now, I wonder—"

"He was taking the money. He had it in his hand when I struck a match. That was after you had gone upstairs."

He strode off at that. Beryl rose swiftly and followed him straight to the main living room and to the fireplace. No servant had come into this part of the house as yet; on the stone mantel were the coins that Jerry had slammed down there. There, also, was the candle he had removed from the bracketed candlestick.

"What the devil!" muttered Costa, puzzled.

Last night Beryl, in her agitation, had paid no heed to those other things on the mantel; now their utter incongruity drew her eyes along with Costa's. A flashlight; that was easily enough explained. But a heavy screwdriver?

"He had a bad bump on the head, did he not?" said the perplexed Costa. "To go roaming around another man's house in the dark, armed with a thing like that!"

For an instant Beryl actually hoped that there was some truth in what he implied; for no reason which she would admit, she would have snatched eagerly at some excuse for Jerry's behavior. But strangely as Jerry had acted—yes, and spoken and written!—she knew that his was no aberration due to an injury.

"Our mysterious stranger came here to get something," said Costa after the fashion of a man starting with what is obvious, seeking to pass from step to step and so come at an explanation of what puzzles him. "He came in the dark, *no?* Else I, being as you tell me, in the room at the same time would have seen. All in the dark he found his way to this spot! Is that so?"

"Yes! I did not think of that last night—I just heard someone moving—"

"He found his way in the dark. All right. And you did not think of that? Still, the thing is interesting! In the dark, in a strange house, he goes straight where he wants to go. Now, here is what he does: He takes down the big candle from the candlestick and lays it carefully on the mantelpiece. Then he scoops out the coins; he has them in his hand when you strike a match— What did he say, my dear?"

"He said 'Damn!'" Beryl told him. "That was when I told him he was about to drop a gold piece!"

Costa's stern face twitched, and for a second she thought that he was going to smile. But as sharply as he had spoken before he demanded:

"After that, what did he say?"

"What could he say? What would any man say?" She looked scornful. "He said that he was no thief, of course. He said he could explain—then he floundered and said he couldn't explain, that things were in such a tangle."

"That was all that he said?"

"For good-night he said one more damn and went upstairs."

He nodded absently. This thing puzzled him and, though he had remarked that mysteries were enchanting, he had perhaps meant only those mysteries to which he had the key. He did not like being puzzled. Frowning at the mantel and the articles on it he said thoughtfully:

"If he wanted just this money, then why did he take the candle down and put it here? And why did he bring a screwdriver? A screwdriver makes one think of screws, and screws— Eh? What is it?" He broke off at a little gasp from her.

"He came to take the candlesticks themselves! They are very old, aren't they? Perhaps they are very valuable?"

Costa pondered. A second time she fancied he was about to smile and again she was mistaken.

"No doubt," he said and shrugged carelessly. "What does it matter?" He put the candle back on its spike, restored the coins to their receptacle and took up the flashlight and the homely tool which had started so much surmise. "Let us forget this, too, Beryl. The man has gone; he has taken nothing. Yes, we'll forget it."

The old fellow was rather an accomplished actor when he drew deep upon his Southern talents, but it happened that this morning he had to do with an unusually astute Beryl. Not Elmer Blodgett himself was ever more alive to darting suspicions. It flashed over her that all of a sudden her grandfather was snatching somewhat hastily at what was after all an absurd explanation. Stealing two enormous old iron candlesticks! Also what on earth did Señor Costa mean by gathering up things himself? He never did things like that. With a houseful of servants, it was more like him to ring for someone to brush a fallen cigarette ash off his sleeve. What was he going to do with the screwdriver, for instance?

"Grandfather!"

"Yes, Beryl?"

"Will you let me have that screwdriver a moment?"

"But, of course! Surely you do not mean to treasure it as a keepsake?"

Beryl promptly applied it to the head of one of the two screws holding the plaque in place on the wall.

"Ah!" said Costa. He appeared to hesitate, then added indifferently: "Don't you think it would be better—"

"I am simply dying of curiosity!" cried Beryl, hard at work. "You know as well as I do that he wasn't trying to steal a candlestick!"

He turned without a word and went to the door; there he beckoned a housemaid, instructed her that he and Miss Beryl wished to be alone, closed the door and returned to watch the busy screwdriver.

The screws were long, bedded in two horizontal bars of wood which were let into the adobe wall; they complained at first, but, once started, twirled with obliging ease. Down came the sconce, Señor Costa lending a very willing hand. In the wall, between the wooden bars, was a round hole five or six inches in diameter. Beryl's hand darted into this inviting cavity and came out almost immediately grasping a small packet.

"Bank notes! Gold, too!"

Costa's swift gesture partook almost of the nature of a pounce. He secured the packet, tore off the string knotted about it and regarded it with sparkling eyes.

"A treasure! There are several thousand dollars here. Let's see; one, two, three—"

"There is something else," said Beryl, groping again. She drew it out. "A letter. See, it is sealed; addressed to, 'My son, Gerald Sommers.' Dated nearly five years ago. The twenty-second of June, 1926. And a memorandum: 'Whoever finds this, I beg you to give it without delay to my son, Gerald Hand Sommers.' And—"

"What date did you say?" demanded Costa, looking up sharply from the money in his hand.

"June twenty-second, 19— Oh!"

"Yes; that was the day the poor fellow was killed."

Both were thinking the same thing. Sommers had lived here about ten years. How did it chance that, of some three thousand days, he had selected, for the one to write and hide a letter here, the one day that was to mark his tragic passing? Coincidence or—

Beryl's big gray eyes widened as she clutched the letter.

"Don't you see? In this letter he tells who it was that killed him!"

"Yes? And now you look like a prima donna who is going to die on a high C. Are you thinking? He was shot through the head; he expired like that." He snapped thumb and finger. "Did he then jump up and write his letter and hide it here?"

"I don't care—I don't understand— Why, then, did he write it that very day?"

He could only shrug.

"Perhaps you had better give me the letter, my Little One," he said and extended his hand for it.

"No," said Beryl warmly. "It came into my hand; it is for Gerald Sommers—and I am the one to take it to him. He called yesterday and I— Well, I was rather unkind I am afraid. Now—"

She did not say the rest, did not even formulate it definitely for herself, yet there it was, though vaguely, in her consciousness. She had drawn back from Red Handsome these last few days; she had, if in ever so little, leaned laughingly toward Jerry Boyne. It was almost with a feeling of eagerness now that she again swayed toward Red Handsome, since to do so was to lean as far as the pole from Jerry.

"This money—" began Costa, and paused, looking sharply at her.

"I had forgotten it! Why, it, too, must belong to Gerald Sommers."

He turned the packet over in his hand and then slipped it into his pocket, smiling curiously.

"What is that quaint saying you children have: 'Finders, keepers'?"

"Grandfather!"

"Your emotions run away with you like a lot of wild horses! Oh, you Americans! We of the older civilizations are more phlegmatic. Now let me ask you this,

Little Miss: Whose house is this? Aha! Mine. I bought it, did I not, from the unfortunate Mr. Sommers? With all that it contained, eh? Should we be entirely logical and—that word 'phlegmatic' is a nice one; I use it again—why then, is it not a fact that the letter, too, is mine?"

She clutched it all the tighter, looking at him with an expression in which a sort of horror mingled with incredulity.

"You would not take money that did not belong to you!"

He laughed at her.

"Shall we say that I am merely borrowing it? I am always borrowing money, you know, *querida*. I am good at that. Oh, how tragic you are!"

"I don't know what has happened to you! You are different! At least, grandfather," she said stubbornly, "I shall carry this letter immediately to Gerald; I have not the least doubt that the money in your pocket is referred to in these last lines Mr. Sommers wrote to his son. In any case I shall tell Gerald—"

"It is a very, very long time—not since you were a little, little girl—that I have locked you in your room—"

Her cheeks had warmed in the excitement of her discoveries and now went scarlet; her eyes flashed danger signals.

"It was so long ago that I had hoped we could both forget," she cried hotly. "It will never be again."

"So be it," he said, and once more smiled. "I ask you not to hurry with that letter to Señor Red Handsome.

You will, of course, suit yourself. Now shall we replace the candlestick, having satisfied ourselves concerning the motives of our recent guest, that most interesting Mr. Jerry Boyne?"

Beryl had forgotten all about Jerry.

"Jerry Boyne!" she exclaimed as the new light flooding her understanding revealed much and, as strong lights are always doing, caused black shadows in certain quarters. "Of course. It was not the candlestick and not the few coins— But how could he know? How could anyone know? And Jerry Boyne, a stranger, just arrived—"

Antonio Costa amazed her with his cryptic reply:

"When you see an old rooster standing over a new-laid egg, my dear, you will just know he is up to something shady!"

CHAPTER X

WITH LITTLE MESA LYING MIDWAY BETWEEN High Mesa and the Alamo Springs ranch, Beryl, though in haste, stopped at Bob Kingsbury's to ask concerning the wounded man's progress. As she drew near the ranch house a man who had heard the lively clatter of Silvermane's hurrying hoofs came out on the front porch. Beryl brought her mount down from a gallop to a sudden stop at the foot of the steps; a cloud of dust rose and thinned and drifted away, and she saw clearly who it was that had come out to meet her.

"You!" she gasped involuntarily.

"None other," Jerry laughed back into her surprised face. "And if you came hurrying along in order to apologize—"

"I did not, and you know it."

"Ah, well! Then if you are hunting stolen horses, the one I rode from High Mesa has already been turned over to one of your grandfather's men—"

"I did not have any idea you were here," said Beryl in her most icy manner. "Had I suspected, I should not have stopped."

"Ouch!" said Jerry, his hand clutching his side. "Stabbed with an icicle!"

For he, too, had breakfasted and he had had a good talk with certain friends within, and his mood was a high one. True, there were clouds everywhere along his horizon, but a natural gayety of outlook was his and he had a feeling—just one of those feelings—that everything was quite all right with a very satisfactory world.

Beryl, doing her level best to fill her expressive eyes with a rare blend of scorn and hate, was just swinging Silvermane's head about to be on her way to Alamo Springs, when the door opened again and an old friend looked out.

"Uncle Doctor!" she cried eagerly. "Will you come here? I want to see you."

"Comin' a-runnin', Miss Beryl." He hurried out and ran down the steps, put a quieting hand on the rein of the restive Silvermane and looked up smiling into Beryl's frowning eyes. Just then the door opened the third time and the round face of Elmer Blodgett looked out, taking everything in with bright, inquisitive eyes.

Beryl sniffed so that those who were not near enough to hear could at least guess from her expression that she did sniff.

"Shall we draw off a few steps?" she said quickly. "There are so many about."

Jerry went back into the house at that, carrying a faintly resisting Elmer Blodgett along with him; this time when the door closed it banged. Beryl, looking down into the bright eyes turned up to hers, almost smiled then.

"I was just riding by and stopped to ask about Mr. Kingsbury."

"Doin' fine. Tougher'n the sort of sole leather they used to put in shoes when they made good shoes. He wants to thank you for all the goodies you sent over." He grinned and added, "Jerry, he ate most of 'em for breakfast."

"Jerry?" She lifted her brows disdainfully. "You seem to have grown mighty familiar with him all of a sudden!"

"Shucks, he ain't no stranger to me. I've knowed that boy half his natural life."

"Known Jerry Boyne?" She did not realize how eager she was; she would have said that she was "simply curious." Then, remembering last night, she said stiffly: "He's a common thief."

When Uncle Doctor only laughed and again said, "Shucks!" he set her wondering. Before she could remark, he added quickly:

"Which way so early, Miss Beryl? Just takin' a little ride or goin' some place?"

"I am on my way to Alamo Springs," she said absently. "I have to see Mr. Sommers; it's rather urgent—"

Again he surprised her, saying in a waspish way that was his at times when things didn't go just right:

"The less you see that Red Han'some guy, the better, Miss Beryl. He's a polecat."

"Uncle Doctor! Why, what's come over you? You never said a word against him in your life! What's happened?"

"A heap," he muttered, and put his head down, briefly engaged with digging a hole in the dirt with the toe of his boot. "I'll tell you some time. If you got any business with him, better let me take it on for you."

"You weren't a bit surprised when I told you Jerry Boyne was a common thief!" She frowned, groped, rose swiftly to sheer inspiration. "He has told you about last night!"

"An' laughed his ol' head off! That kid wasn't stealin' anything, Miss Beryl. He just ain't that kind."

"Where did you know him so well?"

"Oh, places. I knowed him, to begin with, as a kid; that was before I come to High Mesa—"

"Fifteen years ago! Don't you suppose a boy, growing on into a man, changes any in that time? Never mind; I'll tell you something, Uncle Doctor—"

And the tale came with a rush, completing the affair of the old iron candlestick.

"An' you're on your way now like a streak to hand that letter over? Don't you do it!"

"I don't understand you this morning! Don't you understand that the letter is from his own father, written the very day he was killed?"

His hand that had rested so carelessly on her rein, froze hard.

"Better let me take it," was the best he could think of saying.

"No! I found it and I feel a responsibility."

"Sure, I know." Still he clung tight to the rein. Then, hard-driven, he jerked up his head and looked her straight in the eyes and lied as he had never thought to lie to Miss Beryl the longest day he lived. "Too bad, but he'll have to wait for his letter after all. He rode by here about an hour ago, headed down to the border. Said he wouldn't be back for three days. Cattle deal, I think. He's buyin' stock right along, you know."

After that there was nothing left for Beryl to do but turn back.

"Better let me take the letter, Miss Beryl; I'll sure see that Gerald Sommers gets it the first possible minute."

Beryl shook her head.

"Send one of the men over to Alamo Springs and leave word for him to call at High Mesa as soon as he comes home," she called back to him out of a new dust cloud.

Uncle Doctor stood frowning after her departure, scratched his head, swore a little and went clumping heavily up the steps and into the house.

"Jerry, you bum burglar," he snapped, "the fat's in the

170

fire, the milk's spilt an' the cat's got the canary. Nex' time you start out to do a housebreakin' job, finish it or else go bury your tools."

"Sounds interesting," retorted Jerry. "What's the rest of it?"

He had arrived at Little Mesa in the middle of the night and had found his old friend and Elmer Blodgett sitting up playing cribbage. Explanations were forthcoming, and while at it he told everything. For the first time Elmer, his mouth opening wider and wider by startled jerks, his eyes as round and about the size of silver dollars, learned that Jerry had meant every word he said that time that he had remarked, "I happen to be Gerald Sommers myself." At first Elmer refused to believe a word of it; he merely grew sly looking and murmured admiringly very much as he had that other time: "What a game, what a game! If you could only get away with it!" But in due course the truth was driven in on him, and there never was a more delighted man than Mr. Elmer Blodgett. Here were happenings of a sort to satisfy his propensities from hidden root to lofty branch.

"To think," he murmured in a sort of ecstasy, "of a guy being the son of a daddy that owned a ranch worth two hundred and fifty grand, and said guy off combing the seven seas and hobnobbing with ordinary roughnecks like me! Can you beat it? Well, I see now why you're so all-fired set on having the lowest low-down on that other red-head. Will I go get it for my new millionaire pal? I will!"

Last night while the three were talking in hushed

tones, deeming Bob Kingsbury asleep in the adjoining room, there had come a thumping on the thin partition-wall, followed by Bob's voice saying bluntly:

"I've been listenin' to your gabble. Better come on in an' spill the whole sack o' beans, hadn't you?"

Bob, who had appeared to take such a deal of killing, was staging a come-back which surprised even the case-hardened old Doc. With every passing day he grew stronger and more determined to live. The time had come when they had had to tell him about his brother. He asked details quietly, wanted to know where they had buried him, nodded his appreciation when they told him that Dick was taking his last rest right here on Little Mesa, and at the end said only: "Me, I'll be up an' around real soon." He never mentioned his brother again. When he just said grimly, looking up at them with agonized dry eyes, "Me, I'll be up an' around real soon," he said as much as many men would have needed a thousand words to say.

At his request they "spilled the whole sack o' beans." He would have to know sooner or later; further, Jerry judged, here was a counter-irritant for his grief over his brother's death; and finally:

"You're not going to lose a dollar on it, old-timer," Jerry vowed warmly.

Bob shrugged indifferently.

"Losin' a few thousand bucks an' a ranch—that's nothin'," he said. "I've got no business with money anyhow; never had any before; just a streak of fool's luck, oil of course, on some grazin' land an' a flare of prosperity. Let her come, let her go—"

"You're not going to lose a cent if I can help it," Jerry insisted. "And I think I can. We're going slow and we're going to find out a lot of things. Before I spring anything we're going to know a whole lot about that pretty boy with the red hair. He's got some money left, maybe the whole amount that he shook Antonio Costa down for. You'll get yours back, don't you fear; or you'll keep Little Mesa and I'll get mine."

Now that Uncle Doctor foamed over with the news he had had from Beryl, the three men went into Kingsbury's room to discuss it. Propped up against his pillows, smoking a cigarette and looking more like a man recuperating from a single night's spree than one who had coquetted with death, Bob took as keen an interest as any.

"Let's get it straight," he said. "You knew where your old man kep' a chunk of money? You nosed down in the dark an' the girl caught you red handed? Then you dropped things and flew the coop?"

"Dropped things is right, Bob," said Uncle Doctor scathingly, boring with accusing eyes at Jerry. "The pup lef' a screwdriver right where anybody'd see the screws it was headed for, an' now Don Antonio's got the chunk of money. Pretty near as bad as that an' maybe worse, Miss Beryl's got a letter that Jerry's dad wrote the same day he was done in, an' seein' how that letter's addressed to Gerald Sommers, she's off on the runnin' lope to fork it over to that ring-tailed skunk over to Alamo Springs."

"Something funny about that same ring-tail," said Bob Kingsbury, his eyes speculative through his cigarette smoke. "I been thinkin' about it since Jerry tol' me he was a four-flushin' impostor. Maybe it don't amount to nothin' but it's sort of funny, though."

"Let's have it," said Jerry impatiently, for Bob appeared to be in doubt whether to put his thought into words.

"It's this: I've never laid eyes on him."

Elmer Blodgett had been so tense, leaning forward precariously in his chair lest some word might elude him, that it was only with a quick shifting of his weight that he saved himself from a spill.

"I never saw Henry Ford, the Duke of York or the King of Siam," he said sarcastically. "Still I never went around saying what funny birds they were because of that!"

"Shut up, Elmer," said Jerry. "Go ahead, Bob."

"It's only lately I've kinda noticed it," said Bob, and still was hesitant. "Look at it this way: One day I rode down Alamo Springs way, jus' happenin' that direction an', feelin' frien'ly, I moseyed on up to the house. There was a feller settin' on the porch; he stood up when I swung 'round the corral; then he ducked into the house. I didn't get much of a look at him; a long, stringy man, I'd say. Well, I rode up to the house an' a breed, not the same feller a-tall, popped out. No, he said, Mr. Sommers wasn't home."

Elmer was inclined to jeer again, having listened in open-mouthed attention only to be disappointed at the end.

"I don't say it was this Red Han'some person that skipped out of range," continued Bob evenly, "but from what I've heard of the way he looks, it might be. But here's the other barrel: He's a neighbor, an' he's never popped in. He goes pretty reg'lar to High Mesa, don't he? An' the shortes' road between Alamo Springs an' High Mesa runs right by my place, don't it? Still, all an' all, I've never set my eyes on him. That's the tale, boys."

"It *is* kind of funny," Elmer was the first to concede, his eyes darting from face to face. With a sudden whoop, his every-ready suspicions in full flight, he exclaimed: "I'll bet you this same Red, under some other name, killed a whole string of folks—some other place—where Bob was, too—and Bob saw the dastardly deed—and could swing him for it—and Mr. Red's hiding out, scared to death!"

Old Uncle Doctor chuckled.

"I'm beginnin' to cotton to this Elmer party," he declared. "Now, if he'd jus' figgered Red to have wiped out a man or two, shucks, anybody could think that up. But Elmer's got to have a whole string of folks unlawfully removed."

"Think of any red-headed men you've known, Bob," cut in Jerry, intrigued. "It's just possible, you know—"

"Layin' here with nothin' to do but think, I've thought of a good many things," said Bob gravely. "What you mean, I've thought of that, too. No; I can't remember any red-head I ever knew that fits the pitchure as folks make it for me, tellin' me what this jasper looks like. I've moved round, like mos' boys do, driftin'; I've worked here an' there an' had me a little ranch one place an' another; some place I might have known him. I'd

175

have to see him to tell."

"Of course you'd know him!" insisted the enthusiastic Blodgett. "Else why should he dodge you? You must have known him for a crook, too, or he wouldn't be so darned shy."

"That doesn't follow," said Jerry thoughtfully. "Just for Bob to know him and to know that he isn't Gerald Sommers would be enough to explain his keeping out of sight."

"Let's go get him!" cried Elmer and surged to his feet. "Where's my hat? Let's go get him and bring him in for Bob to look him over."

That there was meat in that suggestion was promptly conceded.

"Later," said Jerry. "But before we tip him off that there's anything in the wind let's find out a bit more about him. Elmer's going out on the trail like a good old police dog today. We're going to get Bob up and around, too; if we can arrange for Bob to look the Alamo Springs gent over without Bob himself being seen, that's what we want. And there's something else."

He went to the door and looked out, catching a glimpse of Beryl in the distance, going up into the rocky hills near Indian Gully.

"There's that letter! I've got to have it," he said, coming back from the window. "There must be some significance in the fact that it was written on Dad's last day. I've got to have it, but how the deuce I am going to get it, I don't see."

"She's all set to fork it over to Red Han'some,"

176

grumbled Uncle Doctor.

"I got it!" cried Elmer. "We wait till it gets dark. Then we chase a boy over to Alamo Springs and he takes a message to Red that the lady of his dreams is crazy to see him in a great big rush. He burns the wind getting to her. She hands him the letter, telling him all about it. And then what does he do?"

"What's your idea, Elmer?" demanded Jerry. "The last thing I want is to have him get it."

"Do you think he'll open it right there and read it to her?" challenged Elmer. "He's walking on crackly ice all the time, ain't he? He'll be sort of flabbergasted a minute, won't he? He'll think as fast as he can, and I guess he's a pretty fast thinker, seeing how he's managed things so far. Why, he'll just stuff that letter into his pocket and drill for home, to read it in the privacy of his own boudoir! And as he comes bulging out the hacienda portals, there's the crowd of us ready to pounce on him, and the letter's ours! Just exactly like pulling rabbits out of a hat. Easy when the big magician, that's me, shows you how."

He actually blushed under the approving looks turned upon him.

CHAPTER XI

BUT MATTERS DID NOT WORK OUT AS SIMPLY AND expeditiously as planned. To begin with, that monumental lie which turned Beryl back at Little Mesa, proved to be not much of a lie after all except, of course, in intention. The pseudo Gerald Sommers was not at home when sought at the Alamo Springs; he was off somewhere below the border and he did not return for several days.

"God wouldn't stand for me lyin' to her," said Uncle Doctor solemnly. "Instead of strikin' me dead, He jus' made it come true." He looked accusingly at his young friend. "After this, Jerry, ol' trouble-maker," he said with emphasis, "you do your own lyin'."

He departed for High Mesa, undertaking to keep an eye open at all hours, and to send immediate word if Red Han'some showed. Elmer Blodgett, too, went on his way, tremendously taken with his task of "nosing around and getting the low-down on the other red-head." Jerry and Bob Kingsbury had Little Mesa to themselves during quiet, peaceful days filled with speculation. Kingsbury's convalescence, thanks both to a splendid body and to the determined will to be strong again and about his single purpose, was rapid; he was sitting up when one late afternoon Elmer returned.

"Is it a sweet tangle?" he asked by way of greeting. "Say, if I was an expert accountant with a couple of boys like Einstein punching the clock regular under my eagle eye, why, then I'd have it all figured out in no time at all—say, seven years! Hello, Bob; you're looking like the Fourth of July. Jerry, my millionaire pal, shake. I've found out a considerable good deal."

He hung his natty straw hat, a brand-new one, on a nail, preëmpted two chairs in order to bestow his bright yellow shoes in one, clasped his chubby hands behind his head and beamed. Bob in cushioned ease in a rocker, Jerry more alert looking as he bestrode a rawhide-bottomed chair as though it were a horse, the two gave ear and Elmer told his tale.

"I went straight to the county seat, that's San Juan, and there I stayed most of the time; best room in the San Juan Hotel and all signs of prosperity hung out. You're paying expenses, too, ain't you, Jerry? O.K. In San Juan they'll tell you that Mr. Elmer Blodgett is a good little spender, a fair hand at poker and the advance guard of big things to come to the great sandy outdoors! Large projects, ambitious development, reclamation on a noble scale. And San Juan will rare up like a man and tell you that Mr. Blodgett is nobody's fool, but a man to look the ground over careful, a man whose head absorbs statistics like a sponge soaks up water. Bankers shook me by the hand and the courthouse opened its doors, its books and its mouth.

"Did I learn things? The answer is Yes. After flitting hither and yon, working above ground and likewise mole-fashion, I bring you my gleanings.

"Ready for figures? All right. Costa paid two hundred fifty thousand to Red Handsome for High Mesa. Sure we knew that; I'm confirming what we knew. That price, by the way, included Little Mesa, since sold to

179

Bob here for fifty thousand. I'm using round numbers all the way through; you can have the nickles if you want them. Costa blew the fifty thousand; he's good at that. Plowed part back into High Mesa, developing water and extending fields, adding to his stock and so on; got rid of the rest the easiest way, mostly gambling. Then he mortgaged High Mesa for another fifty thousand."

"A mortgage, huh?" said Bob in surprise. "I thought the old boy had no end of money."

"And the mortgage is held," announced Blodgett with relish, "by no less a financial genius than old lady Fernandez of the Empire! Kind of funny, ain't it? If she knew that Costa's deed was bogus, would she put out good money on a mortgage? But I'll go ahead with statistics.

"Red Handsome, getting the cash for High Mesa, stepped out and bought him Alamo Springs. It's quite an outfit and in round numbers again, with the stock now on it, set him back pretty close to one hundred thousand. He blew money around for a spell as a man would; maybe as much as fifty thousand, at a guess. That left him, let's say, about one more hundred thousand. Guess where that went?"

"To the Empress, if we're right in assuming that she was in on the deal with him at the beginning," offered Jerry.

"Maybe. Not direct, though. It went first of all to a banker down in Mexico, and that banker is a friend of old Mrs. Fernandez', and he was one of the men who stepped to the bat and swore that Red Handsome was well known to him to be Mr. Gerald Sommers. If the Mex banker turned the mazuma over to the Empress, saving for what might have stuck to his fingers, anyhow it don't show on anybody's books as going from Red to her. See the play?

"On top of these amounts there's the other you was wondering about, Jerry. Your dad left about a hundred thousand in securities; Red grabbed it, of course, and it would seem that he has left it as it was. So when you land on him for an accounting he ought to have that where you can tie it up. Counting that and the Alamo Springs place, Red ought to be worth about two hundred thousand."

Jerry's pencil was busy.

"If I did land on him right now," he said when he looked up, "and proved my case, I'd lose nothing. But where would Costa get off? And Bob here? On the other hand, if I let them cut in on Red's stake first, I'd be losing a good deal more money to that jasper than I have any notion of donating to him."

"I've figured the way you're doing," nodded Elmer. "Looks like somebody was about to lose some money. There's you and Bob and the old caballero all standing in line saying, 'Gimme'; and there's Red who hasn't got enough to go around. Costa can't give back the fifty grand he got from Bob, and Bob hasn't even got the ranch he stands on! Then there's the little lady who used to fling her heels on Broadway; she cut a hundred thousand velvet on the deal, then was fool enough to soak back fifty in a mortgage."

"Can you turn any light on the break between the

Empress and Red?" Jerry asked.

"Nobody knows just what happened, though most folks opine that those two would like to poison each other. But here's a guess: It's our bet that she put Red into the place where all the cream was. Around three hundred and fifty grand, as we've figured it. And we're guessing that he forked over a measly one hundred thousand to her! Like as not she'd counted on a fifty-fifty split. It's a chance he found the going so dead easy that he got uppity and cock-sure and let her down. Fair guess? Well, that's about all we'll know until I can go do some more nosing."

But in that final statement he was in error.

Darkness had just shut down and Jerry was lighting a lamp when they had as visitor the last man they would have thought of seeing at Little Mesa. No sound of a horse's hoofs announced him; there was only a sudden clank of spurs on the porch and the door was thrown open with no preliminary knocking. On the threshold, his hands on his hips, stood that border ruffian, Frank Smith, better known as El Bravo.

He reeked with bravado. Crossed belts were about his thick middle and his hands were never far from the butts of the two old-fashioned Colt 45's that he wore prominently thrust forward. His cold repellent eyes were narrowed watchfully; his whole manner bespoke a truculent readiness for carnage were any here minded to precipitate it.

"Howdy, boys," he said coolly. "I'm here on business; peaceable, if that suits you."

He stepped to one side only far enough to have the

wall at his back and left the door wide open. Jerry, setting down his lamp, stared wonderingly at the man, then glanced hastily to Kingsbury. Bob, tired after his long sitting up, was leaning back among pillows, looking pale and nerveless. Of a sudden he jerked stiffly erect and red splotches came into his cheeks. His own eyes, quitting El Bravo's, slashed across the room to his gun lying on a table. Elmer Blodgett, dawdling near that same table, appeared for one instant to harbor the wild impulse to snatch up Kingsbury's weapon, but instantly thought better of the matter and put both hands into his pockets.

Bob, his eyes wild with desperation, held himself rigid where he sat.

"Come to finish the job, Smith?" he demanded.

"Come to talk business, like I said," returned El Bravo.

"You're the man, they tell me, that found my brother—dead—"

"Yes," said El Bravo. "What of it?"

"You damned murderin' dog!"

"Peaceable, I said, too," said El Bravo. "If you'll have it that way."

"Better get me, Smith, while the gettin's good. Understand?"

"Bob!" said Jerry sharply. "Hold your horses, will you? Now is no time to start anything. Suppose you hear what he has to say?"

"I'll see him in hell before I truck with him!" cried Bob angrily. With that he put his hands on the arms of his chair, meaning to rise and start on that impossible

183

journey across the room to the table. Jerry caught him by the shoulders and forced him back.

"Don't be an idiot!" he commanded. "If Mr. Smith wanted to take you up on your nice little sporting offer to bang away at each other, you'd never last to travel two steps." He turned on their caller. "Why not speak your piece, if you're set on it, and then fork your pony for somewhere else?"

El Bravo nodded.

"I'm sent here by Señora Fernandez to talk turkey with Kingsbury. Can't very well ask for a private confab, can I?" What went for a smile with him, a still further narrowing of the eyes and a faint suggestion of a sneer on his broad mouth, accompanied the words: "She wants to be friendly."

Jerry's fingers dug savagely into Kingsbury's shoulder. But Bob no longer required a check upon recklessness. Of a sudden he was as cold and watchful and repressed as El Bravo himself. He told himself grimly that if he knew anything on earth it was that here before him stood the man who had led the recent destructive attack on Little Mesa, who was responsible for Bob's own invalided condition—most of all, confronting him was the man who had shot Dick Kingsbury down in cold blood. It was murder crying to heaven for retribution; it was murder dictated by that merciless wretch of a woman who now wanted "to be friendly!" All very true; equally true, to lift a finger now was to lose for all time the chance to bring about that retribution.

"I'm listenin' fine, Smith," he said indifferently, and

sank back loosely in his chair.

El Bravo chuckled. Perhaps he was not altogether sober; certainly he brought with him a rich aroma reminiscent of the southern side of the border. Drunkenness with El Bravo did not impair his steadiness, did not dim his cold, shrewd eyes, but did stimulate his peculiar brand of humor.

"She says remind you how Little Mesa got raided the other night," he said as coolly as though speaking of the weather. "She says she guesses you'd remember it anyhow, but to ask whether you have had time to figure out that what happened once might happen again? She says that would be too bad, and she'd be awful sorry—seeing as how she'd like to buy Little Mesa herself and don't want it all messed up. Talk like a book, don't I?"

"Do you mind makin' it short?"

"Good enough. Everybody knows that there are always bandit gangs whooping it up along the border, and that there's one operating now that's raising partic'lar hell. Tough hombres, breeds mixed with bad Apache, so they say. They've been cutting it wide and rich. The authorities, sheriffs and border officials, pop out now and then and can't find anything much to do but clean up after the show's over. That's all so, ain't it? All right. Now Señora Fernandez says that she's a notion to take a hand herself. Looks like she could protect this place; she could throw a hundred men into the game, five hundred if she liked. You sell out to her pronto; her offer of thirty thousand still stands; and she'll take Little Mesa under her wing. You stand pat, and she'll do the same. In which case, most likely there'll be another raid and you'll get wiped out. Looks like it might be thirty thousand or nothing, don't it?"

"Thirty thousand? Half of what I've sunk in this place?"

"Just thirty thousand better than nothing," said El Bravo.

"She seems pretty sure that that bandit gang you're talkin' about is comin' back to see me. Knows all about 'em, huh?" Bob fought with his anger; then snapped viciously: "Funny they never get gay with her ranch, Smith!"

"Not so funny," said El Bravo with his heavy shrug. "They've had too much sense to monkey with her; she's got too much power. That is, they've had too much sense until lately; they're beginning to get heady with success, looks like. They raided her last night."

When three pairs of eyes regarded him incredulously he indulged for a second time in his chuckle.

"They swept down, about fifty strong, on her own little town, right at the Empire and under her nose. Burned, looted and rode off."

"And, strange to say," jeered Kingsbury, seeing in the event a crude effort on the Empress's part to quiet suspicion, "nobody got hurt! Huh? How about it?"

"Three dead," said El Bravo and actually grinned. "One was a girl, too; a skirt that Charlie Fernandez fancied for a while and then threw back into the dirt he'd raked her out of; viperish, she'd got, and I guess she's just as happy now playing her harp. One was an Injun kid named Juan; used to ride races for the Empire and lost not long ago to Red Handsome. The other was a

186

fellow that used to be a guard at the hacienda gates. Funny; happens to have been the one that let your kid brother through that time he showed up looking for you. Oh, sure; it was an honest-to-God raid all right; all the trimmings."

Elmer Blodgett gasped and a shiver shook his chubby body; Jerry felt a cold horror settle upon him. As for Bob Kingsbury, not a muscle twitched, not a flicker came into his eyes.

"There you've got the layout," El Bravo went on. "Señora Fernandez has got her dander up; she's certainly going to protect her own interests. She'll protect Little Mesa, too, if she buys it; can do. Of course, if you refuse to sell, it's none of her business. Now what's the answer?"

It must have been perfectly clear to Bob Kingsbury that, since he did not really own Little Mesa, here was a chance; take the Empress's thirty thousand dollars and let her have a worthless deed. Yet other things were not nearly so clear. To begin with, she must know as well as he knew that she was risking her thirty thousand dollars.

He did not long hesitate. It was enough for him that the woman and El Bravo wanted him to sell and that they threatened. As far as he was concerned, thirty thousand dollars could go to the devil before he would deal, except with guns, with either one of them.

"Tell the lady I said to go to hell," he rasped out hotly. "The same to you. And the next time you show up, come shootin'; I'll have my gun handy and I'll be waitin'."

"Bueno." El Bravo was of no mood to argue; he had come not to debate matters but merely to issue an ultimatum and receive an answer. His eyes cut across to Jerry.

"I want a word with you, Boyne," he said curtly. "Alone. Step outside with me a minute, will you?"

"Right," returned Jerry promptly.

El Bravo backed out through the door, whirled and ran to the end of the porch and the clank of his spurs told where he had jumped down in the dark. As Jerry, his curiosity rampant, started to follow, Elmer caught him by the arm.

"You Crazy Fool!" cried Blodgett nervously. "Don't go outside with that killer! He'd burn a man down just to keep in practice."

Jerry shook him off and went out to El Bravo, finding him at the corner of the house, his back to the wall.

"Señora Fernandez told me to get in touch with you, too," El Bravo said quickly but in an undertone which could not carry to the men in the house. "She hinted at a job for you that first day you blew in. You hedged. Now she says that if you're standing off for big pay there's no use keeping it up. Here's her offer: Ten thousand cash to you the minute you run down and sign on with her; ninety thousand when the job's done. A round hundred thousand in all. What's the answer?"

"What's the job?" asked Jerry, utterly mystified.

"Does a man ask what the job is when he's offered a pile like that?" growled El Bravo disgustedly. "It's yes or no."

"What's the job?" repeated Jerry.

"It's to pull Red Handsome down, if you're bound to know. He's no friend of yours, is he? You'd just as lieve gouge him, wouldn't you? And get paid big money for doing it?"

"What does she want me to do? Go out and pop a bullet in him?"

"Hell, no! The old lady's free with her money, but she don't pay a hundred thousand for a hundred dollar job! She wants to pull him down, to bust him flat, to put him afoot without two coppers to clink."

"How the deuce does she think I can do a thing like that?" demanded Jerry.

"Step along with me over to where my horse is," grunted El Bravo. "If we're going to talk all night I'd just as lieve get away from the house."

He turned and led the way and Jerry followed. Behind a stone outhouse standing lonely in a black smudge left by the recent raid, he stopped and faced about.

"What I'm telling you," said El Bravo pointedly, "is between just the two of us. Later, if you get funny, you can't prove I said anything, as I'll just naturally say you're a damn liar. So, since I'm in a hurry, I'll come straight out in the open. This Red Handsome party, now: When he blew in here five years ago he had some little trouble proving that he was Gerald Sommers and heir to High Mesa. The Empress fell for him; he had no money and she kicked in and staked him. Also she helped him prove who he was. No, she didn't say that she knew him! Oh, no; not old lady Fernandez! Ever see anything green about her? But she had friends down in Mexico; big bozos, whose word helped. They swore they knew Red and that he was Sommers, and the thing was done."

"You mean," said Jerry softly, "that he isn't really Gerald Sommers at all?"

"I mean that whether he is or ain't has got nothing to do with this one sure thing: The old lady is sore and she's ready to go to the bat a second time, this time to prove that Red fooled her and that he's no more Jerry Sommers than you are. Got that?"

"I sure got it!" Jerry grinned in the dark. "Go on. I find you strangely interesting."

"It happens," said El Bravo, "that you're a red-head. It happens that you're about the right age. It happens on top of that that Señora Fernandez figures she can read a man like a school kid reads his lesson book. She thinks you're born for a job like this."

"Maybe I am," said Jerry. "Maybe I am!"

"You'll show up tomorrow and talk to her?"

"Did I say I would? Look here, how's she going to prove that Red Handsome was playing a part?"

"I told you how he got in, didn't I? Mostly through the say-so of two big guns down in Mexico. Well, their word don't stand so high just now. One of 'em, a banker, skipped to Europe not so long ago and took most of the bank with him. The other hombre was smeared with the same tar and things don't look too good for him now; he's seeing the world through bars. Ought to be easy to start suspicion, oughtn't it?"

"And to prove—to prove that I am Gerald Sommers?"

"Leave it to her. Now, what's the answer?"

"Here's something to think about: If I did play, and if we get away with it, what about Little Mesa? We'd be proving Red Handsome an impostor; that would prove that he never owned High Mesa and Little Mesa; then the deeds he signed would be no good—and Bob Kingsbury's title would be worthless! So, if I chip in, I take it that her offer to buy Little Mesa is withdrawn?"

"I can't see that that's any of your business," said El Bravo promptly. "Just the same, the old lady said to talk things out friendly with you. Yes, her offer stands just the same. For one thing, it would take time to prove your identity, and she's in a hurry; she wants this place now; she needs the water and she's got other reasons. For the other thing, what's thirty thousand to her? She'd more than make it back, wouldn't she? And if folks suspected later that she had been in on a queer-smelling deal, it would clean her up some, wouldn't it, to show how in good faith she had bought Little Mesa with cold cash?"

"Then things stand with Kingsbury just as they are?"

"They stand. If he's a friend of yours, go and blab to him all you like. I'll say you lied. You might tip him off he'd better sell—or start somewhere else damned quick. He's going to get burned up one way or another."

He had untied his horse while talking and now climbed up into the saddle.

"I'm on my way," he said, curbing a restless mount. "What's the answer for the old lady?"

"Tell her," returned Jerry, and of a sudden his grin was so broad that El Bravo caught the glint of his teeth in the starlight, "that you had a good, heart-to-heart with

191

Gerald Sommers—meaning me! Now hold your mustang a minute! Tell her that I was already looking for a way to kick the props out from under Mr. Red Handsome. But tell her that I am saying nothing of all this to the big round world for a while. There are reasons; she'll know later. I'll hope to see her before the skies fall; in the meantime she can bet all her blue chips on one shining fact: The only real, genuine Gerald Sommers—that's me!"

"*Bueno.* You're on the payroll, kid. Then, since she can use a live man and has no use for a dead one, here's a tip: Dig out of this place in a hurry! *¿Sabe?* I've a hunch it's going to be damned unhealthy around this dump real soon. *Adios.*"

"Hold on there! What do you mean by 'soon'? A day—a week?"

"If I was you I wouldn't be here ten minutes from now," muttered El Bravo. "I've got a hunch— Aha!" he broke off, and a shadowy arm was swung up, pointing out across the rolling hills. "Looks like those Apache Injuns I was talking about were having a party. That would be at Alamo Springs, wouldn't it? Well, *adios;* it's Red Handsome's surprise party, not mine."

He hunched forward in the saddle and his horse shot away with him. Jerry stared not after him but out toward the five-mile-distant Alamo Springs ranch. Above a sudden warm glow in the sky rose a wavering column of fire. For a moment, fascinated with the thing and its significance, he stood spellbound; then he whirled and ran back to the house.

CHAPTER XII

BURSTING IN UPON KINGSBURY AND BLODGETT, Jerry told them hurriedly all that was afoot; what was already occurring at the Alamo Springs ranch and what was at any moment to be expected here at Little Mesa.

"The first thing to do is get Bob out of it," he concluded sharply. "He's in no shape—"

"Here I am and here I stick," said Bob, spots of color in his cheeks and the bright fires of anger burning hot in his eyes. "Elmer, if you'll bring me a rifle and plenty of shells I'll squat back and pray for that bunch to come runnin'."

He was not to be turned from his intention, but in the end he did see reason in compromising with Jerry's suggestion. If an attack was made here tonight it would no doubt concentrate on the ranch house. So if Bob could be elsewhere, yet close enough to take a hand in the game, that hand might be played to greater advantage. Close behind the house the rugged hills broke down in a field of crags and bowlders; there was a spot there where Bob could lie under cover and concern himself with such of the unwary raiders as swooped down on the house.

"If you two boys will give me a hand that far? It's only a step."

Five minutes later Jerry and Elmer had installed Bob in his vantage place, a sort of rocky grotto protected on all sides save that which looked down the short slope

193

to the ranch house.

"Regular Colonel Bowie," grunted Elmer nervously as they lowered Bob to a bed of folded quilts and gave him his rifle and box of ammunition.

Jerry, facing out across the hills to the fire flaming up from the Alamo Springs ranch, demanded of Kingsbury:

"How many men with Red Handsome over there?"

"Dunno, Jerry. He's got a Chinaman in the house. Hires outside help as he needs it, maybe a couple of Mexicans."

"Bob—"

"Yeah?"

"You can keep out of this fight if you want to; they'll never dig you out if you have sense enough just to lie low. What's more, it's natural to suppose that there'll be no attack here until they've finished at Alamo Springs. All right. I'm going to hop in Elmer's car and go over."

"You?" gasped Elmer. "Ain't things bad enough for you right here? What do you want over there? Crazy Fool!"

Jerry shrugged.

"Alamo Springs as good as belongs to me, doesn't it? Think I'm going to stand off and let a handful of the Empress's night-howling pups wipe it off the face of the earth? In Elmer's car I can be over there before the riders get fed up watching the fire they've started. And if I have any luck I'll be back here before they can hit this place."

"You'll never be back," muttered Elmer, but Bob said eagerly:

194

"Good idea! Get my old 30-30 hangin' up in the kitchen; there's a full cartridge belt along with it. Ride lucky, Jerry. And if we don't meet-up here any more— Well, who said there wasn't no other place? *Adios, Jerry.*"

Jerry ran back to the house, snatched rifle and cartridge belt down from the wall, ran out to the car and was off at such speed that Elmer, who had elected to remain with Kingsbury, exclaimed fervently:

"Thank the Lord I'm not riding with that lunatic; he drives like he thought he was back in his old flying machine. Looks like here's where I lose a darned good car."

The road was as bad as Jerry had expected to find it, rutty, sandy, steep up and steep down and here and there full of kinks through the hills, but he hung tight to the wheel and established a new record between the two ranches. As he crested the last hill he snapped out his lights; if not already seen there was no advantage in announcing his arrival, and the hissing flare of a burning haystack gave him all the light he needed.

Beyond the fire in a field at the rear of the house he made out several moving figures, men on horses; and above the roar of the flames he heard voices shouting. The red light flashed on the weapons the raiders carried and struck silvery gleams from bridles and spurs.

There was a grove of cottonwoods in front of the house and it was in their shadow that Jerry jammed on his brakes and jumped down, hoping that he had not been seen and that the sound of his motor had been lost in the noise of the conflagration. An outhouse was bursting into flame, and from the rear of the house a rifle cracked a dozen times. He dragged rifle and belt out from the car and dashed to the house, taking the front steps at two bounds. The door was locked; he pounded on it, clamoring for entrance. Running steps inside answered him; a voice at the door demanded:

"Who's there? What do you want?"

"It's Jerry Boyne. Snap into it; get the door opened. I'm here to lend a hand."

Obviously the man within was puzzled and briefly undecided what to do. Certainly he had not looked to Jerry Boyne for aid at a time like this. But just as clearly he was in no position to stand long debating when a man came offering help. A bolt was shot back and the door jerked open and Jerry as he entered found a rifle barrel jammed in his middle.

"Shut the door, Ping-pong," rasped a voice. A Chinaman, carrying a gun, shuffled from a shadowy corner and shot the bolt. Jerry glared into the red-brown eyes glaring into his own.

"Pull your gun out of my ribs," he grunted, and shoved the rifle-barrel aside. "Didn't you hear me say I came to lend a hand?"

A coal-oil lamp on a table, smoking one side of its chimney yet shining undimmed upon the clean side, gave adequate light. The two men fronting each other could read each other's eyes. Suddenly the usurper laughed.

"I'd have expected the devil before I'd look for you jumping into my scrap," he said frankly. "As long as you're here, come ahead; I've no time to waste asking whether you've gone crazy recently or were born that way."

He turned and ran back through the house and to a small, high window. Jerry hastened to his side as the Chinaman came into the room and closed the door after him, plunging the room into darkness.

"You and the Chinaman alone?" demanded Jerry.

"Just me and Ping-pong; he's a damn' fine heathen and a high class little fighting man. There were a couple of greasers messing around the ranch; they've vanished. Looks like they'd been tipped off in advance that trouble was coming. How'd you get here so soon? Where'd you come from?"

"Little Mesa. Came by car. Saw the fire as it started—"

He whipped up his rifle and blazed away as a man on horseback, waving his hat over his head and whooping joyously, appeared just beyond the burning haystack.

"Missed him clean," he observed as the rider swerved and rode back out of sight.

From the far end of the room came another shot. The Chinaman, lying flat with his rifle nosing through a door which stood open a meager two inches, had fired and now began a soft chuckling.

"Get him, Ping-pong?"

"All samee knock um clazy, belly-side, think so; him flop-flop, no can git up," chortled the Oriental. "Come see, Mis' Sommers; look funny! Go flop-flop, try run, no can do." His words died away in a giggle of pure delight.

"How many of them?" asked Jerry.

"More than I expected. Twenty, maybe. There the rats go!" He began firing and both Jerry and Ping-pong joined in as a dozen or more riders made a dash from the illuminated field to take up their places behind the barn which as yet was untouched. "Too far; devil of a light for shooting, isn't it? Just flicker, flicker, flicker. We didn't get a man that time."

"Think-so plenty mo' fire now bimeby," muttered the Chinaman.

"Then El Bravo's a bigger fool than I ever took him to be," said Red Handsome, and sounded puzzled. "If he means to do a good clean-up job, why all the illumination outside before he tackles the house? We'll burn a whole raft of them down in all that light."

"El Bravo?" said Jerry. "He isn't out there. He was over at Little Mesa on horseback when I left. Ride as hard as he likes, he can't get here for another ten minutes at best."

"That so?" And when Jerry nodded: "Then it's that young ass Charlie Fernandez that's running this show. I'll bet El Bravo told him to wait and the bloodthirsty whelp couldn't keep his hands off. That idiot that was whooping and waving his hat was Prince Charlie, for a bet."

"If they're going to fire the barn why wait for them here? Why not slip out, hunt the dark places and even up the odds a bit?"

"May have to do that later," snapped Red Handsome. "Just now I've got an ace in the hole. See any of 'em, Ping?"

"No can see. Think-so, all one pile behind barn, talkee, talkee, talkee—"

"Damn it, I wanted to see the pack fly to glory! Why'd they have to flock there first? Well, here goes. Watch good, Ping; I'll give 'em the first volley!"

Jerry wondered what it was all about. He saw vaguely how Red Handsome ran along the wall and dropped on his knees; he saw him fumbling at the floor. Then there was a flare of a match and in its light he saw a trap opened and glimpsed wires. There was a second, tinier blue spurt, just a crackling electric spark and of a sudden the outside silence was broken with a dull booming roar. Red Handsome leaped up and came running back; the Chinaman writhed on the floor in a paroxysm of glee.

"I've been expecting these visitors for six months," said Red Handsome coolly. "That's not my biggest mine by any means, but I'll bet it told them something."

"Touched off by a battery here at the house!" gasped Jerry.

Since the explosion had taken place behind the barn, there was no knowing definitely how much havoc it had wrought; certainly it had hurled consternation among the men grouped under shelter. Dark dots went racing out in both directions, men fleeing in terror.

"They'll go slow for a minute or so now," said Red Handsome with grim satisfaction. "They won't know where the next spot is with the lid ready to blow off hell. This time I'd bet a man they wait for El Bravo. Hope so. I'd sure like to drop that hunk of beef."

From afar a voice reached them, a voice high-pitched

in excitement, railing, screaming curses, shrieking com-mands—and breaking off in wild, taunting laughter. Out across the field, lighted up by the burning haystack, was a gentle knoll; dimly seen was a horseman on its top, waving his hat, yelling his unattended words.

"That's that cowardly little shrimp, Prince Charlie," said Red Handsome disgustedly.

"He acts like a madman!"

"Mad? For blood letting, yes, provided he's in the clear all the while. The nastiest little coward on earth. His mamma has done everything she could to make a man of him, but he won't take a dozen steps without a bodyguard. Watch him hold off! Afraid of guns and will faint at the sight of steel—yet must have his gore! The Empress taught him how to shoot and how to use a knife. She had a knife-man spar with him, and Charlie wouldn't play unless his trainer used a rubber dagger and let him have a knife—and in his play he cut the fellow's throat! There was a girl he fancied— Here goes, just for luck."

He took deliberate aim and fired, but the distance was overgreat in the uncertain light. The whooping, gesticu-lating horseman must have heard the whine of the bullet though, for he whirled his horse and vanished in the dark beyond the knoll.

"It would be real obliging," suggested Jerry, "if these visitors of yours would stroll about to the various places you've planted your explosives. But what makes you think they will?"

"I knew they'd fire the haystack, and had a nice one there for them, but they pulled that trick before I knew anything was up. I've got three more charges about the barn, one at each side, one in front. And when they come swooping down on the house—" He shrugged. "They'll be taking chances, and by now I guess they know it."

"And so they'll wait for El Bravo?"

"You said it. Want a drink?"

"No, thank you, damn you," said Jerry coolly. "I don't drink with you."

"No? Suit yourself, Boyne. But why the devil you're willing to fight for a man you won't drink with— Well, that's your business. Hi, Ping-pong, whisky?"

The two drank together and thereafter in the gloom Jerry saw how the tall man clapped the little man on the shoulder. That done they returned to their posts.

There was an alarm clock somewhere in the kitchen and after a while Jerry became conscious of the thing ticking away in its thoroughly businesslike manner. Its matter-of-fact clicking and the hiss and crackle of the burning haystack were the only sounds. The silence lasted for several minutes. When at last it was broken, it was by a bullet crashing through a window. All three in the kitchen ducked involuntarily. It was Jerry who was first to see the flashes outside when further shots came, and he answered them with a will.

"Better run to the front room and take a look-see," called Red Handsome, once more back at the high narrow window. "Put the light out this time; in the dark here we'll have it as good as they will."

Ping-pong pattered out. Jerry saw a man on foot jump up from a place of shadows, running, bent double, to gain the shelter of a hay wagon, and sent a stream of lead buzzing after him. The fellow made a headlong dive out of sight behind the wagon and Jerry could only hope that he had felt the sting of a bullet. The Chinaman came shuffling back.

"Can see, 'way off, mo' men, come slow, scatter all over," he told them. "Better so we all same scatter."

"El Bravo," said Red Handsome, and his voice appeared eager. "Yes, Ping; we scatter all same. One man to the kitchen; I'll stay here. You skip to the front; give the high-sign if I'm to let 'em have the next crack o' doom! You, Boyne—"

"Go ahead," said Jerry crisply. "I'm with you. I don't know the layout here; which room?"

"Here, I'll go show you; get a move on."

He led and Jerry kept close behind. There was a door, a short hall, a bedroom beyond.

"Only two outside doors," he was informed. "Ping will watch the front and I'll take care of the back. From this window you can keep an eye on all that breaks on this side. You're a funny guy! Even if we don't drink together—thanks, old-timer."

"Glad to be along," said Jerry, and grinned in the dark.

Out of his window there was nothing to see except a wide field flooded with wavering light and in the distance a herd of cattle milling about in a fence corner. Beyond the frightened cattle, upon a gentle rise, he made out a solitary horseman—Prince Charlie, no doubt. He was at a safe distance, so Jerry held his fire and his eyes went everywhere in the nearer foreground, questing. So keen eyed was he that he noted where a shadow stirred among other shadows, something moving where tall grass edged an irrigating ditch. He whipped up his rifle and let drive. A sharp outcry of pain or of rage answered him.

"Burned one!" he yelled for his fellow defenders to hear.

"Good boy, Jerry!" Red Handsome shouted back at him, and his own rifle cracked. "The devils are closing in. Aha! Got one, Jerry!"

"Good man, Red!" Jerry sang out to him. "Lucky for us they lit the haystack!"

"It's burning fast. My bad hombres are stopping. How many on your side?"

"Can't see any now. Along the ditch, you know; it is a ditch, isn't it?"

"Yeah. Wish I'd turned the water in. What's doing, Ping?"

Ping-pong applied certain epithets to the attackers which they needed to be lower than scum to merit, and added in his sing-song:

"All stoppee now. El Blavo, think-so him come. Too muchee light. Bimeby hay all burn, come some more."

As he spoke the flames flared high, a little wind caught them and they flickered like tattered banners, then sank and dimmed. A weird, tremulous light flooded the level lands about the house, growing paler, with shadows conquering and spreading out over everything. Again the flames seethed high as some fresh hay pocket among the black char caught fire, and again died down save for erratic spurts and tongues of flickering orange and red.

Red Handsome deserted his post long enough to come running to Jerry.

"They're on foot and sneaking close," he said hurriedly. "Looks like they'd come at us from all sides. I'm back to my batteries. The minute you see any of 'em ducking in close to the house yell your head off and I'll get busy; of course as long as you can pick 'em off with a rifle, we save powder that way."

"Right," said Jerry, and heard the hurrying retreat of boots on the bare floor.

Perhaps a quarter of an hour passed in deep silence, and all this while it grew darker; there was only a dying hot glow where the old haystack had stood. There was no moon, yet the night was fine and clear and starlit. Watchful eyes, were the watcher lucky, might catch a glimpse of a man wriggling toward the house; on the other hand, were the luck all the wriggler's, he might approach unseen.

A yell of warning from the Chinaman shattered the silence. At the same moment Jerry saw several men leap up from the ground where they had lain merged in the dark and dash toward the corner of the house. He began firing as they ran and joined his warning cry to Ping-pong's.

"Red!" he shouted. "They're on top of us. Give 'em the works!"

"The works it is, kid!" came the answering yell. "Hold your hair on!"

With the last word came three explosions which

shook the house, three deafening detonations which, so close did they come together, merged almost into one. Jerry, staggered by the concussion, saw a great fountain of dirt and debris shoot up above the house corner; objects that might have been mangled men or scraps of porch flooring were flung high and far out; rocks and gravel rained on the roof; windows were shattered and glass fell tinkling. Through the din following the first dull boomings came a squeal of hysterical ecstasy from the Chinaman.

For an instant Jerry allowed himself the hope that those mines had sent those of the raiders who survived scurrying to shelter at some respectful distance. But a voice which he recognized as El Bravo's immediately set him right.

"They've shot their wad," roared El Bravo somewhere very near at hand.

"Ping-pong! Jerry! This way you two."

Jerry could see no one through his window. He heard the Chinaman running and himself dashed through the hall and to the kitchen. As he ran he could hear many men on the front porch; they were battering the door down; they surrounded the building like a wolf pack; above all the uproar rose a voice pitched high in excitement, breaking into shrill laughter. It was at a safe distance where no doubt Prince Charlie thrilled to a moment charged with that type of palpitant drama on which his misshapen soul fed.

In the dark kitchen Jerry careened into Ping-pong and both hurtled into Red Handsome. He caught them close and whispered:

"We've done our stunt here. When I yank this door open, you two shove your guns through and fire a volley sweeping right and left. Then we'll take our chances on streaking toward the barn. There's a gully behind it; if we can get that far I'll show you how we can slip out of this. Ready? Here goes."

He drew a bolt noiselessly, then jerked the door open. Jerry and Ping-pong delivered their volley with hearty thoroughness, and the three leaped through. As they gained the tiny kitchen porch, the front door fell and the house filled with El Bravo's men.

But for the moment the three ignored what lay at the rear. They saw figures here and there before them; rifles cracked and spurted fire from three or four places; they jerked their own guns up and fired back as fast as finger could work trigger. Ping-pong kept up a fearful jabbering, mingling incomprehensible yet surely unholy Chinese with the vilest epithets which ever the border knew. Then shots began booming in the house and the three broke into a run, down the kitchen steps and across the yard.

They turned the corner of the barn and there Ping-pong fell sprawling. Jerry, nearest him, caught him up, demanding anxiously:

"Hurt?"

His only answer was unintelligible, virulent Chinese. Ping-pong paused just long enough to fire a single shot back toward the house and they ran on.

"Watch your step! Down!" yelled Red Handsome.

They had reached the dry gully and went tumbling down into it. Along this they made their way for fifty yards or so; then, upon rough, uneven ground, they climbed out on the bank farthest from pursuit.

"Dead easy from now on," grunted Red Handsome. "In the dark they could comb the hills all night and be damned. I know my way here in pitch black and they don't. Nor can they use horses to advantage. Crawl, now, you bozos. See those black hummocky things? There's a field of bowlders there, crisscrossed with wash-outs. We'll cozy up there and try some sharp-shooting."

Behind them El Bravo began bellowing orders. They halted to listen and caught a word now and then. He was calling his men back. A shriller voice rose protesting wildly. El Bravo's roar came again, furious and threatening, and the shrill utterances ceased.

They dropped down on the rugged hillside. Jerry saw how the Chinaman went quietly to work making himself a bandage, tearing his shirt into strips and binding up his leg. All the while Ping-pong, in a murmurous undertone, relieved his feelings with strange and fearful words which gave Jerry a new respect for the Oriental tongue.

A chuckle came from Red Handsome.

"They're rounding up my fancy herd! Now they'll be streaking for home and mother!"

"I'll say," snapped Jerry, "that you're a cool sort of cucumber. A man would think that nothing pleased you more than seeing that bandit outfit haze your stock down across the border."

"Right you are," came the mirthful rejoinder. "Hey, Ping-pong, you Chinese devil?"

Ping-pong began giggling.

"It's this way," explained Red Handsome. "It's a special herd I've had ready for 'em. Hear of the rumor of a foot-and-mouth disease scare over at San Juan? Not all rumor, either. Well, when the Empress, bless her dear soul, scatters my herd among hers, blotting the brands nicely and figuring that no man on earth could pick out a handful of cows spread among her thousands— Nice idea of mine, huh?"

A sort of icy horror sickened Jerry as his imagination caught the full significance of this "nice idea." As far as retribution aimed at the Empress went, well enough. But epidemics were no respecters of boundaries. How many thousands of poor beasts were by this move condemned; how many small ranchers were to go to the wall?

Yet there was nothing he could do. He heard rather than saw as El Bravo's following gathered the stricken cattle and began herding them south.

"I'm on my way," he said curtly. "If our visitors by any chance overlooked Elmer's car I'm in it streaking back for the Little Mesa. I left a couple of friends there—and that place, too, was due for a raid tonight. Maybe we upset their plans—"

"I'll go with you," said Red Handsome, and leaped up. "Come ahead, Ping-pong; we'll look your leg over by lamplight and maybe I'll cut it off for you! Let's drift."

"You allee same go hell, Mis' Sommers," grunted the Celestial. "This good place; me stay."

Jerry led the way to the car which had been disre-

208

garded or overlooked among the cottonwoods, and a moment later he and Red Handsome were speeding back to Little Mesa. Only as they started did it dawn on Jerry that it was curious that Red Handsome, who had always given Kingsbury's ranch so wide a berth, was voluntarily going to it tonight.

CHAPTER XIII

T HE FIVE MILES LYING BETWEEN ALAMO SPRINGS and Little Mesa were traveled in haste and almost in silence. Once, just after Jerry sent the car racing away from the scene of the raid, his companion observed, as though amused by the thought:

"El Bravo sort of lost his head, what with my blowing some of his men clean from here up to the pearly gates; for if he had mowed me down for good and all, what a cussing-out he'd have got from the old lady when he turned in his report!"

"Señora Fernandez? I didn't think that she'd mourn your loss."

"She would though, if I passed away prematurely. The scheming old cat thinks I've got some worldly goods that might as well be hers. With me dead, they'd be out of her reach, while as long as I'm alive she's in hopes of talking me around to doing nobly by her."

Jerry made no reply and they sped on, each occupied with his own speculations. Jerry was thinking: "Now we'll have the answer to one question. Bob's going to have his chance to look this fellow over and figure out whether he has ever known him." He sent his car swooping down a grade and into a dark hollow, then crawling up a steep climb to a hill-top. As he rounded a curve, the headlights of another car flashed out some two or three miles away to the south.

"Old Costa coming home," surmised Red Handsome. "I saw him over at San Juan today hanging around the telegraph office. He'll make faster time on that road than we can up here in the hills, and will be at High Mesa well ahead of us."

"We're not going to High Mesa," said Jerry curtly. "Little Mesa is the end of this run."

"That's so; I forgot." And again they were content with silence and their own thoughts.

Sandy stretches of road fell away behind them. A field of cactus glistened faintly in the starlight. The loose boards of a bridge rumbled under the wheels where a shallow barranca gouged an arid area of rocks and sparse desert growth, and suddenly, as they came up on the gentle table-land, the ranch house of Little Mesa loomed a black stolid mass before them. All was dark and intensely quiet yet of a sudden a sense of disaster spread its apprehensive chill over Jerry Boyne.

From a little distance he heard a voice calling: "That you, Jerry?"

"Yes. What is it, Elmer? What's happened?"

He could hear the sounds of Elmer's unsteady advance, stumbling over the uneven ground at the rear of the house.

"Bob—Bob's gone," said Elmer's voice brokenly.

Jerry jumped down and ran to meet him.

"Gone? What do you mean? Not—"

"He's dead, Jerry," said Elmer with tears of rage and grief in his voice. "They got him, Jerry."

Jerry stood as if stunned. So good old Bob, who had made so valiant a fight, who had held his head so high and had looked with so steady an eye straight into the eye of death itself, was dead. And Jerry had been away, throwing in his luck with a fraud, an impostor and a crook, instead of standing here at a friend's side. He groaned in his bitterness. Blodgett, his senses quickened by the tragedy through which he had lived, must have caught something of Jerry's self-accusation, for he said swiftly:

"You couldn't have helped here, Jerry. He—why, man, he just went out and asked for it! I guess he wanted to go all the time, Jerry; you and me will never know how something busted inside that boy when he found out that his kid brother was dead. He kept on living, but it was only to get the man that killed Dick Kingsbury. And he got him and— Damn it, Jerry, he was grinning when he died!"

"You say Bob got the man who killed his brother?"

"El Bravo. It was like this: Me and Bob was hid up where you left us. A gang jumped the place a few minutes later. About six or eight of the devils. We'd have been all right, holed-up in the rocks, and they'd never found hide nor hair of us, but when we saw the bunch, all vague and shadowy and sort of blurred, Bob heaved up and I heard his teeth click. There was one man among the others that you could see bulk big over the rest. He was bossing the gang, and Bob cocked his ear, listening. 'That's El Bravo, Elmer,' he says to me. Never another word out of him. He shook me off and started; he crept closer and closer, dodging among the rocks. Then the gang swerved and rode down to the house. Bob let out a yell, then and busted out into the open and went running down on 'em. They begun shooting; so did he. I just turned cold and watched. I saw the big bozo wabble and do a nosedive out of his saddle; his horse started to run and somebody stopped it. Rifles was going like corn popping. God, man, it was fierce. Then I heard Bob laugh; you could have heard him a mile. That was just as they rode him down. He knew he'd got El Bravo and he blinked out happy— The party broke up then; they got El Bravo across a saddle and vamoosed. I went out to Bob— He's lying there now, Jerry, on his back, his face up to the stars. I brought the quilt and put over him—then, damn it, I pulled it down off his face—he's looking up at the stars, I tell you!

"It's like this, Jerry." Elmer dabbed at his eyes, then caught Jerry by the arm, holding him in a tense grip. "When you was outside talking with El Bravo, do you know what Bob was doing? He knew then; he just got a flash, sort of, like some folks knows a day ahead it's going to rain! 'There's paper in that table drawer, Elmer,' he said to me before you and El Bravo went out. 'Gimme your pen, Elmer,' he says, 'and stand over me while I write.' He sort of laughed, Jerry, and said: 'You can help spell the hard words and can witness what I'm writin'.' It was his will. Don't I tell you he knew? Him and his brother Dick—Bob wouldn't talk about him, did you notice? But I come on him once looking at a picture; a snapshot it was, and he hid it in his pocket.

"And here's what he wrote," Elmer went on as he showed Jerry a folded paper. "I read over his shoulder; it went something like this: 'This is my last will and testament, so help me God. Having no kin left on earth, and having the hot tip I'm about to blink out, I hereby give back to Antonio Costa all the Little Mesa ranch that I bought from him, along with all stock and other jiggers that goes with it.' At first, Jerry, I thought it was a joke, him giving away what we both knew didn't belong to him. But he was all there, that kid! This will simply means, don't it, that he throws off the fifty thousand dollar debt that old Costa would owe somebody—"

"I should have stayed here—"

"Don't be an egg! You couldn't have done any more than I did. There wasn't any call for him dying—it was just that the kid was all washed-up here, I guess. He was all lit-up, old man. He was ready to strike out for—for some Other Place. Do you know, I've always been scared stiff of dying and— Sounds funny, don't it?" He blew his nose and tried to laugh. "I'm going to remember, when my time comes, just the same! Why, that boy ran into it like a kid running to its mamma."

For a little while Jerry stood silent; his hat was in his hands, his head was lifted, his eyes like those other eyes which Elmer had left uncovered, looked straight up into the high vault of heaven—a great dark void yet one shot through with the light of the stars.

"Yes, Bob knew," he said softly. "Knew when he told me *'Adios.'* Let's hope, Elmer old horse, that already he and his kid brother are laughing it all over together—in Bob's Some Other Place."

"Amen," said Elmer fervently. And then, almost in violence: "God, I could do with a drink. He got El Bravo, though, Jerry."

"Let's bring him to the house," said Jerry. "No, my boy; he did not get El Bravo after all. Old Snake-eye was over at Alamo Springs. It was just some one of his gang that had the bad luck to resemble him."

"Which is sure bad news," grunted Elmer disgustedly. "Just the same," and he brightened, "Bob thought it was him."

An irrelevant thought came to Jerry. All this while he had forgotten the man he had left in the car; queer the way the fellow held back. There had been no sound from him. Jerry's thought was: "And after all we'll never know whether Bob knew him under his real name."

One thought whipped up another. It was rather more than merely queer that Red Handsome had sat back there with never a word at a time like this. Jerry ran back to the spot where he had left the car.

It was gone. Gone without any whisper of sound reaching him and Elmer so short a distance away. That, too, was odd, but almost immediately he guessed the explanation. There had been no need to start the motor; the car was on level ground and could easily be rolled on thirty or forty feet where the road began sloping downward from the mesa. He struck matches, looking at tracks and found them leading straight ahead down the road to High Mesa.

Elmer, when told how matters stood, was quick to voice the suspicion which came so naturally to him and which was already beginning to stir in Jerry.

"Most likely word was left for him at his ranch to come on over," he said. "And he's on his way to get that letter your dad wrote. After you go over to help him kill his rats like you just did he steals the car and lets you down like that!"

A few minutes later, leaving Elmer keeping vigil in the hushed house, Jerry struck out for High Mesa on foot—and at a run. The raiders had scattered all stock; it was foot or not at all. He threw aside his rifle, took his old 45 with him and made his start across the three miles of hills. Of course he could not hope to overtake the car; but he was determined to meet it coming back.

CHAPTER XIV

TO HIGH MESA SPED MORE THAN THE TWO RED-heads. That car which Jerry and his companion had glimpsed once on the lower road, and which they had so casually mistaken for Señor Costa's, returning from San Juan, was in reality a big touring car from the Empire Ranch; in it went Prince Charlie and his two bodyguards. Prince Charlie had driven to the Alamo Springs ranch; he had left the car hidden and had taken one of the raiders' horses in order to have a hand in the night's happenings. With the episode closed there, at El Bravo's angry orders, Charlie Fernandez had scurried back to his car. He was in such state as his men, used as they were to his uncontrollable fits of passion, had never seen him. In a girl his behavior would have been accounted plain hysteria and passed over at that. He shrilled invective; he burst into wild laughter; what ailed him was that he was drunk on excitement, keyed up to the last notch, desperate, unsatisfied—reckless after his own cowardly fashion.

"High Mesa!" He snapped out his orders as he drew his cloak about him and sat huddled in the back seat. "In the devil's name, get started! Hurry, *hombre!*"

Beryl, expecting her grandfather, saw the headlights flash around a curve at the foot of the table-land. The car swept on up the tortuous short grade, disappearing beyond the thick trees of the garden. She went through the house, telling a servant to have supper ready, and on out to the terrace. From among the shadows a man started up before her; she did not think even to ask herself who it was, so quickly did his words come and so did they frighten her:

"Señor Costa has been hurt. You are to come to the car—"

She started to run, envisioning all imaginable horrors. At the moment, like some bright guardian angel turning a flood of light on the pathway she was about to tread, someone in the house opened a door so that a brightly lighted room poured its illumination out in a broad lane of light across the garden. She saw another man, this one wrapped about in a coat and with a broad black hat pulled low. Startled, she stopped abruptly, for, despite cloak and hat, she knew the man instantly. She knew, too, that in another half-dozen running steps she would have been in his arms.

What crack-brained madness drove Charlie Fernandez that night? He had unleashed all the dark passions in his murky soul, had been transported, lived for some crashing moments like some evil, warped god upon some dizzy mountain of Olympus.

"Beryl!"

She whirled at the sound of his voice and ran back to the house. Only at the open door did she stop. Her eyes blazing, her breast rising and falling furiously, she cried angrily:

"Charles Fernandez! What do you want here? Why do you send a man to lie to me about my grandfather? Why do you come slinking to High Mesa like a coyote?"

She heard him muttering indistinctly. A shadow slipped by him, vanishing toward the garden gates; there went the man who had lied to her about Costa.

Young Fernandez came forward eagerly; he swept his hat off in a wide, grandiose flourish, bowing deeply.

"Beryl! I am mad for you. I cannot sleep for thinking of you! Tonight my soul broke loose from its chains. I had to come. I adore you!"

It all came wildly, brokenly and—to give Prince Charlie his due—sincerely. Beryl drew back across the threshold and into the deeply recessed door, frightened. Yet above fear rose anger.

"And, knowing that I did not love you, you came to steal me away! Came like the thief that you are! Are you mad?"

"Am I mad? You drive me mad!" he cried brokenly.

She saw the white flash of his teeth, saw even the wild glimmer of his eyes.

"It is that cursed Gerald Sommers, that red-headed son of hell!" he fumed. "You would have loved me; you were on the way to love me—and he came. To love a man like that! A liar, a crook, a thief, a miserable pretender. What if I unmask him for you? What if I show you what he really is?"

"You have been drinking too much," said Beryl, and thought that she spoke the bare truth. "You had better go now."

She withdrew still further and closed and locked the door. Then she ran to a darkened window, crept up on the broad sill and peeped out into the garden.

Charlie Fernandez stood irresolutely; he crumpled his hat in his hand and beat his thigh with it. Then he turned and went swiftly. She lost sight of him among the shrubbery but a moment later heard his voice, sharp and querulous. The motor started. She could hear the wheels crunching in gravel. She sped to another window from which she could look out on the road. She saw the car, starting slowly, winding down to the lower lands, and marked wonderingly that its lights had been turned off. It went in darkness and, somewhere down below the mesa, she lost all sight of it. She threw open the window, listening; she heard the purring motor a moment longer, then it died away and everything was very still about High Mesa.

She stared out into the starlit night and shivered. What on earth could the man think to gain by constraining, by forcibly carrying her away? Things like that were no longer done—

Ah, but were they not? Did not the great Empire Rancho throw a fat, evil, black shadow across miles and miles and still other miles? Did not that vile Fernandez woman dare anything and everything? And was not her son, though far less bold, every whit as evil?

Her imagination was over-stimulated; such fantastic horrors were stirring in her soul that when a little maid came seeking her, saying softly: "S'ñor Geral' Sommaires has come," she leaped up not so much in gladness as in a sort of tingling relief. Never had Red Handsome found it so easy to capture her two hands as tonight.

She found herself pouring out her incredible story to him, and had begun to tremble before she was half way through. His red-brown eyes caught fire and flashed angrily.

"Charlie Fernandez here? It was his car then that I saw! He came straight from Alamo Springs to you!"

His own tale was poured out scarcely less swiftly than hers; her eyes, already fearful, widened with horror.

"How can things like this be? I thought that the day had long passed when men did or could do such things."

"Gangsters will be gangsters," he said grimly, "and that's what we're dealing with. It's hard to prove anything against this crowd; maybe it's even impossible. They come in the dark; we say that we know who they are but we have to admit we didn't even see their faces! Just the same—"

"And Jerry Boyne came to help you?" she asked

breathlessly. For he had told of things just as they happened.

"Yes. Funny guy, that Boyne. Up to something of his own, and I don't know what. No love between us but— Well, I owe him something for tonight."

"He is a—" She had started to say, "a thief," yet without in the least knowing why she stopped short. "Wait," she said hurriedly. "I have something for you; something you will be very, very glad to have."

Leaving him wondering, she ran lightly up the winding stone stairs and to her room. Almost immediately she was back, smiling yet with some baffling tender sympathy in her eyes.

"It is a letter, Gerald," she said softly; "one we found where it had lain hidden for nearly five years." She held it out to him while he stared speechless and mystified. "From your father."

"From my father?" he muttered, still puzzled. At a glance he read what was written on the envelope. Hastily he turned it over. When he saw that it was sealed a breath of relief escaped him. Still for a moment he seemed strangely confused. Obviously he felt that something should be said, and the simple and natural little thing which should have risen at a time like this to his lips did not come.

Beryl chose to attribute his silence and that quick flush in his face to such an emotion as was to be expected when a son was about to be reached so unexpectedly by the voice of a dead father. While he stood silent, his brows puckered in his uncertainty, she told him briefly of finding the letter. She told him, too, of the money. Oddly, Red Handsome did not appear particularly interested in this part of her tale. Nor did he even think to ask how it chanced that the discovery had been made. Thus Beryl found it quite unnecessary to mention Jerry Boyne.

"Beryl," he said when he did speak, and suddenly thrust the unopened envelope in his pocket, "I am, as it happens, in a tremendous hurry. I got the word you left, for me to come at the first possible moment. I piled into a car and burned the air getting here. Now I've got to get back to my ranch in just as big a rush. If you'll lend me a horse—seems like I'm always borrowing horses from you, doesn't it?" he ended lightly.

"Why, of course. But your car?"

"It let me down half way between Little Mesa and your home. I'd forgot, in the rush, to fill the tank. I haven't thanked you for my letter, have I?" he added hastily. "It's rather—well, almost like a shock, isn't it? You'll understand—"

"Of course," said Beryl a second time; yet it did seem strange to her that he was not more eager to read it; how impatient she would have been in his place! "And you are going right back? Is that not running into unnecessary danger? Can you be sure they have gone?"

"Oh, that crowd will want to be on its way. It's not the simplest thing in the world to smuggle a herd of cattle across the border, even with Señora Fernandez owning land all along for miles; they'll want the stock across, scattered and tracks wiped out by another herd. And they've altogether finished at Alamo Springs for the time being. Yes, I'd better step along."

The more he explained, the greater was she perplexed by his haste, for which she saw no crying need. She watched him go through the garden; he was running before he reached the barn. She returned to a front window and heard him riding swiftly down the winding road. When the rapid hoof-beats grew faint on a sandy stretch, she stepped out upon the high terrace. It was not alone of him that she was thinking now. She found herself speculating with no lessening of perplexity upon Jerry Boyne and on the fact that he had hurried over to lend a hand at Alamo Springs. The thing stirred her lively imagination.

Into her troubled musings burst sudden voices, voices which came from a distance somewhere down at the foot of the mesa where the road plunged into a gloom too deep for her eyes to penetrate, too far away for the words to mean anything to her. But there was a vibrant quality in the crisp utterances which spoke clearly of anger.

It was merely that a meeting had taken place which Red Handsome had been anxious to avoid and toward which Jerry Boyne had labored doggedly. When Jerry came on the abandoned car he experienced a little fillip of triumph; he took a deep breath and ran on. When he came to the foot of the mesa he saw a lantern moving through the stable yard. From this distance he heard men's voices, then the rattle of hoofs. So, allowing himself to hope that here came his man, he placed himself in the thick shadows under a high bank and waited.

The horseman swept down toward him at a gallop. Jerry leaped out in the middle of the road, arms waving, and shouted a command to stop. Willy-nilly the rider stopped, so was the horse frightened. The animal would have whirled and run but that Jerry's hand had caught the reins.

"Why don't you fall off?" growled Jerry and shifted his grip to grasp the other around the middle. "Don't you always spill when your horse jumps?"

The horse lunged wildly, Jerry clung with all his might and the two men rolled in the sandy road.

"What the hell's eating you, Boyne?" came an angry roar. "I didn't steal your damn car."

"Let's have that letter—you've got a letter on you, so don't lie to me."

They surged to their feet, breaking apart. Red Handsome groped for the rifle which had flown from his grasp. He was lucky enough to chance on it and snatched it up with a grunt of satisfaction. But before his hands could lock hard about it, it was jerked from his grasp and sent flying.

"Guns out," snapped Jerry. "Hand me that letter."

What was handed him was a blow meant for his face but which merely grazed the side of his head. In a clinch the two men stumbled and rolled again in the loose sand. Jerry felt his head rock backward under a vicious short-arm jab, and in hearty exchange he drove his fist between the eyes he could no longer see, so did rising dust thicken the already thick dark. Battering at each other, they rolled apart.

Jerry was the swifter to rise but he trod on the edge of a stone and stumbled. Red Handsome, with a short, eager cry, took full advantage of the moment and struck at the stumbling body; struck not with his fist this time but with his boot. Jerry threw himself sideways; the boot heel, meant for his middle, went harmlessly by his thigh. This time it was Red Handsome who lost balance, if ever so briefly. But before he could pull himself about Jerry got in the one blow he was yearning for since its very twin had stretched him on the landing field in Nacional. His fist came up from his side, gathering the power of momentum, and Red Handsome took it upon the point of the chin and went down as under a pole-ax. And now it was his time to lie still and nerveless, lost to consciousness. Not the impact of Jerry's fist alone, but the very stone which had caused Jerry to stumble now amply made up matters to him; Red Handsome's head struck against it and lay upon it without stirring.

"Now," grunted Jerry and squatted over him, rifling his pockets. It was the matter of a moment to come upon the envelope. Jerry sat back and wiped the blood from his eyes. There was a cut, bleeding freely, on his forehead at the roots of his hair. He struck a match and made out the writing in his father's hand: "My son, Gerald Sommers."

"Got it!" growled Jerry with savage satisfaction.

He put it away carefully in his pocket, lighted a second match and stared down at his fallen antagonist.

"Crooked cuss, from start to finish," he muttered. "Anything to win, with a guy like him, gun or boot or what's handy. Well, he's taken one good plastering he'll remember."

Like his own face, the one turned up to him was

grimy and blood-smeared. When Red Handsome knew anything whatever, he would know he had been in a fight. Jerry broke the dead match and tossed it away. Then he started to make the brief journey up to the mesa top. He wanted to see Uncle Doctor and arrange to have the unconscious man cared for; he wanted to sit by a lantern and read his letter. It was of the letter, after all, that he was thinking most when he came to the top of the grade. And here already came a lantern to meet him, swinging along briskly, making a pool of light in which a pair of legs came hurrying. What was more, they were unmistakably Uncle Doctor's legs in high boots.

"Hi, there!" came the sharp challenge. "Who the devil are you? What's the row?"

"It's Jerry. Come ahead with your lantern, old-timer."

Only then did Jerry become aware of Beryl's nearness. She had held back an instant on first hearing his tread. Jerry reached for his hat only to discover himself to be bare headed.

"You!" Beryl gasped.

Uncle Doctor swung his lantern high. He snorted and the girl shivered as they saw Jerry's face. A little blood had gone a long way toward rendering his grimy countenance grewsome in such pallid yellow light as was emitted from the smoky lantern, and it was small wonder that Beryl shrank away from him.

"Somebody step on your face, Jerry?" asked the more matter-of-fact Uncle Doctor.

"I've just had a little run-in with a gent who thought it needed changing," Jerry retorted. "Come ahead with

225

your lantern, Doc, and we'll look him over; he's down there in the road."

"You have killed him!" cried Beryl.

"No such luck. I simply had the breaks this trip and have handed him back what he loaned me in Nacional. Shall we—"

The three were startled by a sudden flare of lights like two enormous eyes blazing up at them from the lower road. And with the unexpected lights came a flurry of voices and a rush of feet, all down there at the foot of the mesa.

"It's Charlie Fernandez!" Beryl explained. "That's his car. He shut off his lights and was hanging around and—"

While they stared down at the headlights and the black silhouettes of hurrying figures, momentarily revealed then lost again, wondering what it was all about, the car backed, partly turned, went forward again, stopped, backed and completed its turning. Then there was a roar of the motor and a bobbing red tail-light. The red light vanished suddenly about a curve in the road and the sound of the racing motor died away in the distance.

"What on earth?" muttered Jerry, at his wit's ends.

"It's Charlie Fernandez and his bodyguards," Beryl told them, fear in her voice. "He tried to trick me into his car—he went away in the dark—he was waiting for something—"

"For you!" said Jerry angrily. "And instead— Good Lord, they've grabbed Red Handsome and made off with him!"

"Come ahead, Jerry," said Uncle Doctor, not in the least perturbed. "Let's go make sure. Maybe he's down there yet."

The lantern led the way, casting monstrous shadows. When the three reached the spot where the big tires had left the marks of the cramped turn, they saw those other marks of the recent scuffle here, but nothing of the man whom Jerry had left lying unconscious.

"It is you," an overwrought Beryl accused Jerry, "who waylaid him and struck him down and left him lying here helpless, to fall into their hands! If they kill him, as I think they will, you will be as guilty of murder as they!"

Jerry stiffened with anger.

"You are the freest young woman with your accusations that I ever had the supreme joy of meeting," he said in a sort of cold fury. "You called me a thief once; now, just because I give a dirty crook a dose of his own medicine—"

"How manly," she flung at him scornfully, "to call him names when he isn't here to defend himself!"

"How womanly," he snapped back, "to call a man a thief and a murderer when you hide behind the barriers of your sex and know he can't defend himself."

"Sh! Sh!" chided the friend of both. "Don't be a pair of wildcats if you can help it. If there's anything to be done—"

"If Mr. Boyne had one little scrap of decency left in him," said Beryl in her best manner of the ice queen, "he would follow straight after those men. They are going to the Empire Ranch, of course, where Mr.

Boyne's dear friend, Señora Fernandez—"

"Damn Señora Fernandez!" cut in Jerry soulfully.

"Don't talk nonsense, Miss Beryl," said old Uncle Doctor sharply, inclined to forget the respect which he usually paid her.

"Listen, Doc," said Jerry, making a bid for calmness. "There's been the devil to pay tonight. El Bravo led a raid on Alamo Springs. He must have split his gang of cutthroats in two; he left one crowd to attack Little Mesa. They got poor Bob—"

"Go slow, kid!" A hard old hand bit into his arm, and two fierce old eyes glared at him as the lantern was swung high. "They got Bob, huh?"

"Yes. Bob jumped into the open to fight it out with them, crazy to get El Bravo for his brother's murder— and they killed him."

"Murderers all!" moaned Beryl. "And now they've got Gerald Sommers—"

"That infernal impostor—"

"What did you say, Mr. Boyne?"

"Nothing."

"I don't understand! Charlie Fernandez called him a 'pretender,' and said that he could unmask him! Oh! You are hand and glove with Charlie Fernandez! I might have known! You came with him—"

Jerry's teeth clicked; there he cut off a hot retort.

"Doc," he said swiftly, "get some men out and haze over to Little Mesa; you'll take care of poor old Bob, won't you? He'd want to take his long sleep alongside his kid brother. Elmer Blodgett will be glad to see you; he's no doubt got the willies already—"

"What about you, Jerry?" queried the old fellow anxiously, sensing some new folly from his young friend.

"Me? I'm off to see a lady friend! Sure, Señora Fernandez. Beryl here wants her little playmate back, and by thunder, I'll go get him for her. There's a horse prowling around somewhere near here, all saddled and ready to breeze. Hand me a can of gasoline. I'll ride back to where that red-headed son of iniquity, Beryl's noble hero, left it when he swiped it from me and did a big sneak to get a letter that— I'll pile into said car and burn the road south."

"You're crazy!"

"Don't I know it? Help me find that horse."

"That bunch down at the Empire will make cat-meat out of you! Of all the asses—"

Of a sudden Jerry began to laugh. The laughter was for Beryl.

"Listen, Doc," he said, and kept his eyes on Beryl. "The Empress is a friend of mine. Sure. Sent me word only tonight by El Bravo. Says she, she's got it in for this hombre Red Handsome; says she, she'll step to the bat and spend money to prove he's no more Gerald Sommers than—than I am!"

"You *are* crazy!"

"Like a fox. Listen some more. She says she'll kick Red Handsome out and put another heir presumptive in. Who's to be the lucky man? Lift your lantern and look at him! Having red hair, I'm her candidate. Now help me find that horse. There he is. Whoa, pony—"

The horse, with reins tangled in a thorny bush, stood

still, head upflung, nostrils distended. Jerry went up into the saddle, and raced back up the road to the garage, seeking a can of gasoline.

"You heard him!" said Beryl, thunderstruck.

The old fellow swung about with never a word and hurried after Jerry. Beryl watched and listened; she heard the two men talking, but they spoke in undertones now. Then a blur in the darkness swept by her; there went Jerry, riding in such haste that he had even forgotten his hat!

"Uncle Doctor! Uncle Doctor!" she cried sharply, and ran seeking him. "I'm all in a terrible fog—I don't understand—"

"Best go in the house, Miss Beryl," he told her, not at all his usual patient self. "God only knows what's up or what's coming out of it. Better go inside. You've done enough mischief for one night!"

"What do you mean? What have I done that is wrong? You mean—"

"Yes, and you know it. What's more, you don't even like to put a name to it. You and that skunk that calls himself— Never mind; I'm only praying, Miss Beryl, that that fool Jerry comes out of this alive, the hotheaded, nit-witted lunatic that he is."

"If there is any danger, it's not for him—"

"There you go again! Didn't I say you'd best step along inside? And take this with you to remember: If you and your old granddad ever had a true friend, it's that same harumscarum Jerry! If there ever was a fine boy, an upstanding, two-fisted, square-shooting kid, it's that same Jerry. Why, he's worth any ten thousand of a sneaking hunk like that pretty boy he's risking his life for."

"But you heard him say that he and Señora Fernandez—"

"Hmf! Why, girl, when you come to know the truth about him you'll just go down on both your knees and thank God there's men like him left in a world that seems to me is going to the dogs fast. I only hope you won't have to say it all with flowers."

Beyond that he would not go, but stalked off to the men's quarters, rousing them with sharp orders. And to Beryl it seemed that if the world had not gone to the dogs, at least it had gone tumbling into a blacker, denser fog than ever—one shot through with murky red gleams, one in which she could only wander despairingly. She who so "hated mysteries!"

"I knew all along that he was fine! There is something that I cannot understand, something that Uncle Doctor knows. And Jerry—Jerry—"

She lifted her face to the stars.

"God bring him back in safety," she whispered.

She did not specify who was to be brought back to her. The fairest possible surmise is that she referred to—a red-haired chap just now on his way to the border.

CHAPTER XV

RRIVED AT ELMER'S ABANDONED CAR, JERRY first of all removed his horse's bridle, hung it over the saddle horn and gave the animal a hearty thwack across the rump to start it on its homeward way to High Mesa. Next he emptied his five-gallon can of gasoline into the tank. This done, deciding that if Red Handsome was not already riddled with bullets he was safe enough for the moment, he switched on his headlights and stood before them to read his father's letter.

A glance at it, however, decided him that a careful perusal would have to await a time of greater leisure. There were several sheets, written on both sides, and the well-known script was, as always, none too readily decipherable. As it was he skimmed the contents hurriedly, and when he had done his jaw was set and his eyes stern and bright with an unalterable purpose. There was much here about a woman calling herself the Empress, much about a man named Frank Smith, generally known as El Bravo. . . . There had been strife between High Mesa and the Empire Ranch . . . Sommers had had his eyes opened to the high-handed lawlessness . . . There had been a clash . . . If he lived he meant to make her pay in full for an atrocity which cried to Heaven . . . There was a fish-eyed reptilian, the killer, El Bravo . . . Sommers addressed his son in this way, leaving the letter in the Sure-enough Money place, since he had not heard from him for three years. "If they do get me, my boy, you'll know who—"

"Good old Dad," groaned Jerry. He folded the letter with an almost tender care. "And I wasn't here when the time came—just as I wasn't with Bob. Why am I always running off from the place where later I'll wish I had stayed? Right now—chasing off like a long-eared jackass after a man who ought to be kicked into the pen. Well, he's properly a jailbird, but at that I don't know that he deserves to have his throat cut. Anyway, if Beryl wants the pup—or wants anything else that I can go get for her—" He jumped into the car, trod angrily on the starter and was on his way.

He was half way to Nacional before it dawned on him that border regulations would stop him from passing into Mexico; the international gates would have been closed long ago. But there were no gates against the passage of the car through the Empire Ranch. That simply meant that he would have to keep an eye open for a road forking off toward the Fernandez ranch which would lead straight to the ranch headquarters without coming under the eyes of two governments. Along some such roadway, to be sure, had El Bravo traveled; that way had he driven off the infected stock from Alamo Springs, inviting no investigation from any authorities.

Forced to drive more slowly lest he miss the way, watchful for any faint track which turned aside, he came presently to a well-defined road branching off in the direction he wanted to travel. He turned into it unquestioningly and picked up all the speed he dared. Here was a desert road upon which, he knew right well, too much haste might carry him into deep, loose sand which would act as a trap to spinning wheels.

"I've got to get me another plane," he muttered in disgust as he fought with a jerking steering wheel and narrowly avoided running into a gulch. "Roads like this were made to look down on from the sky."

He angled through a thicket of mesquite, went down into a dry, gravelly sink, negotiated a difficult way up on the other side and came abruptly to a barbed-wire fence. He threw on his brakes just in time to save the front tires, and jumped down. The gate was fastened with chain and padlock. He ran back to his car. There were sure to be something in the tool kit that would cut wire.

"*¿Quien es?*" said a sharp, sudden voice. "*¿Y que quiere?*"

Startled, Jerry whirled and stared.

"Doggone your picture," he grunted for answer. "Do you know you could be fined for scaring a man out of his skin? Where'd *you* come from?"

The fellow was muffled in a cloak, his face hidden under a broad, high-peaked sombrero. He stood leaning languidly against one of the sturdy posts of the gateway, both hands hidden under his cloak and resting on the butts of his pistols, Jerry supposed.

A soft crunching in the sandy soil told where another man approached from the right. The fellow whose voice had startled Jerry spoke again. He was sorry, but at this time of night there was no passing. The señor would have to come again during the daytime; between the hours of six and six. These were orders.

"Look here," said Jerry, "you're not government men, are you?"

"Private patrol, Señor, for the Empire Rancho."

Jerry began explaining. He did have business with the Señora Fernandez and it was important. The gatekeeper shook his head. He was sorry but there was no passing. Jerry waxed eloquent, becoming heated as he explained that the thing was not only urgent but a necessity. He hinted that the Empress would thank no man for standing in the way of one who brought such word as Jerry carried, that here was an affair which—

"It has to do with something you may already have heard about," he said shrewdly. "Or were you told anything? When Charlie Fernandez came this way just now, carrying a prisoner—"

There was a brief conference in undertones between two men who were mere vague shadows to him. One of them barked out an order to open the gate, then got into the car at Jerry's side and sat upright and rigid, his hands hidden under his cloak. Jerry was to go ahead, and this man was to go with him. And no stretch of the imagination was required to tell him that only a few inches from his side was the business end of a gun or the keen point of a knife. Jerry drove through the gate as it was jerked open.

"The getting in was all right; how about getting out again?" he wondered.

It was only three miles farther, his companion informed him, to the ranch house. A white road snaked among dusty willows; at a barranca there was the thumping of a wooden bridge under the wheels; then more white road, hard packed, on which a man could drive faster. Sudden lights shone out, dull yellow spots where grimy windows like jaundiced eyes peered out from the Empire pueblo. Brighter lights gleamed above them, were blotted out by the big cottonwood grove, shone out clearly once more, and Jerry's car came to a stop before the high white walls, just in front of one of the iron gates.

The man seated beside him did not stir but called sharply. A dark figure, cloaked like the others, detached itself from the black gate and stepped forward. In a few words the gate keeper was told that a visitor by way of the First North Gate claimed urgent business with Señora Fernandez.

"Tell her it's Jerry Boyne," added Jerry.

He started to get down but the man at his side said curtly:

"It is best to wait, Señor. It will be a minute only."

So Jerry made himself a cigarette, pondered on the high hand of lawlessness, and waited. Light steps went hastening up to the house; they ceased suddenly and there fell a short silence. Light steps, even quicker now, came running back.

"Señora Fernandez is glad that Señor Boyne has come," said a voice, and the way was open.

Jerry got down then; he could have driven on up to the house but he felt that having his car ready outside the gates was rather like having an ace in the hole. For it struck him as entirely possible that he might want to leave this place in a hurry. He went ahead briskly, bending his mind toward shaping the forthcoming interview. Two men fell in close behind him and the three passed under garden trees, among darkly glistening shrubs and to the massive front door. It stood wide open upon a red-carpeted hallway, softly lighted.

"Good boy, Jerry!" cried a well remembered voice. And here, shoving heavy curtains aside from a deep, arched door, came the Empress to meet him. What a woman she was! At the moment she scarcely looked half of her fifty years. Vivid always, she was on the crest of some wave just now and came close to being radiant. Evidently she had only a little while ago returned from some expedition on horseback; a pair of silver-chased spurs still winked on the heels of her high, black boots; there was a big silver buckle at the belt of her modish riding breeches; there was the inevitable flash of crimson in the lining of her cape. Never had the woman looked more vain or arrogant; never so sure of her own glittering destiny.

"Good boy, Jerry!" she said the second time, grasping his hand warmly, and led the way back through the curtains into a big, comfortable room with shaded lights and low, cushiony leather chairs. "So, as El Bravo tells me, you've decided to throw in with me? And, being a man of action, here you are saying, 'Let's get going!' "

With his plans laid, Jerry struck boldly, so boldly in fact that the woman stared at him, first in wonder, then in a sharp suspicion which banished her smile of greeting and drew her brows down.

"So that fool, El Bravo, is back, is he?" was the way he began. "Has the man gone crazy? Did he tell you he came close to slaughtering a man we want very much to keep alive? Did the ass tell you that I had to jump in and risk a life that I think a lot of, chipping in with that same man when your hot-heads raided him? You say I've decided to throw in with you—and I say that that depends!"

"What's all this?" she snapped him up. "Listen to the man rave! You had to chip in, you say, to save somebody's bacon? And you come here blazing out at me— What's wrong with your face? Where's your hat? What the devil have you been up to anyhow?"

"And that precious son of yours!" Once committed to his line, he felt that his only hope lay in making it convincingly thoroughgoing. "What did he butt in for? What has he done with this jasper who calls himself Gerald Sommers?"

"What do you mean?" she rasped out at him, her suspicion livelier than ever. "Calls himself Gerald Sommers, you say? What are you driving at?"

He looked at her with level eyes which told no tales.

"Wasn't it understood—or didn't I get El Bravo right?—that I am the one and only real genuine Gerald Sommers?"

She laughed and looked relieved. But again her face hardened.

"When I invited you to play," she said hotly, "I don't know that I asked you to run the whole show. If you've got any notion that you are indispensable, why then suppose you get to hell out of here!"

"I'll go fast enough and gladly enough," he retorted swiftly, "if the show is going to start with killing any geese that lay golden eggs! What did your son do with Red Handsome?"

She moved to a chair and sat down. On a table near by were cigarettes. She lighted one, blew a puff of smoke ceilingward and then looked at him quite calmly and very shrewdly.

"Let's get what you are driving at," she invited. "Shoot what's on your mind."

"Fair enough. To begin with, that was a crazy play to shoot Red Handsome's place up. He might have blinked out—"

"Admitted," she snapped. "There was a bit too much enthusiasm, and— Well," and she flashed him a side-long glance of purely devilish wickedness, "boys will be boys, you know. A youngster got a little too much pepped up and there you are." She shrugged. "As for a certain red-head who used to call himself Gerald Sommers and whom we'll name Red Handsome, if you like that better, he's alive and doing well, I hear."

"Let's hope so! On the hoof that bird is worth a good two hundred and fifty thousand! There's the Alamo ranch, there's a good hundred thousand in securities—"

"You've found out a thing or two, haven't you?" she leered at him, it may have been approvingly. Jerry hoped so.

"You'd be surprised," he told her coolly, sat down and helped himself to a cigarette.

She surprised him by beginning to laugh, gleefully this time.

"And I asked about your face! Charlie told me. Red pretty near spoiled it for you, didn't he? Well, at that,

239

you marked him so you'll know him next time."

"Never mind that. There are times to overlook the personal equations. This is a big thing—"

"Big, your foot!" she sneered. "Man, you don't know what big things are. But the road's wide open for you to look in and learn. If you play the game with me, and play it square from start to finish, I'll put you so damned high that you can reach up and scoop down stars to wear in your necktie! You'd say the Empire Ranch was a big thing, wouldn't you? Well, I guess it is; but it's nothing to what it's going to be. No, the wind isn't just blowing; I feel like talking and you're lucky. Spread your ears and let something soak into your brain. Oh, you've got one all right and I know it, or I wouldn't be taking you by the hand.

"Big, you say, this little deal of hogging High Mesa? Listen, kid; the Empire Ranch is spreading in all directions and all the time. It's like a kingdom now; you know it and you know who's the king over it. You once said something about the high and the low here; that's little Louise. In time I'm going to have High Mesa and Little Mesa and Alamo Springs—and all the land between them and the Empire! Already I've got options on a hundred thousand acres—and if you want to know who's naming the price and making it stick, why, it's me. Big things? They're on the way.

"Now wait a minute! I'm telling you things. I've got money and I've got power and I've got a way of getting what I'm after. There are big men in Mexico who are afraid to move without asking me. Before you are a hundred years old I'll show you how a woman can pick

240

a man and make him president! I've already named one governor and I've busted another—and I've had money from both! Laugh that off! The law?" She sneered. "Here's what in Swedish they call the crux of the matter: Men are fools and petty crooks, and nations are run by men! And here am I, spreading along the border, spreading north and south. Who'll say what goes back and forth across that same border, when I've got a big hunk of it in the heart of my ranch? Why do they call me the Empress? By God, because that's what I am!"

Not even there did she stop. Jerry, fascinated, striving for the poker face which the situation demanded, sat silent and listened. He came to see, as he had never understood before, the true meaning of inordinate ambition; the stuff was in her soul that made Alexanders and Napoleons. Like them, she was sure of herself. A bit mad on top of it? No madder than anyone who has surrendered utterly to the single, driving idea. He glimpsed dark pathways which she meant to tread yet did not fully point out to him; he saw her defying or bribing or tricking the officials of two nations, trafficking across the border in any illicit venture—provided it was magnificently profitable! Even now she was about to found a new town; and it was to be a wide-open devil-of-a-place, such as silly Americans flocked to to pay high prices for liquor and to drop fortunes on gaming tables.

"This gambling racket," she said with a chuckle, "there's money in it, Jerry. And my little casino is getting famous. Drop in tomorrow night if you want to see some fun. A couple of high-rollers have heard of me and are curious. 'Assure us there'll be plenty of money in sight,' they've written me, 'and we'll look you over.' Who are they? Well, one's old General Benito Valdez, and you know who he is and where he stole his millions? And the other's none other than Ellsworth W. Peters, one of the biggest ship owners on the Pacific Coast. Used to live in Spain. That's where he caught the gambling fever. Look in on us tomorrow night, young man; you'll see a big game rolling. And who'll get the coin?"

She winked a shrewd blue eye and ended as she had begun, chuckling.

Of a sudden she jerked forward in her chair, her hands hardening on its arms, and now her keen blue eyes looked like polished blue jewels.

"Don't get me wrong, kid," she said warningly. "Don't set me down as a fool woman that talks too much and tells everything she knows! Don't jump at conclusions or you're apt to land in a ditch. Go blab all I've told you; where'd it get you? Why, man, you might be anything you please, a border gum-shoe or a prohibition agent. I'm not trusting you with anything that could hurt me, and I'll not trust you until you're in as deep as I am! Once you've gone into court and sworn that you are Gerald Sommers— Then it might be different. Right now if you tried to get funny, I'd name you a liar and simply kick you out of a chance of big money. ¿Sabe?"

"You make it nice and clear," smiled Jerry. "Now suppose I tell you something? Ready for a little shock?

Here it is. This Red Handsome chap is going to be easy to oust for the simple reason that he's no more Gerald Sommers than I am! What do you say to that?"

Those blue jewels that were her eyes told him nothing.

"Bright boy," she said slowly. "What do you mean by that?"

"I mean what I say." He paused a moment, hardening himself. "Bob Kingsbury," he said sternly, "knew this Red Handsome of old, and knew that he was not Gerald Sommers."

"Interesting, if true," she said coolly. "Well, I'm listening."

He shrugged.

"Unfortunately Bob Kingsbury is no longer with us—"

"The fool!" she burst out venomously. "Two fools, those Kingsburys. And where are they now?"

Again he steeled himself and again he shrugged. There would come a time— Well, that time was not now.

"I came," said Jerry, eying her steadily, "less to see you than to have a word with Mr. Red Handsome. Where is he? And am I to have that word?"

"You're damned cool!"

"Would I be here at all if I were not?" he demanded.

"What do you want to see Red for?" And here all her suspicion, ever a watch dog over the perilous paths she walked, came leaping back.

"I want to assure him that no bodily harm will come to him as long as he does what he's told; I want to give him your assurance of that as well as mine. Otherwise he may go taking chances and—well, getting hurt. No, that's not all of it," he continued as her suspicion seemed only to grow sharper. "Not even the best part of it. I want to warn him that when time comes to step out of the shoes he's now wearing, he's to sign over all claim to certain securities and to the Alamo ranch—and that he's to make sure I get my share! That's flat, my dear lady. Otherwise I don't play and you'll simply have to go get yourself another red-head who'll take what scraps you care to chuck to him along with your orders."

"Think you're hard-boiled, don't you?" she muttered.

He baffled her with his best grin.

"And," she added angrily, "you mean that you don't trust—"

"Sh!" he laughed at her. "Is that a word for either of us to use? Shall the next Mr. Gerald Sommers trust the little Louise any more than the little Louise trusts the next Mr. Gerald Sommers?"

That amused her. But she grew grave and thoughtful. Jerry rose quickly, before she could have time to say anything further.

"I'm on my way—"

"You are if I say so!" She, too, sprang to her feet. "I could have you wiped out"—she snapped her strong fingers—"like that!"

"Sure. Idiotic, though, wouldn't it be?"

A quick bright admiration leaped up into her eyes.

"Damn you, Jerry— If you play square with me! El Bravo is an ass, after all. Charles is too young— Yes, I'll let you go and gab with my visitor." A shrewd smile touched her lips. "At that, I guess I've got ample evidence there's no great love between you two! It's carved all over your faces, both yours and his! What a sweet black eye you'll be carrying around to remind you. When will I see you?"

"Not before tomorrow night," he said at random. "I've been known to look in when and where money was changing hands."

He did not know when she had rung for a servant; he did not hear any far bell tinkling, but the curtains parted and a boy in her resplendent livery looked in.

"I want Ramiro," she said commandingly and the boy, with a quick, frightened *"Sí, Señora!"* sped away.

Ramiro, one of her cloaked guards, hawk faced, jade eyed, a leathern visaged Indian, came hurriedly. To him the Empress gave her commands crisply. This señor was to have five minutes, no more, with that other señor in the strong room. And Ramiro was to remember what had happened to a certain confrere of his who not so long ago had allowed a mad Kingsbury to come in uninvited through her gates. Ramiro's eyes narrowed; one might be very sure that he had not forgotten.

"*Adios,* Jerry," said the Empress carelessly. "Ride with me and pick stars. Go your own way, and get nowhere like the rest of the fool men. Or get funny, and drop to hell the shortest way."

"*Adios,* Empress," said Jerry, and followed Ramiro.

They went out at the front door, through the garden at the side of the house and to the rear. In a corner of the high white walls was a small square building of solid masonry. It appeared to be windowless; there was a narrow door under which a dim light seeped. But all was pitch dark about it. An enormous oak spread its branches, thick with foliage, above the low roof and shut out the stars.

"Dim chance I've got," muttered Jerry to himself. "And by now, I'll bet a man, she's got half a dozen ragamuffins on the way to see what's doing."

He made up his mind right then that there was nothing to do but go back and report to Beryl that her little playmate was safe enough for the present and that in a day or so he'd have him free. And at the very instant when sober reason convinced him of the utter impossibility of accomplishing anything, a reckless and quite mad impulse assailed him, and he ceased marching with cold reason and committed himself irrevocably to the mad impulse.

There was a single guard leaning against the wall of the strong room. He should have the key. Jerry saw the glow of his cigarette. He'd be lounging, not particularly concerned with two men coming from the house. Ramiro, with his hands under his cloak, was close at Jerry's side.

In the friendly dark Jerry drew his old 45 Colt out of his pocket. When they were within three steps of the building, Jerry whipped this heavy weapon high above his head and brought it crashing down on Ramiro's skull. As the Indian collapsed, Jerry leaped in upon the guard and drove the muzzle of the revolver hard into his side.

"The key!" he whispered savagely into the fellow's

ear. "One wiggle and I blow you all apart. Quick! *Quick!*"

Had he had time to plan, he would never have attempted so foolhardy a thing. First of all there was every chance that the man had no key!

But a key was already turning in a lock—the door was open—and Red Handsome, starting up from a bench, was staring wonderingly. Jerry drove the guard inside and said hurriedly to the prisoner:

"On our way. We've got only a minute. Tie this fellow up with something and shut his mouth with a handful of rags."

Red Handsome's eyes in the candle-light gleamed savagely.

"There's a quicker way," he grunted, and struck. With all his might he drove his fist into the guard's face, and the man dropped without a gurgle. "On our way? You're damn' right! Wait a shake though. I'll borrow this hombre's cloak and hat. Ready."

They stepped out and closed the door after them. A moment they stood, listening. Not a step was to be heard anywhere. Then, walking swiftly and as silently as they could, they went through the garden and to the front gate.

"It will be easy," whispered Red Handsome. "The damn fool guard will never be looking for trouble coming from the inside."

"Keep your face hidden," commanded Jerry curtly. "There's to be no trouble. Walk along naturally now; let him hear us talking. He let me in with the Empress's orders and he'll let us out."

The gatekeeper turned carelessly. When Jerry said coolly, "Open up, *amigo,*" the man answered, *"Sí, Señor,"* and lifted the iron bar. The two stepped through. Here it would seem went the recently arrived stranger accompanied by the same guard who had escorted him here. The gate clanged shut and Jerry slipped into the seat of his car. Red Handsome wasted no precious moment in climbing in beside him. Smoothly the car rolled out into the road, turning north.

"I wish I could have borrowed the old lady's biplane," began Jerry, "in case of—"

From somewhere in the gardens behind them a sharp voice called out; another voice answered excitedly. There was a babble of sounds, a sudden silence—and then the scream of a siren, as bloodcurdling as the howl of a wolf.

Jerry opened his throttle wide and sent the car leaping along the wavering white ribbon of road.

CHAPTER XVI

HERE'S WHERE WE TAKE A BEAUTIFUL CHANCE OF piling up in a ditch," said Jerry, gathering speed recklessly. "At that we'd be no worse off than if those war-whoops behind closed in on us. Hold your hair on—"

"Look out, man! There's a curve. God! That was close!"

"Don't grab me, you fool!"

"Fool! I'll say I'm a fool! I ought to have stayed— I

wish I was back there, behind bars— I'd have gone free all right; all the old hag wanted out of me was money—"

"Shut up! Help me watch the road ahead."

They skidded around another bend and the headlights showed a straight strip of the narrow white road. Jerry took full advantage of it, jamming his accelerator down to the floor board. He had no eyes for the speedometer but knew from the whining wheels and from the rush of air that Elmer Blodgett's car had its good points.

Suddenly his companion began shouting at him.

"Half a mile ahead there's a road turns off to the left. Take that one. Slow down for it or you'll run by."

"Why?" snapped Jerry. "What's the matter with this road?"

"This is the one they'll be sure we've taken. Also, this leads to her main gate and there are always three or four guards handy to it; they've got a camp there. Swing left, I tell you; we'll have to do with one man only at the gate—if we ever get there!" he groaned, as the front wheels got caught in a sand trap and for a breathless instant threatened to throw the car, swinging perilously, out into a tangle of mesquite.

"Right," retorted Jerry. "Watch for the road fork. Left we go."

Behind them the siren screamed again. At no time is the voice of that diabolical contrivance exactly sweet music to the ear of the speeder; just now it cut through the night with such downright hellishness that it made little prickles along a man's spine. Jerry, with eyes glued to the road and hands glued to his steering wheel, began gradually to lessen the pressure of his boot on the throttle, and when a sharp "Ready!" was called in his ear, he was ready. For a moment, even so, it was pitch-and-toss whether they would make the turn in safety, but fortunately here at the fork there were ruts into which the wheels slipped and which held them from a lateral wandering. Again Jerry stepped up the speed.

"Another mile and we are at the gate!" warned Red Handsome. "Slow down for it. Better give me your gun."

"Slow down for nothing!" said Jerry grimly. "I'll bet the Empress never slows down for gates! Grab the horn and ride it; I'm busy. Hold it down. The gate will be open, all right—as long as we're asking to get out instead of to come in."

"But if it isn't!"

"Swallow your *ifs* and grab the horn! Here we go!"

Red Handsome cursed him for a fool but made haste to obey orders. With a steady blare of the deep-toned horn the car fled with undiminished speed, the steering wheel jerking dangerously in Jerry's tense grip as the spinning tires flung loose sand behind. A tiny light gleamed out straight ahead; there stood a Mexican with his inevitable cigarette. Jerry lifted his voice mightily to aid the command of the horn:

"*Abra la puerta, hombre!* Open up!"

The glowing cigarette-end leaped and vanished. Well, that meant swift action of some sort. A white gate post flashed by, so close that only by an inch or so did the mudguards miss it, and with the Empire Ranch behind,

Jerry drew a first long deep breath.

But though he accounted the main hurdle negotiated, he realized that he was still far from a satisfactory completion of the night's adventure. The road ahead of him was an evil thing, just a track through the sand, turning illogically, never too clearly defined, a road from which an unwary man at any instant might depart to find himself with churning wheels marking time in a sand drift. He was forced to go more slowly, though still at a clip which kept him tense; and he had no taste for any lessening speed, so positive was he that pursuit was in full cry behind him.

"How far on this sort of road?" he demanded. "Any chance of turning into a better one?"

"Three miles. There's a long slope there that comes down from Indian Gully; not much of a road but harder ground underfoot. If you can keep from getting stalled in here—we ought to make it. Better slow down a bit."

All about them was what seemed in the starlight a limitless expanse of sand sparsely dotted with sage, a flat white-gray floor with the domed sky, white-star spangled, coming down to meet the level earth. Only straight ahead was the distant horizon broken by the hills behind High Mesa; between two remote rocky headlands a star burned like a lantern in a deep gorge. That way, still some miles ahead, lay Indian Gully.

They dropped down into a sudden barranca and were in luck not to come by a broken spring or some greater damage. They fought their way up and out on the farther side, Red Handsome jumping down and adding the urge

251

of shoulder power. They crossed a wide sink wherein ghostly big moths fluttered white in the streaming headlights. Leaving this behind, they came to that long slope which gave hard ground underneath and a straight road slanting up toward the mouth of Indian Gully.

"There's a chance they didn't try to follow—or that they took the other road," conceded Red Handsome, staring back. "What I was afraid of—"

"Sh!" commanded Jerry. "What's that?"

A single moment of intent listening told them the answer.

"And that's what I was afraid of," growled Red Handsome. "They're after us in the *Hawk*, and any speed you make will be like a crippled horned toad trying to run away from a road-runner."

"Keep your eye peeled. How far off?"

Jerry snapped off his lights and as a result was forced to slacken speed; he dared go forward only at a crawl now. What a fine thing it would be, he thought longingly, if sage brush grew like oaks so that a man might drive his car under broad sheltering branches. Here about him was nothing that a man himself, let alone a car, might hide under.

"They're following the other road," said Red Handsome presently. As yet he had caught no glimpse of the plane itself, but judged from the sound of its motor. "Poke along while we can. They'll patrol that road for two or three miles, then cut across to this one. Damn it, man, can't you drive any faster than a mile a week?"

"Too bad this car hasn't a back seat for a man with your proclivities," Jerry informed him disgustedly.

"Suppose you just watch out for the plane and leave the driving to me."

The rate at which they were traveling irked him no less than it did his companion, yet even at this crawl he found it hard to keep in the road. Nor did he even consider turning on his lights again; that would invite immediate discovery and, though he hadn't figured out how the plane itself could very well interfere with their progress, yet he did pay the Empress the compliment of fancying that she knew her way about, and was not simply skylarking for the fun of seeing where he was headed.

They inched on. The drone of the motor in the sky grew fainter with distance. The road straightened obligingly in a direct line up the long slope. Jerry went into second gear—for five tormenting minutes he had been in low—and picked up speed. With luck he thought that another five minutes would bring them to the mouth of Indian Gully and into a track among bowlders and some few welcome cottonwoods.

Far off to the right, the way the big biplane had taken, he saw out of the corner of his eye what at the first instant was like a star gone mad and most thoroughly misbehaving, racing off among its fellows—a pale blue star playing comet tricks.

A rocket! A blue rocket for some sort of signal. It vanished in a spray of blue sparks. Almost immediately the purr of the distant motor picked up in distinctness and became a strengthening throb. Louder and clearer and more menacing it grew. Like a great bat the plane itself began cutting across the stars.

"They'll be on us in a minute! Give her the gun, man!"

But already Jerry was "giving her the gun." As a result he ran off the road, yet discovered with a spurt of gratification that there was a hard, solid surface only thinly overlaid with sand, and that his wheels gripped and carried on. Who wanted a road now? He steered straight for the rugged ground ahead, his greatest care now not to crash into a rock or go spilling down into a gulch. The best he could do was to aim for what looked like white open spots ahead and trust that they were what they looked to be.

The plane, coming on at terrific speed, was almost overhead. Surely, he thought, in so much dark the lookout above would fail to see the car running without lights. Just then, as though to tell him how futile such thin hope was, a second rocket went streaking across the sky, so near this time that he heard the hiss of its passage. This time, however, it was a blood-red rocket and it burst in a cascade of red fire. Another followed and still another, as the plane swooped low, banked and curved and came rushing back.

Since it was obvious that he had been sighted he switched on his lights, set his teeth and gave his full attention to driving. It seemed to him then, knowing only what he knew, that another five minutes or less would see the game as good as won. Surely those signals were to bring men after him, yet equally clear was it that he had a good, safe lead—

The biplane, piloted with a skill which drew an involuntary flash of approval from him, came swooping back, lower, still nearer, and of a sudden there broke out, above the roar of the motor, a sound as of two mad riveters in a competition.

"Machine gun!" he gasped, and snapped off his lights again.

"It's that hell-cat driving, and her little beast of a son at his favorite outdoor sport," cried Red Handsome. "Jam on your brakes. We're sunk hell-deep."

"Up-to-date, that old lady!" muttered Jerry. "Well, she said as much—"

With a will then he did slam on his brakes. The plane had roared on and there was a dull boom that seemed to shake the world. Then, from a spot perhaps a hundred yards from them, the earth vomited itself skyward in a great geyser of sand and rubble and rock.

"That's only a warning. The hell-cat would rather have us alive. Put on your lights for her to see that we've stopped."

Already, almost at the first word, Red Handsome had jumped down and run to the front of the car. The thing to do, the only thing to do, so far as he could see, was to turn on the lights and then to stand in front of them, arms up in indication of surrender.

And to Jerry Boyne, sitting rigid, gnawing at his lip in blazing anger, the thing appeared to him in the same light. That bomb was without doubt a mere warning—look out for the next and the next! He tried to shrug and remind himself that it was better to lose a trick in the game than to be blown to pieces.

"It looks like— By the Lord, I've got it! Got it, do you hear me, Red? Come back here—on the jump. Oh, what a hunch! Quick, you snail! Give me your belt—Oh, you ass! No, I haven't gone nuts. Quick, while they're wheeling and coming back. Don't ask questions!" He caught at the belt which finally was held out to him and began getting his own off. All the while he was barking out his orders, and all the while the plane, describing a wide arc, was cleaving its black path across the stars. "Now let some more air out of the rear tires; get them just flat enough to give them all the traction the law allows." He was working feverishly with his two belts now, getting them lashed to the steering wheel, seeking places to tie the other ends. He started his engine as from behind the car came the assurance that the tires were deflated as Jerry had ordered.

And now came Jerry's final amazing order:

"Grab hold of a wheel and help me get the car turned around. She's going to head straight back down the slope toward Mexico!"

For the last time he switched on his lights. Señora Fernandez, if it was she at the controls as Red Handsome swore she was, and her son Prince Charlie at the machine gun, must have accounted the game won, for they swept by again and merely relieved their feelings by dropping a second bomb at an entirely safe distance. Looking down, all they could see was that the car was turning and pointing its lights back toward the south, and what further sign of surrender could that precious two ask?

"Now!" cried Jerry. "Let her flicker!"

He stopped his car, completed the lashings of the steering wheel and opened the door at his side. As he let in his clutch he opened the hand throttle all the way and jumped. Rolling over a couple of times he sat up and watched Elmer Blodgett's car go tearing away down the long slope, making its last run.

The biplane rose sharply, circled and once more swept above the runaway car. Again there was the rattle of gun fire and, as the plane perforce passed the slower earth-bound vehicle a third bomb fell and a cloud of debris was belched skyward. The plane zoomed on; the little roadster, with its steering wheel jerking savagely against two belt straps, carrying no weight but its own, fled on, swishing loose sand backward from its low-pressure tires. From where Jerry sat staring and where Red Handsome stood bemused, nothing of the car was to be seen save its frantically bobbing red tail light.

Down the long slope it gathered momentum; now and then it rushed through patches of sage brush; it encountered areas of deeper, looser sand and went skittering across them. If those straps only held, and the wild thing didn't smash head-on into a bank or turn turtle at a barranca, why then the Empress and her charming son might chase it all the way to the border!

But doubtless the Empress was at the end of all patience, if patience she had ever known. The plane darted down after its scurrying prey again and again, and every time there was the staccato barking of the machine gun and, time after time, an earth-shaking thud as a bomb exploded.

Jerry leaped up shaken with laughter.

"I wouldn't have missed this for a mint of gold pieces!" he choked. "Gosh, if we could only see the finish! She'll blow Elmer's buggy sky high—and then they'll gather round and look for the corpses—and will wonder whether they blew us clean out of the world!"

"Let's go," grunted Red Handsome. "I've seen enough of the show, for one. We've got our chance now while the Fernandez family chase the car."

"On our way, then, though I would like to hang around. Oh, well; a man can't have everything. Here's where we duck on into Indian Gully; we can make our way on up into the higher hills and then across to High Mesa. Let's go."

"Only I'm not on my way to High Mesa," Red Handsome told him as they hurried on, hunting the darker depressions all that they could. "I'll cut across to Little Mesa and then on over to Alamo Springs."

"High Mesa, I said," Jerry told him coolly. "I went and got you according to orders; I'm going to deliver you the same way. We go to High Mesa, first stop. Now, don't let's waste time and breath arguing. I've got a gun on me and you haven't; I'd just as lieve blow a hole in your left hind leg as drink a glass of water with merry little pieces of ice sloshing around in it. Let's move. It's a long, long way to Tipperary yet and I'm right anxious to get a receipt for you."

"What are you driving at? Who sent you for me?"

Jerry ignored the question and the two hurried on. They came to the cleft of Indian Gully and felt safe from pursuit. Jerry politely waved his companion ahead, and used a forty-five for the waving; after that they went on in silence.

It was a long, long walk, how many miles Jerry did

not know, but plenty, he was sure. In due course, foot-sore from rough, steady going, they made their way among the broken hills to a spot whence they saw a light. The light spelled High Mesa, and looked to be still miles away. The light went out. Must be near midnight and time honest lights were out, meditated Jerry. They plodded on. When they startled a herd of horses into full headlong flight, Jerry shook his fist after them; why didn't they come up and ask a man to have a ride? He became, at first vaguely, aware of a new freshness in the air; it was touched with an elusive fragrance and was crisp and sweet. Dawn, that's what it was. You could smell it coming down from the hills. A wee whisper of breeze was stirring; the stars were paling and there was a tremulous light along the horizon. So that was why the light winked out; not for midnight but for a new day. And at High Mesa someone had sat up all night—waiting—

It was full bright dawn when the two men, plodding like automatons, climbed up the last stretch of road to the mesa and passed through the broad gate of the softly glimmering white adobe wall. They heard the plashing of the fountain and the gay bickering of the little garden creek, and were tempted to turn aside here for a drink instead of waiting for one in the house.

In the garden, standing beside what was to be a great heap of cut flowers were Beryl, old Uncle Doctor and the fat Maria. As the two dusty newcomers bore down upon them, the old man saw them first and emitted something like a yelp of joy. Maria, turning swiftly at a considerable risk to her balance, stared at them and murmured, *"Mamma mia!"* Beryl dropped a pair of shears and came running forward, both hands out, crying impulsively:

"Oh, I am so thankful! And I do want to ask forgiveness—from my old playmate—Gerald Sommers!"

Red Handsome did not quite know what it was all about but stepped quickly forward. Somehow she slipped by him when it seemed that she was going straight into his arms, and in another instant Jerry found himself in possession of those two quick impulsive hands, and saw her face lifted up to his and even saw how big and wonderful and altogether starry her eyes were.

"You're a dear, adorable old humbug," were the amazing words she was saying, and such tricks does the very early morning light play that he could have sworn that her eyes were very, very gay and that tears were shining in them. "You're exactly what my grandfather says of you—an incurable Romantic! And I am so ashamed—"

"What's all this?" cried Red Handsome, all at sea.

"Mr. Red Handsome," said Beryl, whirling on him, "meet my old childhood playmate, Mr. Gerald Sommers, sometimes known as Jerry Boyne—a sort of burglar!"

Jerry glared at Uncle Doctor but saw on his face only a look of mystification equal to his own.

"I never let out a cheep," muttered the old fellow. "Don't look at me like that."

"I don't understand," said Jerry. Then he looked to

where Red Handsome stood, his face drawn savagely, strangely stamped with anger and chagrin and, perhaps, an abiding sorrow. "All I know is that I promised Beryl to go get this man for her. Here he is, safe and sound."

"Let him go," said Beryl quickly. "I think he may want to go now—a long way."

But Uncle Doctor had other ideas. He closed his pocket knife with a snap.

"Me and him will go have a little powwow," he said after the fashion of one who meant to allow no opening for argument. "I got a gun in my boot and a bowie knife down the back of my neck, Mr. Red Handsome, so suppose we step?"

Red Handsome stood very still, staring at Beryl. Her eyes met his frankly, levelly. What she read in his look touched her; there was love there, the best thing about the man. And it was that love which had held him here in the neighborhood of High Mesa when, but for it, he would long ago have gone safely—a long way.

Slowly at last she turned away, sighing a little. His head jerked up, he stood an instant erect and rigid like a man facing rifle muzzles and determined not to wince. Then without a word or a backward glance he strode off through the garden with Uncle Doctor watchfully dogging his heels.

And Jerry became fully conscious only then that his hands, which had locked so tight about Beryl's, had never let go!

"I don't understand—" he said a second time.

This time Beryl laughed softly.

"And I called you a thief—and thought it was the candlesticks! And those earrings—look!" Yes, early as was the day she had them on and had worn them for hours. "Maria, run, quick; breakfast for a gentleman who comes home—home, do you hear? After long absence. May I have my hands now, Mr. Sommers? At least one of them. My nose itches!"

There was nothing for Jerry to do but laugh with her and reluctantly to release her hands.

"I'll tell you all about it over coffee," said Beryl. "Before my grandfather and his guests come down."

"He doesn't know?" said Jerry quickly.

She stood on the doorstep looking at him wonderingly.

"No," she said at last, "he doesn't know." But she spoke as though she were thinking of other matters. She kept looking at him in that queer fashion; then just a hint of a grave smile touched her lips. "Jerry Sommers, do you know I believe you're just exactly like a little boy I used to know? Do you remember—"

"I remember everything! How you looked, what you said—"

Maria was watching them, mouth open, eyes incredibly round, with no thought of obeying that command to "run quick." Beryl laughed at her, repeated the command and led the way into the big house just awaking to a new day—and to a cozy breakfast table—and most of all to a deal of explanation on both sides.

CHAPTER XVII

"HOW ON EARTH DID YOU FIND OUT?" JERRY ASKED his bright-eyed vis-à-vis across the table.

"I didn't find out! I was told. Forty wee sma' voices dinned it into my deaf ears before I would listen to any one of them. Last night when Charlie Fernandez in a rage called—him—a pretender, and said he could unmask him, it meant nothing to me. On top of that the word slipped from you, 'impostor.' The two coming together started me, I guess. Then what a landslide, if you don't mind your metaphors mixed. You said the day we met at the Empire that you had known me a long time ago; you knew my name. You gave me these." Her finger tip set an earring brushing her cheek. "Uncle Doctor let out that he had known you, when you were a little boy. You had red hair; my, what red hair! You knew your way in the dark to the place the letter and money were hidden. Dear me, what a 'Mysterious Stranger' all along! On top of this, once the light was let in just a crack, it was strange how that other man, whom I guess we'll have to call Red Handsome for want of another name, had forgotten so much that I remembered. Really the only odd thing is that I didn't know almost from the beginning; but the thing was too incredible for one even to suspect."

"By the way," he said abruptly, "the poor devil must be as hungry as I am—"

"While you were making yourself beautiful to come to breakfast, Maria loaded a tray and sent it out to him.

But you haven't told me how you managed to bring him back. I suppose that all you had to do was go to your charming friend, Señora Fernandez and—"

"Wait till I tell you! If you could only have seen her plane roaring along after an empty car, like a mad hornet chasing a—oh, say chasing a knight in armor drest!"

Beryl listened in sheer wonderment and, before the tale was done, shivered.

"Is there no wickedness that terrible woman does not dare?" she cried hotly. "What is to be the end? Is she to go on and on, from crime to crime, with so many of us knowing her for what she is, yet beyond the reach of the law? Dick Kingsbury's death and now Bob's; raids on both Little Mesa and the Alamo Springs—"

"A little later," said Jerry soberly, "I want you to read my father's letter. There is no doubt that she was responsible for his death; in my mind there is equally little doubt that El Bravo, always moving at her command, killed him."

They were in the garden when Antonio Costa came down, Jerry helping her gather the great heap of flowers which presently were to go by wagon to Little Mesa. All that flowers could do toward softening the final grim fact of the tragic end of a man's brief existence was to be accomplished by these fresh, fragrant, dewy blossoms. There was no Kingsbury kin to wait for; the only one waiting was the dead brother lying alone under the pepper trees shading a gentle knoll; all days were alike to Bob now, and it seemed best not to delay that simple ceremony of consigning the quiet body to its ultimate rest. High Mesa men were already at Little Mesa.

Antonio Costa greeted Jerry with gravely smiling courtesy, making no reference to that young man's recent abrupt departure, indicating no surprise at finding him here at so early an hour. He trusted that Mr. Boyne was quite recovered from his recent harrowing experience, and also expressed the wish that he would honor High Mesa with his presence again and still longer.

"I have two of my very good friends staying with me for the day," he said on turning back to the house. "When you and Beryl have finished here you will come in and meet them?"

Between Beryl and Jerry it had been agreed that nothing of Beryl's discovery was to be told Costa for the present. At least nothing would be said until after his guests had gone; Beryl promised that willingly enough.

"But then," she said firmly, "he must know. We have no right to keep such knowledge from him. Of course I recognized the disturbing fact immediately that you are the real owner of High Mesa. And you will have to be like the villain in the old melodrama and evict the poor old man and his lovely little granddaughter. What *was* your idea? Would you have gone on and on and on, wondering how you could break the news to us?"

He strove to explain. There was no haste, and he had wanted to see what could be salvaged for Señor Costa; Red Handsome still had money, and there was that other money which it appeared he had paid to the Empress to secure her aid. If she would but be patient—

Señor Costa beckoned from a window. His friends were about and could not start their day aright without a bright morning smile from Beryl; also they wanted to shake Mr. Boyne by the hand. Jerry was presented to the two, General Valdez, an elderly Mexican, very soldierly with bristling white mustachios and the air of a grand duke; Mr. Peters, a man of sixty, a successful American business man, from the cut of his clothes to the cut of his eye. The names, Valdez and Peters, were vaguely familiar; he felt that he had heard them recently, but with Beryl ready to start—she had promised that she would ride with him to Little Mesa, leaving the wagon to follow—he gave really very little thought to the two elderly gentlemen. Such individuals existed; one could not but be conscious of the fact. But they did not matter in the least.

At Little Mesa, Elmer Blodgett, seeing them coming, met them and was clearly relieved to have them arrive. The flowers came in the wagon from the ranch; Beryl, carrying an armful, went into the house. Jerry in a few words told his old friend of the night's happenings. Elmer heard him out without a word, merely grunting now and then, and at the end remarked drily:

"Struck you as funny, didn't it, the old lady and her nice little boy chasing after my car and no doubt blowing it all to pieces about the size of your finger nail? I guess it would be funny—with another man's car!"

Later when all was in readiness Antonio Costa came

to pay his last respects to a neighbor. None here had known Bob Kingsbury long, yet when at last they turned away from the flowery hillock covering two companionable graves, there was in each heart a little monument of kindly thoughts and memories. And there were quiet tears from over-full hearts. Elmer Blodgett cleared his throat and hurried after Costa who had gone ahead, head down and profoundly thoughtful.

"Mr. Costa," said Elmer. "He—Bob, you know—left something for you. I guess I'd better fork it over."

He gave the scrap of paper to Costa who took it wonderingly and read it in growing wonder.

"But he returns Little Mesa to me! I do not understand, Señor Blodgett!"

"There are a good many things which take a lot of understanding," Elmer conceded. "Well, things most generally come out in the wash."

"Eh?" said Costa. "Oh, yes." He looked Elmer over keenly and in the end appeared moved toward a sudden new friendliness. With a faint smile he invited: "Your friend Mr. Boyne is staying with us at High Mesa. I hope you, too, will honor us? Both my granddaughter and I will be delighted."

"Me, too!" said Elmer.

That afternoon in the cool, pleasant patio, Jerry, at Beryl's insistence, told the others something of his last night's adventures. No reference was made to the fact that a certain individual who had passed himself off among them as Gerald Sommers was at present immured in the stone grain house, very much under Uncle Doctor's eagle eye; but the Empress's high-hand methods were made sufficiently clear. That she had been responsible for the raids on the two neighboring ranches was touched on; that she had attacked the two fugitives from the Empire with machine gun and bombs was added, that there might be no doubt as to the sort of thing she would do being given provocation and opportunity.

General Valdez' mustachios bristled more than ever and his black eyes snapped.

"Even in Mexico City I have heard of this lady," he said drily. "It would appear that she is very—let us say that she is very resourceful. But this story of raids and murders! Of coming after a car into United States territory and throwing bombs at it—"

He lifted his immaculate hands in a way eloquent of disbelief. Jerry flushed.

"The car itself ought to be Exhibit A," he said briefly. "I've no doubt that a short drive would show it to you in such condition that even the incredulous would see the truth."

"It was insured for fire, theft, transportation and collision," said Elmer lugubriously. "I thought the feller that wrote the insurance stuck everything in it he could think of, but he forgot machine guns and dynamite!"

It was in the dusk that Jerry and Beryl went treasure-hunting. Out in the pasture all one had to do was start at a certain old tree, take nine steps due north, four steps due east, five steps north again—and unearth an ancient tin tobacco box containing not a cent less than forty-three pennies! It had been Costa himself, though not definitely specifying what they should do, who had hinted that the two might find it more pleasant outside than in the house; it appeared that he wanted a few words alone with his old friends, and Jerry jumped at the opportunity to go on this errand with Beryl, reviving old memories.

"It ought to be right here," said Jerry, looking up from the hole he had shoveled. "And it's gone! Robber! You came and lifted the treasure!"

"Goose!" Beryl promptly named him. "It's the wrong place."

"It's not. I remembered every number and direction—"

"And forgot that a man six feet high and maybe higher takes a longer step than a little boy a dozen years old!"

Together they unearthed the "treasure."

"Forty-three there'll be," he said, shaking the box for her to hear.

"Forty-three is right," said Beryl, her eyes dancing at him in the dusk.

"Though originally, when a boy and girl I used to know brought them here, there were forty-five."

"Yes," said Beryl nodding, her eyes dancing more than ever.

"The boy took out one and gave it to the little girl; the little girl took out one and gave it to the boy." He pulled out his wallet and from its depths produced a penny. She opened a hand which she had kept all the while tight shut and the two pennies, of even date, which had traveled so far apart during fifteen years, once again chinked ever so merrily together.

"Why, there goes the car from the garage," exclaimed Beryl suddenly. "Grandfather is taking his friends somewhere—the rascal! He got us out of the way so he could run out on me!"

"Never mind," laughed Jerry. "Give the boys a chance. We haven't counted all our wealth to make sure of it."

"He is up to something," Beryl insisted. "He did send us out of his way. That was because he knew I'd stop him—"

At the house they learned that Costa and his friends had left word and excuses. Also there was a brief little note for Beryl:

"My Little One: Do not be worried if we are late. My friends have a curiosity to look in at the casino at the Empire. I, too, shall play a little, for I feel sure that this time I am going to win a lot of money to buy my Little One nice things with. Excuse me to our good friend Jerry.

A. A. C.

"Great Scott!" said Jerry.

"You don't think that they are going into danger! Oh, Jerry, I am afraid!"

"Not physical danger," he reassured her promptly and with conviction. "Men like your grandfather and his friends—this general from Mexico—no, they're all

270

right. But it's mere dollars and cents I am thinking about. Do you know if Señor Costa has any considerable sum available for ready squandering?"

There was that money, several thousands, which he had taken from behind the candlestick! If he staked that—and lost it! Of late her grandfather puzzled and worried her.

"Look here," Jerry went on when he saw her hesitation. "He and his friends, both of whom I'll warrant are plungers, once they get going, are up against a crooked wheel down there at the Casino, and I don't for a minute doubt it. There's nothing simpler on earth than fixing a roulette table so that its owner simply can't lose. And do you suppose that the Empress, when it's a question of big money, is going to overlook a bet? Not for a moment. Your grandfather—"

He broke off sharply. All of a sudden, now that his mind was open to suggestions connected with roulette, he remembered where he had recently heard the two names, General Valdez and Mr. Peters. He had had them only last night from the Empress herself; she had invited him to look in "tomorrow night" and see how a couple of high-rollers paid handsome toll for their moment of pleasure across her table. That last wink of hers had told volumes.

"I'm going along," he concluded almost savagely, for it struck him that already old Antonio Costa had lost enough at this woman's hands; if a warning could stop the trio of old sports, that warning was going to be given.

"But for you it would be plunging headlong into

danger!" she cried nervously. "Remember last night. No, you mustn't go; better that they lose some money and maybe learn a lesson."

"I'm going," said Jerry stubbornly, "but I'm going to run no chances. The world begins to look to me to be too nice a place, a regular jim-dandy inhabited by a most bewilderingly, amazingly, adorably—"

"Sh!" she laughed at him.

"I'll try to overtake them; you'll stake me to a car, won't you? Oh, I'll promise not to get it all blown up like Elmer's. And I'm taking little old Elmer along, and old Doc—and we'll just bristle all over with rifles, shot-guns, pistols, butcher knives and so on, like—like old General Valdez' mustaches!"

There was a two-seater at his disposal, and Beryl watched the car whizz away into the night. Though it did not bristle in the porcupinish way which Jerry had prophesied, still she knew that the men hurrying south in it were fully, if discreetly, armed. They were three men whom she judged eminently capable of taking care of themselves; then, too, her grandfather, the old General and Mr. Peters knew their own ways about. Further, with the General always there went two men who looked like prizefighters, and Mr. Peters was accompanied by his "secretary" who was a very alert and muscular young man. Nine men all together, and every one of them would have his eyes open. Beryl decided that everything was all right, and prepared for another night of vigil.

CHAPTER XVIII

A ND THE NINE DID ENTER THE GATES AT THE Empire together. Jerry had driven the second car and made every endeavor to overhaul the first, but it grew evident that the three old men on their way to their rendezvous with my Lady Luck, or Maid Misfortune, were as ardent as so many Romeos. It was only as they were alighting at their journey's end that Jerry caught up with them; the gate was swinging open in the high wall at the Empire Ranch when he hailed them.

"Señor Costa," he called, hurrying forward. "May I have a word with you?"

Costa, all impatience to get ahead with the night's pastime, asked rather curtly what was wanted and did not appear in any way delighted to discover that he had been followed.

"I only thought it fair to warn you," said Jerry bluntly. "That table is as crooked as a dog's hind leg. Now that you know it, and I don't see how you could have thought it anything else, no doubt you will wish to tell your friends. Last night I had a few words with the Empress; it's as clear as—"

"Thank you, Señor," interrupted Costa stiffly. "You are most kind. I am quite sure that you mean well. Nevertheless we have promised Señora Fernandez, and she expects us. We shall be glad to have you come with us—if you judge it wise to put in an appearance here so soon?"

The others, having hung on their heels a moment, were already entering the grounds. Jerry, though he wanted to swear at Costa for his stiff manner, which he put on and off like a starched shirt, beckoned to his two companions and followed the others.

Early as they were, all was ready at the Casino. By the time they had laid aside their coats and had joined Señor Costa at the little bar in a toast to their absent hostess, she was no longer absent but came in at the door to greet them gayly. At her heels came Prince Charlie. It was his gasp which stopped his mother in the first sentence of her welcome, for his prominent eyes had fallen, full of amazement, on Jerry and rested on him in a perplexed, incredulous stare.

The Empress frowned and her cold blue eyes hardened. To her as to her startled son the vanishment of two red-haired men from an automobile under fire had constituted a troublous mystery. The car had been wrecked by a well placed bomb which had blown it literally to bits; all evidence which might have been afforded by two belt straps lashing a steering wheel had been destroyed; that the car had driven itself was not to be thought of. Then where had its occupants flown? Had they been shattered to shreds too small to be located? Not even a boot left hanging on a bush? A thoroughly mystified and angry Empress had spent a day in useless conjecture, and now Jerry's coolly smiling face did nothing to alleviate her feelings.

But hers was not an equilibrium to be turned topsy-turvy as easily as her son's. There was only that quick frown and hardening of the keen blue eyes; then she ignored Jerry quite as she was ignoring the strong-arm men—so obviously only that—who accompanied her guests.

"These two gentlemen, Señora," said Costa affably, "are my best of good friends, the General Benito Valdez and Mr. Ellsworth W. Peters of Pasadena. You expected them, no? They sometimes like to amuse themselves at roulette, and I have assured them," and here he made her his elaborate bow, his hand on his heart, "that here they may be assured of both an adequate bank and fair play."

She waited somewhat impatiently for him to finish.

"I expected them," she said crisply, and looked curiously from the two back to Costa. "They wrote and I've got a bank ready that ought to satisfy them. If they break it, they'll be taking off a wad of money that even Valdez and Peters oughtn't to be ashamed of. I didn't know, though, that they were friends of yours."

"Ah!" was all that Costa said in answer, and both Valdez and Peters merely inclined their heads and looked at the Empress with frank interest. Costa himself was already glancing at the table. "Shall we start?" he asked, smiling. "To begin with, to show my friends how the little table behaves itself, I am of a notion to risk a few thousands myself!"

"A few thousands?" said the Empress and looked at him with new interest. "Fine. Shoot the works. Ortiz," she commanded, all business. "Let's get going."

Ortiz, that same croupier whom Jerry had once already watched here serenely presiding over the vagaries of the small ivory ball and whirring wheel, a dandified young Mexican with "gambler" and "crook" written all over him, took his place at the table. At that moment, and for the first time, Jerry became conscious of El Bravo's presence just within the door; the man had entered at the Empress's heels and stood there, inconspicuous but ready at hand if required. What caused Jerry to note him at all was a sudden start that Uncle Doctor, standing shoulder to shoulder, gave. Uncle Doctor, during the day, had read a certain five-year-old letter entrusted to him by Jerry. For the first time since reading it he looked straight into the cold bleak eyes of the man who, he was as sure as he cared to be, had shot his old friend and employer. Now Uncle Doctor grew as stiff-bodied as a hound quivering at the end of a leash. Yet he held himself very still; he even put a quick hand on Jerry's shoulder and muttered under his breath:

"Not now. But soon, if God is good! That man is mine. Go easy, kid. Steady! Get your eye on the play."

Costa had taken a chair and was putting his money on the table. Jerry, drawing nearer, saw that there were really "a few thousands." Bank notes and some gold pieces. And as he saw, and observed old Costa's placid, guileless, downright innocent old face all wreathed in smiles, he did not know whether he resented more the Empress's merciless exploitation of the old fellow, or Costa's infernally irritating nonchalance as he prepared to squander his "few thousands." However all that Jerry could do was shrug and watch; here was really no affair of his—though had he known that that money on the table was his money, he might have been stirred up enough to make an excuse of that and halt matters at their very beginning.

Costa very coolly, while getting ready, slipped a thousand dollars out on the red and was watching neither the stake nor the ball while this first play was made. Instead he was arranging his funds in such order that he could select each bet without trouble; he did like to have things made easy. He was then lighting his first cigarette when the ball clicked and stopped at the number 36. A red number and he had won his first bet of a thousand dollars. The croupier, Ortiz, gave over nursing his small, pointed mustache long enough to lean across the table and place the amount of the loss with Costa's stake. Then he gave the wheel a spin and the ball a whirl as though in haste to get back to his mustache.

"I feel lucky tonight, Señora," said Costa, smiling up at the Empress who gave him back a bright quick smile.

"Hop to it, Señor," she said lightly. "Me, I'm backing the bank, you know."

Jerry was not in the least surprised that Costa won the first bet; here was the old, come-on system, and there were big fish looking on and waiting to get hooked. Of course the old man would be permitted to win—for a time. That there could be any other than the one inevitable end to the night's play Jerry did not for an instant believe.

Costa had not disturbed the money, now two thousand dollars, on the red.

"I think it will be red again, no?" he said lightly.

"Maybe even it will be the little number 36, repeating itself?"

So on 36 itself he put another "small" wager; only a hundred dollars. The lively little ball which can be so fascinating while it speeds in its gay circles, so like the spoken word of fate when at last it comes to rest, flirted tantalizingly among the numbers and then, most obliging of little fellows, it gleamed up at them from number 36. And Señor Costa had won a second time: two thousand dollars on the red, thirty-five hundred dollars on number 36. All together, in about a minute of play, he had won six thousand five hundred dollars. Just as easy as that!

Jerry looked swiftly at the Empress. She was smiling, untroubled. He glanced at Ortiz; that young man was relinquishing his mustaches in order to submit to the unspeakable ennui of setting the ball going again. Jerry's eyes traveled on and rested briefly on the figure near the door. There was a strange gleam, he thought, in El Bravo's usually lifeless eyes.

Ortiz gave the wheel a deft turn and snapped the ball.

"Make your bet," he invited languidly.

"I like this red color, *amigos*," murmured Señor Costa. He liked it so much that he left the four thousand dollars standing on it; the winnings from number 36 he drew to himself. And the third time in such swift succession the dancing little ball was of Costa's own tastes, and elected to stop on the red. On number 30 this time, separated only by the number 11 from 36. The croupier paid the bet; another four thousand.

Jerry felt something worrying his arm; Elmer Blodgett's fingers were disporting themselves like a pair of steel pincers.

"Ain't the old one a ripper?" whispered Elmer. "Ten thousand five hundred bucks in three flips and never turned a hair!"

Costa merely looked pleased in a simple, childlike way.

"I tell you, I feel lucky tonight," he admitted. "Now, for a little system: The ball stopped once at 36, again at 36; next at 30. The number 11 is just between. What does my system say? Why, here is five hundred dollars on 36, and five hundred on 30—and an even thousand dollars on number 11! It cannot lose. *Vamos a ver!*"

"Good Lord," groaned Jerry within himself. "It cannot win! System! There goes two thousand back where—"

"Click!" said the laughing little ball. Well, wonders do happen now and then. It must have been exactly of Costa's mind, doubtful about both 36 and 30. And with all the rest of the field open to it it snuggled down and went to sleep between those two—on number 11. And Antonio Arenda Costa had won thirty-five thousand dollars, and lost one thousand. A nice little profit of thirty-four thousand on the play.

Elmer was babbling in Jerry's ear:

"Forty-four thousand, five hundred, in three passes! Oh, mamma! Watch him roll. This is his night to howl, and *can* he?"

Jerry shook him off and again his eyes ran like lightning across the faces of three individuals in whom just then he was tremendously interested. The croupier was twisting his mustaches; was he just a little bit swifter about that affair than before, and his hands harder? Certainly there had passed across the Empress's cold blue eyes a faint hint of shadow. Certainly El Bravo's eyes did have life in them.

"I am glad of the opportunity, Señora," said Costa graciously, "to show my friends how kind your table can be."

"The ball's spinning," said the Empress coldly.

"Ah," said Costa. But he merely drew all his winnings to him and made no move to place a bet. The ball circled, hesitated in its skittish way and rested on a black 28. Costa smiled. The croupier gave a rather zestful start to wheel and ball again and the old Spaniard shoved out every cent he had in front of him, upward of fifty thousand dollars to await fate upon a black field.

"I like to play fast," he said ingenuously, and watched with the frankest of interest while the ball and wheel seemed in less haste than ever before to decide a very simple matter.

This time Jerry did not watch the table but was hawk-eyed for the slightest play of expression on the masklike face of Señora Fernandez. He heard at last the familiar, expected click—and saw for a flashing instant a little look almost of horror in her eyes. He whirled to the table. Black it was and Costa had won—the croupier was counting to make sure the exact amount—Costa had won another snug little bet, this time fifty-one thousand seven hundred dollars.

There were men in the room to whom fifty thousand

dollars was a small affair. General Valdez of Mexico City was rated at several millions; Peters of the East and West S.S. Line was worth several of General Valdez. But none the less every man was watching in an interest which had become breathless; here, at least, were large possibilities and here was the goddess Luck in one of her most intriguing phases.

Jerry tried to make the croupier out, and thought— barely suspected, rather—that that young man was a bit nervous. Certainly there was a deal of vigor put into the next speeding of ball and wheel.

And then never was Jerry so beset to fight down one of his heady impulses. It was only a glance, only a suspicion of a glance, but it did pass between Señora Fernandez and her croupier. And it did say: "Enough of this nonsense! Stop it!" Jerry wanted with all his heart to lay both hands on the immaculate shoulders in front of him; to yank old Costa up out of his chair and out of his placid simplicity; to throw him into his car and haul him safely home. Here he had in front of him a good hundred thousand dollars, and the old chap was in debt, mortgaged up to the white eyebrows! Another roll, and he'd lose. It was as sure as fate, as sure as a crooked wheel could make sure. Why he had been allowed to win this much— Well, no doubt the big play was yet to come when Valdez and Peters warmed up and plunged in. As yet they gave no sign of being of a mind to pass beyond the stage of spectatorship.

Jerry fought with his impulse and throttled it. No use. Well, look at it one way, Costa in the end would be losing actually only those "few thousands" with which he had begun.

Costa's shapely old fingers, very steady and insouciant, placed a bet. Saying something about "My system," he put a thousand dollars on number 28, a thousand on each of its neighbors, 7 and 12—and put every other cent he had on the black. It was to be remarked that both 7 and 12 were black numbers, 28 red. That no doubt had something to do with Costa's "system."

And now while ball and wheel went their opposite ways toward a final adjustment which was fraught with very considerable importance, Jerry with difficulty withdrew his gaze from the table and bent it on Ortiz's face. The man was rigid; his fingers were still; there was the hint of perplexity in the black eyes fairly glittering from under lowered lids.

"Click!" said the ball, and Ortiz stiffened and flinched. Elmer Blodgett forgot himself and hurled his hat up to the ceiling and whooped. The most obliging, downright lovable roulette ball in all this world of exasperating roulette tables, had settled itself down as if to stay on number 7. Seven and black! And Antonio Arenda Costa had again, incredible as it seemed, incredible even as luck itself always is, made a fourth consecutive winning—this time to the chiming tune of about one hundred and thirty-five thousand dollars. And if anything beyond this amazing fact was clear, that other thing was that the Empress had paled and was looking bright, naked daggers at Ortiz—and that Ortiz looked frightened.

"Well, Ortiz!" cried the Empress in a sort of contained, throttled fury. "Señor Costa won—I think this time one hundred thirty-six thousand four hundred dollars. Can you count that high? The money is in the drawer."

Ortiz counted swiftly and paid. Then he stepped back.

"Señora," he said in a voice oddly like her own had been, "I am not feeling well. Perhaps you will excuse? And take my place?"

It was like a challenge, that last. She stared at him, then nodded and stepped to the place he vacated.

"Make your plays, gents," she rasped out with a poor attempt at nonchalance.

"Now," cried Costa, and stood up. "We will have some fun, no, Señora? We two are old-timers at roulette, eh?" He made her his delightful bow. "At roulette, Señora, as in love and war we play to win, do we not? Now—"

She sped the wheel one way and snapped the ball the other.

"Make your bet," she said shortly.

He made his bets while the ball rolled, seeming to be in no haste, yet having five wagers staked in time. A thousand dollars each on five numbers. And this time he lost, and the loss cost him an even five thousand dollars. He appeared pleased.

"This is fine!" he cried cheerily. "It was growing monotonous, was it not? Like business and not play! Now we shall see, eh, Señora? You and I."

"You and me; right," she retorted. "Dog eat dog and—let's go!"

The ball started but Costa appeared undecided. He meditated a moment then cried out, "Red once more!" and as cool about the matter as though he were betting a last year's bird's nest, he placed his entire capital on the red. A look—Jerry read it for triumph—flashed up in the Empress's eyes. When the ball stopped she was looking a little tauntingly at Costa's face; she seemed so very sure that she knew that it would not be red again.

But red it was.

The woman actually rubbed her eyes. She stood as still as a statue save for the slight quiver of a lower lip caught between her teeth. Then without a word she counted Costa's bet and paid it.

Paying, she snapped the drawer shut.

"Gents, that'll be all this time," she said rather coolly, all things considered—and Jerry knew that there were other matters to consider beyond her mere financial loss. "Some other time if you say; now, the bank's busted!"

"But surely—" began old General Valdez, both eager and disappointed.

"Nix. No. Not," she snapped at him. "I guess this ends the party, boys. Come again." She went to the door, turning her back on them and stopped, staring straight into El Bravo's strangely bright eyes. "You come along with me, El Bravo. You and me are going to have a talk."

Jerry, with a start coming out of a brief daze, caught Uncle Doctor's arm.

"Let's make it snappy getting these old sports out of here and tucked into bed," he whispered anxiously.

"Maybe the night's work is done—and then again maybe it's not!"

"Right, kid. First, we switch off the lights. Out they go and out we go, same time."

So it was in the dark and in a close-packed little party that the nine men left the Empire casino.

CHAPTER XIX

"A M I DREAMING?" GASPED ELMER WHEN THEY came safely to their parked car. "Did the old Spanish cavalier actually get away with more than two hundred and fifty thousand berries? And is the queen of Sheba pulling in her horns and just waving a smiling farewell to that hefty wad of condensed sunshine?"

"Quick," commanded Jerry. "Pile in. Come on, Doc; we'll scout ahead a bit. Like Elmer, I seem to feel we're dreaming. It's too easy!"

At the wheel he waited only until he heard the motor of Costa's limousine, then led the way.

"Keep your eyes glued on the road, kid," said Blodgett. "Leave it to me and Doc to watch both sides. You wouldn't think she'd start anything, would you? But did you see her eyes? If ever there was a woman mad enough to explode and blow the whole doggone world up along with her, it's Little Louise! And if you'll hear me, when she stabbed our old pal, El Bravo, with those same eyes of hers—"

"Watch the road," snapped Jerry. He had the uneasy

sensation that history was about to repeat itself, though perhaps with a fresh quirk leading to a new ending; here he was again turning his back on an angry Empress who, he thought, had more reason than before to seek to detain her departing guests.

"If she meant to cut up," said Uncle Doctor thoughtfully, "she'd never have let us ramble this far—"

"Don't be too sure!" Jerry told him swiftly. "She wasn't prepared for what happened, was she? Something went wrong with her table; and it had her guessing right to the finish. Then we made as lively a get-away as the law ever allowed. She had no chance—"

The horn of the car following honked several times and Jerry understood that he was being requested to deliver a burst of speed and very promptly obliged. The two cars, one only a hundred feet behind the other, sped northward along the narrow white road among the dusty willows. The tiny Empire village was just yonder, off to the left, twinkling through the scattering trees; at its edge, between village and race course, was the hangar where the *Hawk* was kept. And Jerry, without turning his head aside, was conscious of a single light racing across the field, lantern or flashlight borne swiftly along. He set his teeth and jammed down his accelerator.

"Hear it!" cried Elmer, and his hand grasped Jerry's shoulder. "That's the whirr of her damned biplane."

Jerry heard—hesitated—slowed down and came to a stop with a chauffeur behind him cursing him roundly and jamming on his own brakes barely in time to avoid a collision. Jerry paid him not the slightest attention but jumped down and ran back to Costa's car.

"She's getting her plane out already," he barked out as several faces stared out at him wonderingly through the dark. "Think she'd let you trot off this way with a quarter of a million on you? This time there'll be no warning bombs. If there's anything certain on earth it is this: The Empress and Charlie are out for big game, and they'll simply blow both cars up."

"My dear boy," said Costa in a tone which made Jerry feel that he was actually smiling, "I am sure that you are allowing yourself—"

"I know!" cried Jerry angrily. "Our only chance, if we've got any at all, is to pile out and take to cover on foot. You'll not forget that it was only last night that I was in this very same sort of a plight. Do I want to repeat the experience? No, thanks! But if we leave the cars—"

"Señor," said Costa, still patiently but with somewhat sharper emphasis, "you are mistaken. The plane will not follow us. You may take it from me that I know what I am saying."

There was so much conviction in his tone that for an instant Jerry was ready to believe that Costa knew whereof he spoke and that the sensible thing to do therefore was to get back into his car and lead on. But by now Elmer and Uncle Doctor had both run back to him and Elmer began worrying his arm and muttering:

"Shut up! Listen! Sure it's the plane; they're going up."

At that Costa stepped down and peered off toward the hangar, listening as intently as they did. When he spoke it was in a troubled voice:

"I—I don't understand! I had every assurance— Ah! Yes, it is the plane and— Gentlemen! *Amigos!* I very much fear I have led you into a very great danger. Look! You can see it! And I was so sure, so confident!"

"I think the young man is quite right," said Ellsworth Peters briskly. "Leave the cars here; they're too sweet a target. We can slip off through the willows; we can be miles away before daylight—"

"It is I who brought my friends into this affair," cried Costa ringingly. "It is I who will draw them safely out of it. If necessary— Yes! I will even give back what I have won."

"No!" rapped out old Benito Valdez, and his mustachios must have bristled then as never before. "*Por Dios,* it would be an infamous thing if we men—"

"There she zooms!" cut in Elmer. "You can see the baby against the sky. Up she goes. And if you gents are going to stand here all night and wait for something to drop on you— *Adios!* I'm going somewhere *pronto!*"

But, fascinated, the others watched, and even Elmer, finding himself alone, stopped and gawked. The *Hawk* taxied down the field and rose gracefully, bending its course into a wide arc when once clear of the ground, cutting back toward the road. Impatient for altitude it rose sharply—

"Good God!" someone cried. "It's falling! Look out!"

Some five hundred feet up there against the stars something had gone wrong. Jerry's thought, from the way the thing flopped crazily sidewise, was that a wing had crumpled. He stood rigid and horrified and helpless. You wanted to drag your eyes away from it and could not; you wanted to lift a hand somehow to check that awful plunge earthward—

There was one long scream, vibrant, terrified, terrible, whether from mother or son no one knew. A great black body falling plummetwise, plunged straight down hissing through the air—the dull thud as so much tonnage of steel and wood impacted with the earth—a roar then as of a battery of cannons, and a great tower of fire rushing fiercely sky high.

"An act of God!" burst out Ellsworth Peters excitedly.

"An act of a man," whispered old Antonio Costa, aghast.

"And those bombs meant for us," cried Elmer Blodgett in a queer hushed voice, "have simply blown clean to hell the one—"

"Sh!" muttered Jerry. "Come. We can do nothing here—and I think we had better go. There still remains El Bravo."

At High Mesa, Señor Costa, coming slowly down the winding stone staircase, was confronted by two young people who jumped up and came to meet him, full of expectancy. Both General Valdez and Ellsworth Peters had gone to their rooms, escorted by their friend Costa himself. Jerry and Beryl, left alone in the big living room, had talked with never a pause and at times both together, and now Beryl, still gripped by the horror of the thing which she had listened to, ran to her grandfather demanding eagerly:

"Now tell us! Tell us quickly! Everything! I am dying to know."

"Yes, yes," he said, and seemed curiously tense. "I have promised to tell you and now I shall. We are going to sit down, though. This night, filled as it has been with happenings, holds yet other things still to happen. Are we ever to sleep like honest folk at High Mesa again?" He pinched Beryl's cheek. "Last night you never closed an eye, my Little One. Tonight, too, you are like a little owl! Will you run and bring us something to drink? Then we will talk."

He frowned, not irritably yet with profound concentration, while Beryl brought decanter and glasses. He poured himself a brimming glass of red wine, looked up sharply and, as he raised his glass to his lips, bent his eyes steadily on Jerry and said gravely:

"With all sincerity I drink to your health, Gerald Sommers!"

Both Jerry and Beryl gasped.

"You knew!"

Costa smiled and sipped.

"From the beginning almost. From that first day when our good young friend here was so eager to know about his father—when I saw so strange an agony in his eyes—when I said to myself, 'Here comes one to whom Gerald Hand Sommers meant a very, very great deal!'—from that instant I groped. You, my dear," he smiled at Beryl, "say you hate mysteries; that is the Americano of you! I, a Spaniard, I love them!"

"But—" began Beryl, finding herself merely more mystified than before.

"No *buts,* my dear. We are now explaining things, telling a fine tale while we wait for— Never mind. I pondered that day; I watched and listened; I even thought back to all that I had heard and seen. This young man called himself Jerry Boyne. He had red hair. He said to my little granddaughter, 'Why, your name is Beryl!' She thought that he was what you call fresh, trying to flirt. I saw that he was in earnest about everything he did. I said, 'Jerry might be Gerald.' But why 'Boyne'?"

"My mother's name," said Jerry. "When, fool kid that I was, I flew off the handle—"

"I know. Yes, your mother's name. I have a very good memory, Mr. Jerry; I remember names. I had friends who long ago knew the Boynes of Santa Barbara very well, so you see the name itself came to me. And then I recalled that your father, whom I knew slightly before he bought High Mesa from me, had lived a long while in Santa Barbara. Then there were other small matters—"

"Of course," nodded Beryl. "I am afraid poor Jerry isn't much of a mystery-man after all; we both smoked out his secret!"

"Knowing him to be Gerald Sommers," continued Costa, meditatively twirling his glass, "I of course realized that I had ample time to strive to adjust matters—"

"You could not tell what he might do," protested Beryl.

"Ah, but I could! All I had to do was say to myself: 'This boy is fine; I see that in his eye. Also he is the son of a very splendid father and of a mother of fine family.

So, what will he do? Why, he will do as I, were I in his place, would do!' Would I, Beryl, or would you turn out a poor old gentleman and his so adorable little big-eyed owl of a pretty granddaughter for the hungry coyotes to eat? Did I not tell you long ago this young man was a Romantic? *Bueno!* Who is right now?"

"But," said Beryl falteringly, so hoping to have all things bright and clear, with no tarnishing speck, yet still troubled, "when you took—"

He laughed softly at her.

"I can read your mind in a flash! When I took the money, no? The money which we both knew belonged to Gerald Sommers? It was a loan, that was all; I knew I should return it and I knew, too, that so richly generous a young man would never deny me the use of it. But," and he looked stern and grave all of a sudden, "I took no chances with my honor, my dear. In my room you might find a memorandum; it acknowledges having borrowed that money; it calls attention to the fact that High Mesa will go back to our friend Jerry, improved by at least fifty thousand dollars I have spent on it. That was fair, wasn't it? Oho, I am a business man!"

Beryl decided that he was, and looked brighter. Yet there remained a last perplexity to darken her eyes once again.

"That man—El Bravo," she whispered.

"Now," said Costa, "we come to the big thing."

He put down his glass and grew silent over a cigarette in the meticulous making.

"It is like this," he said at last, evidently having taken

the moment to get his thoughts in proper sequence "One thing—many silly people who think themselves wise say that we Spaniards are fools about money. That perhaps, is merely because there are other things we care more for; we like money, yes, but we like other things more. Among those other things is pride. Yes, we are proud; we have reason and, even if we did not have reason, still would we have pride. And I found that unfortunate woman, Señora Fernandez, treating me like a fool; a certain Señor Red Handsome treating me like a fool. It was my pride that would not tolerate such a thing! I said to myself that I would show some people a few Americano tricks! Aha!

"I began with Frank Smith. This El Bravo, say you, is a bad man? If a man knows a, b and c he knows that. He is not one to trust; he is absolutely no-good. Eh? *Bueno.* A man like that is for sale. I bought him. I put him in my pocket. I had him come here two times, two times only—and it would seem that both times this little miss knew all about him coming! I must be careful. If ever I have a love affair—"

"Grandfather," commanded Beryl, all impatience and strengthening hope, "please!"

"I said to Mr. El Bravo, 'You all think me a fool, no? You think that I, who all my life have been playing games of chance, have not come to have my suspicions about Señora Fernandez' roulette table?' I laughed at him and he wondered what it was all about. I told him; you would have taken us for two mighty fine friends— Antonio Arenda Costa and El Bravo! Uf!—I told him that I was no mechanic or anything of that kind and

did not know and did not care to know what electro-
magnetic currents or wires were. But that I did know the
wheel down there at the Casino was manipulated; that it
could be controlled all very simply by the croupier; and
that what had been done sub rosa to make it a dishonest
wheel could be undone—"

Beryl, who had found it hard to contain herself,
clapped her hands now.

"You bribed him to make the wheel work for you!"

"*Chiquitita!*" he reproved her, and looked horrified.
"Are you a child then, to speak like that? Or is it that
girls do not understand? No! El Bravo, when I bought
him and put him into my pocket, wanted to make the
wheel work for me. I employed self-control, a virtue
which you Americanos must learn yet from us
Spaniards; I did not kick him down the steps. But I told
him that I wanted an honest wheel; that was all. He must
tear out the wires or magnets or whatever it was; he
must arrange so that no one could control what was
going to happen. That was all that I wanted, all that any
man of honor could ever want. I knew my cause was
just; I knew God would be with me. And—I won! You
see?"

He paused for a chuckle, then spoke again swiftly:

"I am glad that I won no more than I did. It was really
owing me, or at least most of it. All that I was cheated
out of by Red Handsome and the Empress came back to
me from Señora Fernandez. And a *little* more"—he
shrugged and chuckled again—"for interest and my
trouble!"

"If it had not chanced that your friends, General

Valdez and Mr. Peters, came to play, there would not have been so much money in the bank and—"

"You see the hand of providence as Señor Peters saw it when the plane crashed? No, Señor; no now as there. It was I who begged my two friends to come and make the appointment. It was I who asked them to warn Señora Fernandez that it would be necessary to have plenty of money to make it worth their whiles. Aha! American tricks, no?"

Jerry and Beryl looked at each other.

"I'd say," grinned Jerry, "pure Latin guile! What gets me is that you could trust El Bravo, even having bought him!"

"I gave him, in his hand, five thousand dollars. He has cold eyes, but I think they burned holes in the night. Then I told him that I would play for big money, maybe a hundred thousand, maybe more, and that he was per-fectly welcome to one dollar out of every ten that I made! You see? Mr. El Bravo makes altogether above thirty thousand dollars."

Jerry got up abruptly and walked restlessly up and down the long room. Costa, watching him narrowly, said a quiet "Sh" to Beryl. Jerry turned to a window as though his need were to commune with the outside night; but all curtains were closely drawn. He glanced through an open door and saw Elmer Blodgett standing over a small round table, idly shuffling a deck of cards; he had forgotten Elmer. He came back slowly and stood looking down into Costa's face.

"El Bravo killed my father," he said quietly.

"Ah! And I trafficked with this same El Bravo."

Costa rose slowly to his feet. He put his hands on Jerry's shoulders. "My son—" he began, then broke off sharply. With an almost incredible swiftness those two agile white hands of his darted under Jerry's coat and in an instant he had whipped the old forty-five out of its loose holster.

"Listen to me!" cried Costa then, springing back. He was of a sudden as stern as an inexorable fate. "Listen, I tell you! I did not know this when I traded with El Bravo. I knew him for a villain but not for all that he is. Nevertheless I traded with him, and I gave him my word—and, Señor, my word is my word, no matter to whom it is given. Do you understand? Is that clear?"

"El Bravo is coming here—now," said Jerry.

"El Bravo, when his time comes, will sink straight down to hell with the weight of his crimes! You are to listen, I tell you! I feared that that plane might follow— I spoke to El Bravo of it. And he promised me that it would not follow—he would put it out of commission so that it would take hours to fix it. By that time he meant to have his money and be far away. And—"

A cry of horror burst from Beryl. And a look of horror was in Jerry's eyes as he said sternly:

"And, knowing that she would discover that he had double-crossed her and would hunt him down to the ends of the earth—he weakened the wings' struts or did some such devilish thing! And you—"

Jerry's anger was flaring up. Costa stepped back, his old hand hard on the pistol butt.

"El Bravo is coming. Yes, now! I gave him my promise, Señor, my very sacred word of honor that he

should come assured of my good faith. And now I tel
you this: I would die, Señor, now, this very night—or i
need be I would shoot you down, my dearest goo
friend—rather than betray even one like El Bravo! I
that clear?"

"Good!" said El Bravo, and sneered.

The three started and whirled. El Bravo had come i
quietly at the window left open for him, entering a
once before both Jerry and Beryl had known him t
enter. He stood just inside, bulky and burly, stooped
little, balanced almost on his toes. Both of his big hair
hands were at his hips and locked hard about the grip
of his two weapons which were very much in evidence

"The money, Costa!" he said sharply. "Make
snappy. I'm on my way."

Costa without a word drew a packet from his pocke
and tossed it into the big paw that was lightning quic
to catch it.

"I have given you exactly ten percent," said Cost
curtly. "You have it there. We have finished, you and
Now— *Go, hombre!*"

El Bravo's cold eyes flashed.

"Go!" cried Costa.

"You'll keep your promise?"

"Are you crazy? My word is my word. I will take n
step to pursue you; I will do all in my power to protec
you. But you had best go."

"All right." El Bravo stuffed the packet into hi
pocket, dropped his hand back to his pistol-grip an
backed out of the window. "Give me an hour," h
snapped. "I've a car here and I'll be—"

"Go!" cried Costa angrily.

The curtain dropped, blotting out the brutal face. El Bravo had gone, no doubt running. And had gone enriched by above thirty thousand dollars, ample enough no doubt, to his way of thinking, to repay him for all that he had done to both table and plane.

"Now, will you give me my gun?" demanded Jerry sternly.

"Are you, too, mad!" Costa flung back at him. "You heard me—"

Jerry gathered himself to spring, but before he could move there came from the garden a voice that shattered the silence with all the abruptness and sinister import of a pistol shot. It was Uncle Doctor's voice, ringing clearly:

"Go for your gun, El Bravo! For killin' Jerry's dad—"

Then came the shots themselves, until it seemed that not two men alone but a dozen were firing out there. Those in the house who heard without seeing could imagine El Bravo, crouching in the shadows, blazing away desperately with both hands; they could visualize Uncle Doctor, grim and methodical and very accurate. Costa was taken all aback and was like a man who watches all the stars tumbling down from their places; Jerry, seeing him off his guard, was quick to spring upon him and snatch the weapon from his hand, and to leap out through the window.

"Come back!" cried Beryl in an agony of fear, and Costa leaped to the window and shouted: "Come back! I tell you, come back!"

The shooting ceased as abruptly as it had begun an
very soon Jerry did come back to them.

"Doc killed him," he said sternly. "Yet your honor i
safe, Señor. You did all that you promised, all that yo
could do. For you could have no suspicion that Doc
wily old boy that he is, was patrolling the premises an
meant to do so all night. He had it in his mind that, wit
so much money in the house, we still ran a lively chanc
of hearing from the Empire."

"I am glad that it was not you—that it was not at you
hand," murmured the white-faced girl.

"Doc loved my dad," said Jerry simply. "Yes, it wa
best that way."

Elmer had come running, excitedly demanding a
particulars; before he could be fully satisfied Uncl
Doctor jerked open the front door and stood looking a
them with a curious expression stamped on his face.

"My man's got away," he said sharply. When the
stared at him, naturally misunderstanding, he adde
curtly: "No, not El Bravo. I'm talkin' about that othe
jasper I had shut up in the grain house. Red Handsome.
His brows corrugated angrily. "While we were awa
tonight, down to the Empire, some low-lifed varmin
went and pried the padlock off and let him loose
Anyway, he's clean gone. But when I get my two hand
on that scaly scoundrel that set him free, there's goin' t
be a new hide nailed to my barn door! Of all the—"

"Uncle Doctor!" said Beryl.

"Now, Miss Beryl! I've been mindful you was pre
sent, and so I haven't said one half of what I meant
When I used a nice little parlor word like scaly—"

"I let him go," confessed Beryl and in such tones that onfession became defiance. "By this time he is very far way, and we will never see him again."

"You! You let that polecat go!"

"Good thing, too," said Jerry promptly, and Beryl ashed him a look full of appreciation. "He can't take nything with him, neither the Alamo Springs ranch nor et whatever funds and securities he has in the San Juan Bank; we'll have those tied up before he can move a and toward them. Besides, he wouldn't dare. As Beryl ays, he'll be a long way from here by now."

Beryl went to Uncle Doctor and put her two hands on is shoulders. On tiptoe she whispered into his ear:

"Please, Uncle Doctor! I don't want— You know! That barn door of yours!"

"Shucks!" he said. He stood looking at her as though roping for further words, and added: "Shucks!" Then e patted her hands and turned to go. Over his shoulder e said: "I'll have a man in San Juan by sun-up with vord to old Judge Colter and the district attorney and he bank. 'Night, folks. You can sleep safe, Miss Beryl; 'll forgive you this time."

All this while the old Spaniard had stood blank-faced nd motionless. Now a shadowy hint of a smile played bout his sensitive lips.

"Señor Elmer," he said graciously, "shall we, just you nd I, go into the little room where you were—where he round table is so handy and the cards are? We all row nicely into the habit of going without sleep, no? Perhaps if we amused ourselves— You suggested, I believe, that even two-handed poker—"

Blodgett brightened, allowed Costa to lead the way, closed one eye craftily for Jerry's edification and followed his host, softly whistling "The Spanish Cavalier." The moment for which he had waited so long had arrived!

As for Jerry and Beryl, they slowly gravitated to a deep, cushiony window seat. To be sure, this was their second night without sleep, but Beryl's eyes were inordinately bright and lovely, the soft flush had returned to her cheeks and she seemed absolutely to thrive on continued staying wide awake, while to Jerry it seemed a crime for a man to lose a single delicious moment of life in the blank unconsciousness of slumber. But a little later, perhaps a couple of hours after that little game of poker started "just for fun," when Elmer came into the room he saw that Beryl's head was nodding so that a pink earring seemed to rest on Jerry's shoulder.

"Ahem!" said Elmer Blodgett. "I—I just stepped in," he continued hastily, growing apologetic as two pairs of eyes regarded him curiously, quite as though two richly contented young people wondered who he was and whence he came and why. "I—I just stepped in, you know, Jerry, to see if you could lend me some money? didn't want to butt in, you know, but—things haven't gone so well with me; Don Antonio has sure had a run of luck tonight! But if I—"

Jerry continued to look at him as though still in doubt whether the man was real or merely an unwelcome vision. Elmer shifted and snorted and finally muttered "Sure, that's all right!" and oozed out. By the time he reached the door he was whistling again—though downright dolefully now—"The Spanish Cavalier."

Beryl sighed.

"I wonder who is winning in there?" she said dreamily.

"Oh!" said Jerry. "That's so; those two are playing cards, aren't they? I don't know why they have to interrupt us so often, do you? There is so much we have to tell each other—"

But then, another way of looking at it was that they had all the rest of their lives in which to get so many important things said. Just now it was imperative for Jerry to tell her about her eyes.